The Catalpa Tree Fairy

and other stories

by Jennifer P. Tanabe

Contents

The Catalpa Tree Fairy

Naida woke up feeling very excited. Today was the day all the new fairies were to be assigned their trees. At last almost all the snow had melted. The sun was rising higher in the sky and warming the earth, preparing it to support growth and new life.

A few days ago the fairies had finally been able to go outside again after all the cold, dark months they had spent cooped up at home. Their cozy cave on the rock face overlooking the forest had kept them warm and snug all winter long, but they had had limited opportunities to fly and play. In fact, most of their time had been spent learning how to take care of the trees. Now the day had come when they were to put it all into practice.

"Jayda, are you ready?" she asked her friend.

"I don't know," Jayda hesitated. "It was so much fun to be able to play outside these past few days so I'm glad the winter is almost over. But I'm a bit worried about taking care of a tree by myself."

Naida nodded. "I wish we could go together too."

Lara, another member of their little group, came over to join them. "It would be nice to go together, but I don't think it works that way. Each tree is different and so are we, so we get matched up together with trees that fit our personality."

"That makes sense," Naida agreed.

"But it's still a bit scary to imagine what kind of tree we'll each get." Jayda added.

"We'll find out soon enough." Lara said. "Look, Merida's here!"

All the young fairies quickly gathered around Merida, their leader. "Now, you all remember your responsibilities, I hope. Your first task is to gently encourage your tree to wake up. Don't push, just let it know that winter is almost over and it is time to awaken."

The tree fairies all nodded, looking seriously at Merida. They knew this was a vital role that they played in their tree's cycle of life. A tree that awoke too early was in danger of freezing to death. A tree that slept too long would miss the warmth of spring and not be able to complete its growing cycle before the frosts came back in the late fall. Of course, the fairies were not yet able to decide it was time to wake the trees. That responsibility lay with the elders. But they were the ones who were to carry out the order – how exciting!

Merida continued, "I will take you individually to your assigned trees. Everyone be patient, and wait for your turn. Focus your energy and prepare to be attuned to your tree's life spirit. Once you're attuned to your tree, you are connected for the rest of your life. When your tree's life is over, your life is over too. So this is a serious day."

The young fairies looked at each other, the finality of this moment dawning on them. The trio who were always together – Sylvia, Sophia and Sandra – began whispering to each other. "What's the matter?" Merida asked, firmly but kindly for she was a wise leader and understood that some new fairies found this day very challenging.

Sandra looked up and hesitatingly asked, "Did our trees have fairies last year? I mean, are they new trees so they weren't around last year to wake up?"

Sylvia joined in, "But I thought you told us we are getting big trees, so they must have been woken up last year. What happened to those fairies?"

Merida smiled. "That's a good question. Does anyone know the answer?"

All the fairies looked around at each other. They thought this question must have been answered sometime in their studies, but they couldn't remember. Suddenly Naida recalled the day when a special fairy had come to speak to them at their group meeting. "Is it because these trees are ready to have fairies now, but before they were too wild?"

"Well done, Naida! That's very close," Merida smiled at her student. "That's certainly one way that older trees get new fairies. But this is a different situation."

Then Jayda remembered something. "It's the Big Ones who are ready. The Big Ones that live with the trees. They are ready for us to help with their trees. Is that it?"

"Good, Jayda, that's correct. The Big Ones have progressed to a level where we can go and help them. Last year they weren't ready, they were too wild if you like. They tried to take care of their trees, though, so now they are ready to receive our help. But be careful, the Big Ones don't understand about fairies yet, and we don't know how they will behave if they find out we're there. Don't be afraid, just stay out of sight when they come around."

All the fairies were fluttering around now in excitement, mixed with a certain amount of fear at the mention of the Big Ones. "Big Ones can't fly, can they? So we're safe if we go high up in our trees?" Lara suggested.

"That's right," Merida agreed. "They can't fly. But some of them will try to climb your tree, especially if it has strong branches. The young Big Ones enjoy climbing, but even they can't go to the top!"

"So, you're saying there is a group of Big Ones that live beside the trees that we will take care of?" Lara asked. "I thought tree fairies got assigned to trees that are far away from where the Big Ones live."

"Yes, Lara, usually the Big Ones are far away. Often a whole group of trees, that's called a forest, grow well together with the animals that live there and we are able to go and help them. In those cases, the fairies usually don't meet any Big Ones."

"So, we're a special group? Maybe I'd like to be in a group that goes to a forest. I'm not sure I want to be around the Big Ones," Alicia was shaking a bit as she said this.

Merida looked at her kindly. "Oh Alicia, you're trembling! Don't worry dear, I know you'll love your tree! And don't be afraid. You will always come home to sleep here every night, and any time if you feel frightened you can come here. And I'll be around to help you."

Merida stood up and addressed her young students. "Fairies, you are a special group. You are chosen to take care of these trees. The spirits of the trees are waiting for you. Don't disappoint them!"

The ten little fairies stood up and made a line. "We're ready, Merida!" they chorused. "Bring us to our trees!"

Merida started taking the fairies one by one to their trees. First to go was Jayda, who turned to look bravely at the others as she prepared to follow Merida. "Good luck!" called Naida to her friend as she flew off.

Merida quickly returned for the next fairy, and Lara stepped forward. "I'm ready."

The others followed in quick succession. Sylvia, Sophia and Sandra tried to go as a group but Merida scolded them and told them they would see each other soon enough. Then it was Daniela, then Tonya, and then Catriona, leaving only Naida and little Alicia.

"Go next, Alicia," said Naida, "you'll be fine."

"And you'll be fine waiting, won't you?" Alicia replied.

"Yes, my turn will come very soon. And we'll all be together again tonight, to share about our trees!"

Still, Naida was trembling almost as much as Alicia by the time Merida came back for her. "You're the last aren't you?" Merida asked her when she came back. "Come on then."

They flew quickly across a stream up a hill to where Naida could see a small building. Everything was still bare, dark and cold looking, as if expecting the winter snow to return at any moment. Most of the trees that were near the building looked quite dead, but Naida knew they were only sleeping. Or at least she hoped so.

"Now remember the way. You should come back when it starts to get dark. There's no need to stay overnight." Merida was explaining the plan to her. "This is your tree, Naida. Come and hold its trunk here."

Naida looked at the tree and shivered. It seemed so big, and so dead looking.

"Come on, don't be afraid. I'm going to attune you to your tree." Merida put her hands over Naida's and began the process. Naida felt a rush of energy coming through her, not just into her hands but into her whole being. It was different from the feeling of the small plants that they had touched during their training. This was a strong, deep and powerful vitality. Naida felt the tree's energy touching her own life spirit, and binding them together.

"This is your tree, Naida. It is a Catalpa tree. Stay with it now and begin the awakening process." And Merida flew away, leaving Naida still holding onto the trunk of her tree.

Naida slowly took her hands from the trunk and looked up at her tree. It was rather a strange shape. The branches weren't very straight; especially the smaller ones where she hoped the buds would soon form. But there were plenty of branches and she soon began to enjoy herself flying around and landing on different spots. The top of the tree was quite high and she could see across the building to where the stream was, and her home.

Wondering how her friends were doing, Naida looked across to the other trees, but they were too far away to see any signs of life. "Right, all our trees are still sleeping, there's nothing to see yet. I should tell my tree it's time to start waking up!"

Remembering the lessons they had been given, Naida returned to a central place on the trunk of her tree and placed her hands on the bark again. Breathing deeply, she began to communicate with the tree, sharing her energy and letting the tree know it was safe to awaken and start to grow again. After a while she let go. Now it was time to fly to the top and begin the process of warming the twigs and branches and energizing the pre-buds that would become leaves and flowers.

Naida had worked on only a small portion of the branches before she noticed that the light was changing. The sun was getting lower in the sky and she knew it was time to stop. She went back to the trunk to say goodbye to her tree. "I'll be back tomorrow," she whispered. "I hope you can start to wake up!"

When Naida reached home it was bustling with excited fairies who had already returned. Everyone was talking at once and it was like a madhouse. Naida looked for her friend Jayda, but couldn't see her. She went over to Lara and asked if she had seen Jayda yet.

"Oh yes," Lara replied with a nod. "She came back and was talking to Merida and then they flew off together."

Naida looked puzzled, so Lara added, "They didn't say anything, just went back outside. Don't worry. I'm sure they'll be back soon."

Naida turned back to the entrance and sure enough the two of them were just alighting on the branch that served as a step in front of their doorway. Before she could move to greet her friend Merida was clapping her hands to get their attention. "What's all this! Quiet down and prepare dinner. There's a lot to do." Seeing the fairies looked rather downcast at the scolding, she softened her tone and added, "I know you're all excited. There will be plenty of time for sharing once we've all sat down to dinner. Come on now, and let's get organized."

The fairies quickly cleared a space and brought out dishes of food and small cups to hold the celebration nectar that Merida had prepared for them. As soon as each fairy had her cup filled Merida raised hers and said, "Thank you all for your commitment today. Now we have ten trees that are connected to the Great Spirit. Congratulations and long life to you and your trees!"

The fairies raised their cups and repeated "Long life to our trees!" After taking a drink they quickly passed the food around the circle, each taking a selection of the delicacies. Once they were all settled and enjoying the feast Merida spoke again. "So now is the time when some of you can share about your experience today, if you wish. We'll begin with Jayda since she has something to show us. Go ahead Jayda."

Jayda smiled at everyone and then turned to Merida. "I don't know why I have this special tree, but thank you Merida." She brought something out from behind her back, "Look everyone, my tree already has leaves!" There was a buzz of excitement as all the fairies leaned forward for a closer look. Jayda lifted up a long, narrow green object and then passed it to Naida who was sitting next to her. "See, it's from my tree. It was already growing these green skinny leaves so I asked Merida and she said they're called needles, pine needles 'cos I have a Pine tree. Isn't it exciting?"

Naida was turning over the leaf and studying it carefully. "It has a sharp point; I can see why it's called a needle. Careful everyone!"

Lara took it next, and admired it while being careful not to injure herself on the sharp point. "It's a bit sticky, isn't it?" she said, wiping her hand which had gotten some sap on it. "Oh, but it smells quite nice, this sticky stuff!"

Jayda laughed, "Yes, the pine sap is very sticky. I should have warned you about that, but I thought I got it all over myself already and there was none left!"

As the fairies passed the pine needle around Merida asked Jayda to explain how her tree had leaves already. "My Pine tree keeps its leaves throughout the whole winter. It's called an evergreen tree, because it always has green leaves. I think it has these special skinny needles, not big wide leaves, so the snow falls straight off!"

"Mmm, and they're kind of hard, too, so maybe they won't freeze up when it gets too cold?" Naida suggested.

"Or be too heavy and break the branches down if the leaves got lots of snow and ice stuck on them!" Tonya added, passing the needle on to Alicia.

Jayda nodded in agreement, "And it grows new ones in the spring too, so I still have to tell it to wake up now and make new needles. I think they'll be small and cute when they first grow, not as hard as this old needle!" At that everyone laughed. "But I still want this one back if everyone's finished looking at it!"

Jayda, Pine Tree Fairy with Pine Needles

"Thank you very much Jayda for showing everyone your Pine needle and explaining about your tree," Merida was nodding her approval. "Tomorrow we will all go and visit Jayda's Pine tree before everyone goes to take care of your own trees. Does anyone else have something special to share about their tree?"

The fairies looked at each other, but no-one seemed ready to share. In fact, some were already yawning. It had been a long day.

"Alright then, off to bed with you," Merida concluded. "You all worked hard today so get a good rest. I'll clean up, but just for tonight!"

"Wow, good job Jayda," Naida said to her friend as they prepared to settle down for the night. "How exciting to have a green needle leaf to show everyone! I'm looking forward to visiting your tree tomorrow. My tree doesn't have any buds or anything yet."

"Don't worry, Naida. I'm sure your tree will get its leaves when it's time. And then we can all visit your tree!"

Just as Merida had promised, in the morning all the fairies flew together to visit Jayda's tree. Her Pine tree had a tall, straight trunk that seemed to reach right up into the sky. There were lots of big branches, each coming from the main trunk. Smaller branches and twigs covered with the sharp green needles lined each branch, and the fairies delighted in flying around and catching hold of the needles. They were careful, though, not to break them off, aware that the tree was a living being and that each green needle was an important part of it.

Soon it was time to say goodbye to Jayda and to go and take care of their own trees. Naida waved to her friend and flew off happily to find her tree. She was thinking how much fun this was, especially now there was a tree that already had its own green leaves; well, still had last year's leaves she corrected herself. "In any case, it really looks like it's alive. I hope my tree wakes up and looks alive soon!"

To her disappointment, Naida's tree looked just as dead as it had the day before. Even though she hunted around all its branches she found no signs of life. Sighing, she realized she should just go to work and send positive "wake up" messages to the tree. Maybe then she would be able to find its first buds.

Before she found anything that looked even remotely like it would become a leaf, the sun was getting ready to set and Naida had to return home. As she flew back she wondered if maybe no-one else had leaves on their tree yet, so they would just eat dinner and maybe sing some songs together. "That would be nice," she thought.

Most of the fairies arrived home at almost the same time and it seemed that they were all shaking their heads and saying "no leaves yet," to each other. Then Tonya came in carrying something. Merida went over to see her and nodded approvingly when she saw what the fairy had in her hands. Jayda turned to Naida and said, "It looks like we'll have another 'show and tell' tonight! I wonder what Tonya has brought."

As soon as everyone had finished eating Tonya picked up the item she had brought home. The fairies leaned forward trying to figure out what it was. "It's not a leaf, is it?" they asked each other.

"Go ahead, Tonya," Merida announced. "Tell everyone what you discovered about your tree."

"Okay, well my tree doesn't have any leaves yet," Tonya began. "But it has this!" and she held up a piece of white paper-like material. "This covers the trunk of my tree. It's white, and so pretty, isn't it? And it looks kind of like paper. It even peels off really easily like rolls of paper! I think it's such a fun tree!" and Tonya laughed a bit self-consciously. "Don't you all love it?" and she passed the piece of 'paper' around the circle.

"So, is your tree called the White Paper tree, or what?" Catriona asked.

"Um, not exactly," Tonya responded. "Merida told me it's a Birch tree, and because it has white bark its name is the White Birch tree. But because the bark looks like paper, it can be called the Paper Birch too. So maybe I'll call it the White Paper Birch!"

"I like that," said Lara as she studied the piece of bark. "The White Paper Birch tree."

"Can we visit Tonya's White Paper Birch tree tomorrow?" Jayda asked, and the trio of Sylvia, Sophia and Sandra all joined in with a chorus of "Yes please!"

"That's a good idea," Merida agreed. "Any time someone has something interesting to show from her tree we can all go and visit it the next morning. Now, does anyone have anything else to share, or are you all ready for bed?"

Tonya, Paper Birch Tree Fairy with Birch Bark

Everyone looked around, but no one seemed to be ready to volunteer to say anything. In fact, Alicia was already yawning and a couple of the others looked quite tired.

"Bed it is, then," Merida said. "But remember to clean up first!"

The next morning the fairies enjoyed their visit to Tonya's tree. As they approached even from a distance it was easy to see her tree with its white trunk. And when they got closer all the fairies were impressed by how the bark looked just like paper peeling off in a roll from the trunk. "Isn't mine such a cool tree?" Tonya exclaimed proudly as she showed off her tree.

Merida was smiling at how much Tonya was enjoying her tree. "Alright, everyone. Thank you, Tonya, for showing us your wonderful tree. Now it's time to go to work."

But before the fairies could leave, Alicia raised her hand. "Merida," she said rather timidly, her voice shaking a little. "Merida, my tree has white on its trunk too, but it doesn't look like this. The white is kind of powdery, and it comes off when I touch it. And there are some big black marks too. Do you, um, do you think my tree might be sick?"

Merida had turned to look at Alicia, and she said gently, "No, Alicia, you have a different kind of tree. The white powder is normal, and yes it will come off easily. It's nothing to worry about. And the black marks, are they like upside down triangles, on the lower part of the trunk?"

"Yes, I think so."

"Well, those are places where a branch used to be. The lower branches of your tree do tend to fall off leaving those black triangles behind. It's all normal for your tree."

"Oh, thank you Merida. I was worried for a moment, especially after seeing Tonya's tree!"

"Well, that's a lesson for you all. Don't compare your trees. What is normal for one may not be healthy for a different tree. Now it's time for everyone to go and take care of their own trees. We can visit Alicia's tree another day!" Merida clapped her hands and the fairies quickly flew off to their own trees.

The day passed quickly for Naida although once again she found no signs of life on her tree. "Not to worry," she thought. "It's just not ready to wake up yet. In any case, I haven't visited all the places where the leaves should come. I need more time!" She flew home at dusk in quite a cheerful mood.

No one had brought anything from their tree so after dinner Merida asked if anyone wanted to say anything about their tree. Naida raised her hand a bit hesitantly. "Go ahead, Naida," Merida encouraged her. "Well, I realized that I hadn't visited all the places where the leaf buds will be, so maybe my tree shouldn't wake up yet? I mean, what happens if the tree wakes up and not all the buds have been warmed up?"

"That's an intelligent question, Naida. I can see you're concerned about your tree. That's good." Merida looked around. "Does anyone have an answer?"

"Well," Lara said slowly, "I guess if the buds haven't been warmed up and the tree wakes up it would start having leaves at the warmed places and then get more leaves as we warmed up the rest. But it's probably good not to take too long to finish the job, or you'd have half a tree with leaves and the other half still bare!"

"Oh, that sounds bad. I hope I can finish warming all my buds in time. I don't want leaves on only half my tree!" Alicia said looking quite worried.

"In my case you wouldn't notice much," said Jayda with a laugh. "I've got pine needles everywhere already!"

Everyone joined in laughing with Jayda about her Pine tree, even Merida. Then she said, "Yes, that's right. But don't worry everyone; your trees know how to wake up. They will make their leaves and flowers when the time is right as long as you gave the tree plenty of good energy. Now, how about a song before we go to bed? Let's sing something that will make us all happy and ready to give lots of energy to our trees tomorrow!"

They sang several songs before Merida clapped her hands and said it was time to say goodnight. "That was fun, wasn't it?" Jayda said to Naida as they headed for bed. "Yes," Naida replied, "I was thinking yesterday maybe we could sing songs after dinner, so I'm glad we got to do that tonight."

The next morning when Naida arrived at her tree she felt a pang of disappointment. It still looked quite dead. She had to remind herself it was only sleeping, but she thought even a sleeping tree could show a bit of life. Sighing she leaned against the trunk and gently put her hands on its bark. She felt the connection to her tree. There was that special vitality that seemed to come from far down in the depths of the tree, maybe in its roots. "Wake up soon my tree," she whispered. "I want to see how beautiful you are when you have your leaves!"

Then she flew upwards to continue giving warmth to each branch and twig, finding all the possible places for buds to form and gently cupping her hands around them. Naida tried to imagine tiny leaves all curled up inside buds that were still hidden in the ends of the small twigs. She was so focused on her work that she didn't notice the time passing. "Oh my goodness, I'm

16

PRAISE FOR Gillian Flynn AND *Dark Places*

A *Weekend TODAY* "Top Summer Read"

One of *The New Yorker*'s Best Books of 2009

One of *Publishers Weekly*'s Best Books of 2009

"Gillian Flynn is the real deal, a sharp, acerbic, and compelling storyteller with a knack for the macabre."

—Stephen King

"Gillian Flynn's writing is compulsively good. I would rather read her than just about any other crime writer."

—Kate Atkinson

"With her blistering debut *Sharp Objects*, Gillian Flynn hit the ground running. *Dark Places* demonstrates that was no fluke."

—Val McDermid

"Love her or loathe her, Libby Day won't be forgotten without a fight . . . [a] nerve-fraying thriller."

—*New York Times Book Review*

"Flynn follows her deliciously creepy *Sharp Objects* with another dark tale. . . . The story, alternating between the 1985 murders and the present, has a tense momentum that works beautifully. And when the truth emerges, it's so macabre [that] not even twisted little Libby Day could see it coming."

—*People* (4 stars)

"Gillian Flynn coolly demolished the notion that little girls are made of sugar and spice in *Sharp Objects,* her sensuous and chilling first thriller. In *Dark Places,* her equally sensuous and chilling follow-up, Flynn . . . has conjured up a whole new crew of feral and troubled young females . . . [a] propulsive and twisty mystery."

—*Entertainment Weekly*

"Gripping thriller."

—*Cosmopolitan*

"The world of this novel is all underside, all hard flinch, and Flynn's razor-sharp prose intensifies this effect as she knuckles in on every sentence. . . . The slick plotting in *Dark Places* will gratify the lover of a good thriller—but so, too, will Flynn's prose, which is ferocious and unrelenting and pure pleasure from word one."

—*Cleveland Plain Dealer*

"Gillian Flynn's second novel, *Dark Places,* proves that her first—*Sharp Objects*—was no fluke . . . tough, surprising crime fiction that dips its toes in the deeper waters of literary fiction."

—*Chicago Sun-Times*

going to be late! Goodbye tree, I'll be back tomorrow!" she announced as she quickly flew away.

Arriving at home Naida was relieved to see that she hadn't missed anything. Several fairies were still preparing the food and Merida was talking to someone at the side of the room. As Naida alighted, Merida turned and smiled. "Good, everyone is here. Let's begin. And tonight Catriona has something to share, but after we eat!"

Naida took her place beside Jayda and they quickly shared the food. "Isn't it exciting, wondering who will bring something from their tree each night?" Jayda said cheerfully.

"Yes, but I wonder when I will have something to share," Naida responded with less enthusiasm.

"Now, don't worry. Merida said not to compare, each tree will produce its leaves in its own good time."

"Easy for you to say, Jayda. You have the evergreen tree; it always has leaves!" Naida couldn't stay morose for long, and was already laughing as she said that to her friend.

Jayda laughed too; glad to see her friend was in good spirits again.

"Now, quiet everyone and let's see what Catriona has brought for us!" Merida announced.

"Wait!" Sylvia stood up suddenly. "I have something to show too. My tree is so beautiful, let me show mine first!"

"Oh, yes, we want to see what Sylvia brought!" Sophia was excited.

"Yes, yes, Sylvia's tree is beautiful. Let's see hers first," Sandra joined in.

Catriona looked doubtfully at Merida. "Well," she began, nervously, "if Sylvia really wants to ..."

"No, Sylvia, Catriona came home first. Let her show what she brought and then you can show yours." Merida was firm.

Sylvia sat down shaking her head, and turned to whisper to her friends.

Catriona looked around, still unsure. The other fairies were looking at each other, unsettled by Sylvia and her trio.

Then Lara spoke up. "Come on Catriona, let's see what you brought. We all want to find out what kind of tree you have."

Catriona slowly reached behind her and brought out something that clearly was not a leaf.

"What is it?" the fairies asked. "That looks funny!" "Is it really from your tree?"

"Yes, it's from my tree. It's kind of like flowers. But they're all grouped together tightly in a bunch and they hang down from the little branch. They look so pretty on my tree!" Catriona was getting quite excited and she was waving her "flower bunch" around so much that powder was flying off it.

"Oh, what's that stuff?" Lara, who was sitting next to her, started sneezing.

"Goodness, Catriona, pass it around so we can see it before you break it!" "Yes, pass it around!" came the chorus.

"But what is it, Catriona?" Lara asked. "It's not a normal flower surely. Does it have a name?"

"Oh yes, I forgot. It's a catkin! Isn't that a great name? Cat-kin. I love it!" Catriona was laughing gleefully.

"But do you have leaves?" Daniela asked. "Don't the leaves come first before the flowers?"

"No, no leaves," Catriona looked a bit downcast. "My tree has catkins first. But it will get leaves later. I'm sure it will get leaves later. At least I hope so," and she looked expectantly at Merida.

"Yes, Catriona. The catkins come first on your tree. Now what is the name of your tree? Do you remember?"

"Oh goodness, I'm just so excited about the catkin I forgot to tell you all that my tree is called a Willow tree. And it has a tall trunk and then all these long branches that hang down and it grows by the water, and it almost looks like it was crying and made a big pool of tears so it's called a Weeping Willow tree. At least I think so." Catriona was smiling as she said all of it in a torrent of words without taking a breath. "But I don't know why I have a weeping tree, I'm a jolly fairy!"

And that made everyone laugh.

Catriona, Weeping Willow Tree Fairy with Catkin

When she finished laughing, Sylvia looked at Merida, "Can I show what I've brought now?"

"Yes, it's your turn now. Everyone pay attention to what Sylvia has brought for us."

Sylvia took something quite small from behind her. The fairies leaned forward trying to see what it was.

"It's a flower!" Sylvia said proudly. "It's not a catkin, it's a real flower. It's red and so pretty. There are bunches of them but I picked just one to show everyone. There are so many of them on my tree today. My tree looks like it has a red dress on!"

She passed the flower to Sophia and Sandra who were sitting beside her as usual. "Oh and my tree is a Maple tree. It has many thick branches reaching up to the sky. It looks so strong, but it's really pretty with all its red flowers! But no leaves yet. I guess the leaves will come after the flowers."

Sylvia, Silver Maple Tree Fairy with Flower

"Thank you, Sylvia. That's a very good description of your tree!" Merida nodded at Sylvia and all the fairies who were busy admiring the red flower. Sylvia smiled contentedly. Her friends Sophia and Sandra were smiling too. Naida could see that they were hoping their trees would produce flowers next.

Since Catriona's and Sylvia's trees had produced flowers, or catkins, before its leaves, the other fairies were wondering about their own trees and whether they would get flowers, or catkins, or leaves first. Merida heard them and smiled. "Don't worry, each tree has its own schedule. Just take care of your own tree and let us know when something happens. Now, shall we visit Catriona's tree tomorrow and see its catkins?" A buzz of enthusiasm ensued.

"Ooh, yes, I want to see the catkins!"

"And I want to see the weeping branches!"

"And afterwards we'll all go to see Sylvia's tree with its beautiful red flowers," Merida added, smiling at Sylvia who immediately responded with a smile of her own.

In the morning they all took off in the direction of Catriona's tree. She was so excited she flew up and down and around the group. "Catriona, calm down, you're making me feel dizzy just watching you!" Merida called out to her.

But the little fairy just laughed and flew faster towards her tree. "Come on everyone, let's see my catkin tree!"

Her tree was easy to recognize as soon as they got closer. It had many long thin branches hanging down, making almost a complete circle around the trunk. As they drew closer they could see the bright yellow catkins hanging down from stems on the branches. It was a lovely sight.

Catriona was even more excited. "Oh there are so many catkins now! Yesterday there were just a few. Look how many catkins there are!"

"Now I know why Catriona is so excited," Naida said to Jayda. "Just look at all those catkins! Aren't they special?"

Some of the fairies were exploring the branches. Sylvia called Sophia and Sandra over to one of the long hanging branches. "Here, let's try holding the end of this branch and flying with it."

Sylvia, Sophia and Sandra swinging on Weeping Willow branch

As they flew the end of the branch came with them. "Now, hold on," Sylvia shouted, "and let's swing!" The three fairies held on to the end of the branch as it swung back to its original position, and further, and then back again. It was swinging like a pendulum!

"Oh, look, they're having so much fun! Let's swing too!" Daniela called out. "Come on, everyone, let's swing this branch!" And a whole group grabbed the end of another branch and made it swing, even further than Sylvia's branch. Of course, not to be outdone, Sylvia called her friends to swing their branch again and they flew so far and high that Merida noticed and called out to them to be careful. "Don't break it, fairies! And be careful you don't crash into another branch, or us!"

Catriona was clapping her hands at all the fun everyone was having. "See, my tree isn't a sad weeping tree at all. It's a fun tree! Don't you all love it?"

"Yes, Catriona, it's a lovely tree. Thank you for showing it to us. But it will be weeping if you all play too much and break its branches," Merida warned. "Let's quickly go and visit Sylvia's tree now."

Sylvia led the way, and stopped a short distance from her tree. The group of fairies hovered looking at her tree, admiring the beautiful red flowers that covered it.

"Ooh, it's so beautiful, Sylvia," Sophia said.

"Yes, it's just like a red dress," Sandra agreed.

Merida smiled. "Let's go closer and take a look at the flowers. But be careful not to break them off," she warned.

With Sylvia leading the way the fairies flew around her tree, noting how the flowers grew in clusters along the twigs. Although there were buds, there was still no sign of leaves. Finally, Merida called them back together and told them it was time to go and work on their own trees. Waving goodbye to Sylvia with a chorus of thank you's for showing them her tree, the other fairies set off happily.

Naida was quite optimistic as she arrived at her tree. She thought it was wonderful the way Catriona had been so excited about her tree, and how everyone had enjoyed playing with the long branches and with the catkins of course, and how beautiful Sylvia's tree was with all those red flowers. "I do hope my tree has something special I can share with everyone," she thought. "But it has to wake up first!"

As the next few days passed Naida tried hard to maintain her enthusiasm and keep smiling. She spent every day warming the ends of the twigs on her tree, and encouraging it to wake up, and every evening she came home to find another of the fairies all excited about their trees.

The other members of the little trio who spent so much time together brought home news from their trees. Sophia came home with a little bunch of green flowers. "It's not a catkin, is it Merida?" she asked.

"No, it's a cluster of flowers attached to that long stem. But they hang down like catkins."

Sophia smiled happily. "And they're really beautiful!"

So everyone wanted to see Sophia's flowers on their hanging stems and the group visited her tree the next morning. Sophia's tree was also a Maple tree, like Sylvia's, but a different kind. Merida explained, "When you see their leaves you'll understand why they're both called Maples, but they are also different."

"Yes, mine has red flowers, and Sophia's are green and hanging on these stem things!" Sylvia said immediately. "Of course they're different!"

"Well, maybe the leaves will be the same, and that's why they're both Maples," Sophia suggested.

"And mine is a kind of Maple too!" added Sandra. "But I'm sure it's different from both of yours as well!"

"So we're like triplets, the same but different!" Sylvia said with a laugh, hugging her two dear friends.

Merida smiled, "Of course!"

"I just wonder what kind of leaves they will all have," Jayda said to Naida.

"Well, at any rate they won't be like your needles!" Naida responded.

Daniela's tree produced greenish colored catkins and also small leaves, so she was very excited. "Look, I've got leaves on my tree, and little catkins! It's called a Red Mulberry, but it's not red, at least not yet!"

Lara's tree produced leaves too, but no flowers. "But look at my leaves, they're such an interesting shape! My tree is the Oak tree. Come and see it everyone!"

Tonya's Birch tree produced catkins, and by the time the group visited it there were also tiny leaves appearing.

And little Alicia's tree also produced catkins, much to her delight. "I do love these catkins," she said. "I'm so glad my Aspen tree has catkins too."

Sylvia's and Sophia's trees produced leaves almost at the same time. They compared their leaves carefully. Each leaf was green with five lobes.

Lara, Oak Tree Fairy with Leaf

"Now I understand why our trees have the same name!" Sophia said. "Look, the leaves are almost the same shape!"

25

"You know, my tree is the Silver Maple," Sylvia said. "I wonder why? I don't see anything silver about my tree."

"Oh look, Sylvia," Sophia said. "Look at the underside of your leaf compared to mine!"

"Oh yes, I see!" Sylvia responded excitedly. "Yours is just a light green underneath but mine has a silvery look to it. Oh, that's it!"

Sophia, Sugar Maple Tree Fairy with Leaf

The two fairies had shown their leaves together at dinner, explaining the difference between their two types of Maple tree. "Good job," Merida had complimented them. "Your trees are related, but they have differences. Shall we go and see both trees tomorrow?"

A few days later Sandra's tree suddenly produced leaves too, but she was a bit worried. "My leaves are so dark, they look strange. Is that right, Merida?" she had asked.

"Yes, Sandra," Merida replied. "Do you remember the name of your tree?"

"Yes, it's a Maple." Sandra said, looking puzzled. "Oh, it's the Crimson King Maple – does that mean it has red leaves?"

"That's right!" Merida said laughing. "Not quite red, but a reddish purple color. I suppose that's what crimson means!"

Sandra, Crimson King Maple Tree Fairy with Leaf

"Oh, let's all visit the Crimson King Maple and see its red colored leaves!" Sylvia said, delighted that the third member of their trio had leaves on their tree too.

When they visited Sandra's tree the fairies all agreed that her leaves were special. Most of them had seen only green leaves before, at least in the spring time when they were young and fresh. Sylvia and Sophia were especially interested since the leaves looked very similar to those on their Maple trees, just a different color.

"Are there more kinds of Maple trees with still more different colored leaves?" Sylvia asked.

"Well," Merida, responded. "There certainly are more kinds of Maple tree, but I don't think they have different colors, more like different shapes. You see your leaves all have quite wide lobes? There's another kind of Maple that has skinny lobes. My friend has one of those trees. It's called a Japanese Maple and it has reddish colored leaves like yours, Sandra."

"Ooh, can we visit it sometime?" Sandra asked eagerly. "I'd like to see another tree with these dark leaves."

"Well, it's quite far away." Merida said hesitantly. "I'm not sure if we can go there this year. But maybe next year," she said quickly, seeing Sandra's disappointed look. "You all have a lot to do to take care of your trees, so let's get back to work now."

Naida's tree was still the same, and she worked diligently to try to encourage it to awaken soon. She realized that almost all the other trees had already woken up, and she was starting to feel somewhat uneasy. "What if my tree never wakes up?" she thought anxiously. However, her concern for her tree was soon forgotten when she arrived home. The trio of Maple tree fairies were all abuzz with excitement.

"There's a bird in Sophia's tree!"

"Yes, a big bird! I think it's building a bed." Sophia was excited but slightly worried at the same time.

"Calm down everyone," Merida's voice was heard above the hubbub. "Let's all settle down in our circle and when we're ready Sophia can share her news."

As soon as they were ready, all eyes turned to Sophia. "Can we hear about the bird now?" Alicia could hardly contain herself and her eyes were big like saucers. "Is it really big and scary?"

"Alright, Sophia," Merida said. "Tell us about your bird."

"Well, it's in my tree." Sophia said. "At least it keeps flying away and coming back carrying things, sticks and leaves and stuff. And it's building something in a fork in a branch. Actually I think there are two of them. One of them does all the building and the other one flies around a lot."

"What kind of bird is it Sophia?" Sylvia asked.

"I don't know what it's called," Sophia said shaking her head. "But it has red color on its front, and it's big, and it sings really loud!"

They all laughed at that. As the laughter died down Merida said "It must be a Robin. They are not very afraid of Big Ones so it could build its nest in one of our trees."

"It's making a nest?" Sophia asked. "Will it come and live in my tree all the time when it's ready?"

"No," Merida replied. "Robins build a nest to put their eggs in. The mother Robin, she's the one building the nest, she'll stay with the eggs till they hatch and then both Robins will feed the babies."

"And baby Robins will come out of the eggs?" Naida had heard the part about putting eggs in the nest. "Goodness, you'll have a tree full of birds, Sophia!"

"Oh dear, I'm a bit scared of that bird." Sophia looked less enthusiastic. "I hope it won't try and eat me!"

"Oh, no, that's terrible!" Alicia was shaking in horror. "Merida, can we chase the bird away? I don't want it to eat Sophia!"

"We'll protect you, Sophia," Sylvia said bravely. "Right, Sandra?"

"Um, sure. Or maybe Sophia can come to my Crimson King Maple tree till the Robins are gone."

"Now, now," Merida tried to calm them all down. "Robins are not bad birds. Just don't get too close and you'll be fine Sophia. The Robin is busy building her nest so she won't bother you if you just focus on taking care of your tree. But when the eggs come let us know and we'll all visit together to take a look."

"Alright, Merida. I'll be careful. But can you come with me tomorrow to make sure it's a Robin and not a dangerous bird?"

"Yes, Sophia, I can do that. Now everyone, that's enough excitement for today. Off to bed with you all!"

The next day Merida went with Sophia as promised. Naida and Jayda watched them leave together. "Sophia must be brave to have a big bird live in her tree, don't you think?" Naida said.

"Hmm, yes, I suppose so. But it's kind of an honor really, don't you think, to have a bird choose your tree to make its nest? I'm not sure birds would like my Pine tree; those needles are kind of sharp!"

"Well my tree doesn't have any leaves at all, so that's not much good either!" Naida responded. And the two friends laughed together before departing for their trees.

That evening Alicia came home clutching a small leaf. "It doesn't look so exciting by itself," she said. "But you have to come and see my tree tomorrow! When all the leaves are on the tree they talk to me!"

The other fairies looked at her in disbelief. "Alicia, come on, leaves don't talk!" they said.

"Well, not really talking like we do. But they kind of shake if there's any breeze at all, and they make this whispering sound. It's lovely!"

"What do they say?" Tonya asked. "I mean, you said they talk to you!"

"Oh, well," Alicia looked confused. "Um, I guess they talk their own language 'cos I don't understand any words. At least not yet," she added.

The fairies were still shaking their heads and passing the small leaf around. "It doesn't make a noise at all when I shake it," said Sylvia. "I think she's imagining it!"

"No, no, I'm not! Don't be mean." Alicia was almost crying. "Just come and see my tree tomorrow." She looked at Merida. "Please, Merida, let's all visit my tree tomorrow. Then you'll all hear my leaves."

Merida smiled at Alicia. "Of course we'll visit your tree tomorrow. Don't worry, I believe you about your leaves."

"Thank you, Merida. I know I didn't imagine it. Everyone can hear them tomorrow."

Alicia, Quaking Aspen Tree Fairy with Leaf

But that night the fairies were awakened by bright lights and loud booming sounds. It was a thunderstorm! As they huddled together, trying not to be afraid each time the lightning flashed and the thunder roared, they began to worry about their trees.

"Merida, will our trees be alright in this storm?" Alicia asked fearfully.

"Well, your leaves should be doing more than whispering tonight!" Sylvia said and everyone laughed.

Merida looked around. "I hope so, our trees are strong. But it is a bad storm. So everyone sit quietly and think of your tree. And send good thoughts to your tree. Remember you are connected to your trees so they will feel the good vibrations you send them."

The group gathered in a circle. They each sat with their legs crossed and their hands clasped together. Merida began to sing quietly, and the others joined in, nervously at first but gradually gaining in confidence.

Suddenly there was an especially bright flash that lit up the sky, followed almost immediately by a loud crack of thunder. And then Jayda screamed! She clutched her arm and fell over gasping and crying.

Naida rushed to her side and put her arms around her. "Jayda, Jayda, what happened? I'm here, it's going to be alright!"

Merida told the other fairies to keep concentrating on their own trees and moved over to Jayda and Naida. "It's my arm," Jayda said between sobs. "Oh my arm, it hurts so much!"

"Let's take her to her bed. Naida help me." Merida looked very serious and Naida quickly helped support her friend over to their bed. "Stay with her, Naida," Merida ordered. "Hold her other hand and share good energy with her. I'll make her a special hot drink."

Naida held on to her friend's hand. She could feel it was cold, so she forced herself to be calm and focus on sending good energy to her. Jayda was looking quite pale, but she managed a smile as Naida began to feel warmth circulating between them.

"Drink this," Merida said as she came back carrying a cup of steaming liquid. "And then sleep."

Jayda took a sip and made a face.

"I know, it doesn't taste good. But drink it down. Naida, stay with her. Make sure she drinks it all! I have to go back and take care of the others now."

As Merida returned to the circle, all the fairies looked at her with worried expressions. "Will she be alright?" was the question they all wanted to ask.

"Is everyone else alright?" was what Merida asked.

"Yes, we're fine," chorused the fairies.

"But will Jayda be alright?" Lara asked.

"I believe so," Merida responded. "She's drinking the special tea I made and Naida is taking care of her. I believe Jayda's tree was struck by lightning and a branch has broken off, that's why her arm hurts. We'll find out in the morning. Now, I think the storm has passed, all I can hear is rain. So we can all go back to bed. And let's be thankful that no-one else is hurt!"

Lara went over to the bed where Jayda was lying, propped up so she could drink the tea. "How is she?" she asked Naida. "Merida seems to think she'll be okay."

"Yes, she's almost finished this drink. Apparently it tastes awful!" Jayda managed a rueful smile as Naida said that.

"I can take the cup back. You are going to sleep here with her aren't you?" said Lara.

"Thanks. Yes, I'm staying here," and Naida helped her friend lie down and then settled down beside her. Naida didn't really expect to sleep, but Jayda fell asleep immediately and so Naida found herself drifting off to sleep too.

It seemed like no time at all had passed before it was already morning. The sun was streaming in to their home. Everything outside seemed to be sparkling as the light caught the raindrops that were all that was left of last night's frightening event.

As the other fairies woke up and busied themselves preparing for the day, Naida sat up carefully and looked at her friend. Jayda was still asleep. Although her face was pale, she seemed to be breathing normally. Naida breathed a sigh of relief, hoping that everything would turn out alright.

Merida came over to check on them and smiled at Naida. "She has slept well, that's good. Sleep is very healing you know. You stay here with her for now while I organize everyone else."

Merida gathered the other fairies around her. First she addressed Alicia, "I'm sorry, Alicia. We won't be visiting your tree this morning. I have to tend to Jayda and her tree."

"Oh, of course, please take care of Jayda," Alicia replied nodding her agreement. "Are you going to see Jayda's tree now?"

"Yes, I will bring Jayda to her tree with Naida's help. Perhaps I need one more?"

"I'm ready to help," Lara volunteered immediately. "I'm strong like my Oak tree. I can help to carry her if we need to!"

"Thank you Lara, that would be very helpful. Now, the rest of you, please go quickly to your trees to make sure they are alright. Comfort them if they seem agitated. You know how to do that, just put your hands on the center of the main trunk and think comforting, warm thoughts. And try to feel calm yourselves. I will come and visit each one of you later in the day. Go now!"

The remaining seven fairies quickly took off towards their trees. Merida noticed that the trio of Sylvia, Sophia and Sandra were flying together and smiled, realizing they were going together to see their trees. Lara saw her watching them and smiled too. "Yes, those three stick together. Is that why you gave them all Maple trees?"

"Yes, that's right. They can help each other today and that's not a bad thing. Come on now, we have a job to do to take care of Jayda and her tree."

Jayda was awake now and Naida had brought her some water to drink.

"Are you ready to go and see your tree Jayda?" Merida asked. "I've got Naida and Lara to help you, so you hardly have to fly at all."

"Ok," Jayda managed a brave smile. "I think I will need some help. My arm feels very strange this morning and I'm quite weak."

The group arranged themselves so that they could fly without causing Jayda additional pain and soon they approached her tree. "Oh," Jayda gasped as they drew closer. "Oh no, there's pieces of my tree on the ground. And, oh, I can see where a whole branch broke off. Oh, my poor tree!" Tears were streaming down her face.

Naida could feel her pain as she held onto her friend. "Merida, what do we do?"

Merida looked around and said, "Let's sit down here on this strong branch, close to the trunk. Naida and Lara, you stay with Jayda, hold on to her so she doesn't fall. I'm going to investigate." Merida flew away, first circling around to where the branch had broken off, and then around the tree looking at the pieces on the ground. She came back to the others to report. "Yes, that big branch broke off, and it brought some other smaller branches down with it. But the main problem is the big branch."

Jayda was looking quite worried. "What do I do? I need to help my tree!"

"Yes, Jayda, you will help your tree. Put your good hand on the trunk and talk to your tree. Naida, Lara, you each put one hand on the trunk and with your other hand hold onto Jayda. That way you will be able to connect to Jayda's tree and send it comforting energy. Alright?"

The three fairies did as Merida directed, and soon they were swaying slightly together as they each had one hand connected to the tree.

"I'm going to look around, and I'll be right back," Merida said and she flew away.

Naida watched her go, wondering what would happen next. "I can feel your tree, Jayda," she said softly. "It feels like it's crying."

"Yes," Jayda whispered. "We're both crying. It hurts."

"Don't worry," Lara said. "I can feel a lot of strength. It's going to be alright."

Just then there was a lot of noise down below and Merida came flying back. "Hold on tight, fairies," she said. "The Big Ones are coming to help!"

"Oh, what are they doing?" Jayda couldn't see them.

"Someone is coming with a big ladder. Oh, they're climbing up to the broken branch!"

Naida's eyes opened wide. "I've never seen a Big One so close before! Are we safe?"

"Yes," Merida said, trying to appear confident although Naida could see she was nervous. "They're going to do something to the broken branch. Oh my goodness, they've got that cutting machine! It will be loud, but don't let go. And try to keep the tree calm!"

As the Big One reached the broken branch he lifted a machine and a roar suddenly started up, seeming even louder than last night's thunder. The fairies cowered against the tree, but they kept holding on tightly and determinedly thinking positive thoughts to the tree. As the chainsaw cut into the branch Jayda's whole body shook and Merida also supported her to prevent her from falling.

"It will be quick, just hold on," she said. And sure enough the terrible noise soon stopped, and a piece of the branch fell to the ground. "See, he's cut off the broken piece. Now it doesn't look so bad."

"He's going back down," said Lara. "But there's another Big One with him, a smaller one. He's carrying something too. Oh my goodness, he's coming up now!"

The smaller of the two was now climbing the ladder. When he reached the branch he took a brush out of the can he was carrying and starting painting the end that had just been cut.

"Oh, that feels good!" Jayda exclaimed. "Is it medicine?"

"Yes, he's putting some medicine on the end of the branch to help it heal. It will seal it up so it won't get infected," Merida was watching him. "You see, the Big Ones here are doing a good job of taking care of these trees, that's why we can come and help them."

"But they don't know we're here, do they?" Naida wondered. "I mean, I'm glad they're doing a good job but they're still awfully big and I'm a bit scared of them."

"Don't worry, they can't see us!" Merida reassured the three fairies. "I've never met a Big One that could see us fairies, although sometimes it seems they can hear us laughing!"

"Should we try it?" Lara suggested. And, of course, that immediately made them all laugh.

"I don't know if they could hear us," Naida said still chuckling. "I was laughing too much to see them!"

"Oh, I think the smaller one that put the medicine on might have heard us," Jayda said. "He looked up when we all started laughing. I hope he did. I wanted to thank him for making me and my tree feel better."

The loud noise started again. Although it was loud, this time it didn't shake the tree. Merida looked down and said they were just cutting up the broken branch that had fallen off the tree. The noise lasted a short while and then there was silence again.

"Oh, look," Naida said. "They're picking up all the pieces of the broken branch and putting them into that cart to take away. And I can see they're taking the smaller branches that fell down too. Isn't that nice?"

"Yes, it's all going to look beautiful here again, thanks to them." Lara was nodding. "Are you feeling better, now Jayda?"

"Yes, thank you. My arm feels a bit strange, but I think it's going to be alright soon. I'll just sit here for the rest of the day, though; I don't think I can fly around yet."

"That's right, Jayda," Merida agreed. "Stay where you are and keep connected to your tree. I'll come back for you at the end of the day and help you fly home. Now, Naida and Lara, thank you very much for your help. You did a great job! It's time for you to go to your own trees now. I'll come and see each of you soon. And tonight you can all report on what happened to Jayda's tree!"

Naida hesitated, but Lara took her hand and pulled her away and the two fairies flew off waving to Jayda as they left.

As she had promised, Merida spent the day visiting each fairy and checking that their trees had not suffered any damage. Of course each tree had a collection of flowers and/or leaves strewn around that had fallen off, and some had some small twigs on the ground beside their trees. But none had sustained any serious injury.

Naida was the last to be visited.

"Everything all right here, Naida?" Merida asked as she flew up. "You did such a good job taking care of Jayda last night and today. I really want to thank you for that. You're a good friend."

"Thanks." Naida said. "She is my friend and I just wanted her to be okay, and her tree too. It will be alright now won't it?"

"Yes, I'm confident it will heal. Don't worry, trees are strong and they are used to storms."

"Is everyone else's tree alright?"

"Yes, thank goodness. And your tree looks like it just lost a few small twigs, nothing serious."

"Right. It feels the same as always. Not very awake." Naida smiled. "I was kind of hoping that noisy storm would wake it up!"

"Well, that's a novel idea!" Merida said as they both laughed. "Alright, it's almost time to go home. Do you want to come with me to Jayda's tree so we can go home together?"

"Oh yes, please! That would be lovely," Naida was already in the air ready to go.

Jayda was looking much better when they reached her Pine tree, but she was grateful to have their support to fly home. When they arrived they saw all the other fairies were already there. As soon as they saw Jayda they all rushed over to find out what had happened. Lara had only said that Jayda and her tree were doing okay when she left them. She wanted Jayda to be able to tell the tale of how the Big Ones had come to help.

Merida immediately told the excited fairies to prepare dinner and be quiet. "Jayda is fine, and she will tell you everything once we have eaten. Now, let's make her a place to sit while everyone else prepares the food."

As soon as they were ready, everyone sat looking expectantly at Jayda, who began to feel rather shy. "Um, is everyone else alright? I mean, did anyone else's tree get damaged?" she asked hesitantly.

"We're all fine!" was the chorus.

"All my flowers were blown away!" said Daniela. "But they would have fallen off soon anyway so my tree wasn't upset."

"My leaves were still shaking a lot," said Alicia. "But you will have to come to see it to hear what my tree was saying!"

"Even my Robin's nest is still there," Sophia replied, looking almost disappointed.

"Good thing it didn't have eggs yet," Sandra said. "The mother Robin would have been scared trying to protect them from the storm."

"Alright, enough already!" Sylvia was impatient. "We want to hear your story, Jayda. Tell us!"

So Jayda told the group about the big broken branch lying on the ground, and how there were a lot of smaller branches that had fallen down too. She explained how Merida had told them all to hold on to the tree and to each other and to send it healing energy, and how they had been doing that while Merida was flying around. Then she looked at the other fairies and said, "And then the Big Ones came!"

There was a big gasp from the group, and several fairies looked terrified. "Big Ones? Oh no! What did they do?"

Jayda laughed and explained how they had brought a ladder and climbed up to help her tree. The smaller one had painted medicine on the end of the broken branch and it had felt so good. She said that they had all laughed when Merida said that Big Ones could sometimes hear fairies laughing, and maybe the smaller one had heard them. But then she looked seriously at the group. "The Big Ones brought a very noisy machine and they cut the broken end of the branch off before they put the medicine on. That hurt, and it was so loud!"

Again the other fairies gasped in horror. This time Lara calmed them by saying that the noise didn't last long and the Big One was quite good at working the machine so there was no danger to them. At least she was trying to believe that.

Then Jayda continued, "And then they cut up the big branch that fell down and put the pieces in a cart to take away. They even cleaned up the branches from the ground too, so it looks all pretty around my tree again. I'm so glad the Big Ones came to help!"

Merida nodded and reminded everyone that they were assigned to these trees because the Big Ones were doing their best to take care of them. "Let's all be thankful that we have good Big Ones to help us care for our trees!"

"Yes, thank you Big Ones," the fairies chorused.

"And now off to bed. That was a very exciting day and we didn't get much sleep last night."

"Can we all visit Jayda's tree tomorrow, and see where the branch broke?" Sylvia asked. "It would be nice to see how the Big Ones helped one of our trees," she said to convince Merida.

"Well," Merida hesitated. "Perhaps it would be a useful lesson. Does everyone want to see Jayda's tree?"

"Oh yes, please!" came the responses immediately. Merida smiled. "I suppose that's the plan then! Jayda, we'll all come with you tomorrow to see your tree. Maybe we can all give it some extra healing energy to help it get well." Then she looked at Alicia. "Oh, Alicia, I'm sorry. We were supposed to visit your tree tomorrow. What shall we do?"

"Oh, that's fine. Let's go to Jayda's tree. And then Jayda won't have to fly all the way to my tree, it's quite far. She probably needs to conserve her strength for her own tree right now. My tree can wait."

"That's very kind of you, Alicia," Merida looked at the little fairy approvingly. "And don't worry; we'll all visit your tree soon! Now quickly clean up and everyone go to sleep."

The next morning as promised they all accompanied Jayda to her Pine tree. The fairies were horrified to see where the branch had broken off, remembering how beautifully symmetrical the tree had been before. But they were fascinated with the perfectly cut edge and the way the special medicine covered the end so it wouldn't get diseased.

"Does it still hurt, Jayda?" asked Daniela.

"A bit," Jayda admitted. "But it feels so much better since the Big Ones came and fixed it."

"I hope the Big Ones won't come back today," Alicia was looking around nervously. "I'm still scared of them, even if they are helping our trees." Sylvia and her friends started laughing just then, and Alicia looked even more worried. "I thought you said they could hear us when we laugh. Better be quiet or they might come to find out what's going on!"

"Oh Alicia, don't worry," Lara said with a smile. "Only the little one seemed to hear us, and that's probably because he was very close to the tree. I'm sure they can't hear us from far away, right Merida?"

"Well, no-one really knows what the Big Ones can hear. But I agree with Lara, if there are no Big Ones close enough for us to see them I'm sure they can't hear us." Merida replied. "Now, let's all make a circle around Jayda's tree and give it some healing energy."

The fairies arranged themselves around the trunk close to the broken branch. Each one held the trunk with one hand and touched the next fairy's shoulder with their other hand. Naida was next to Jayda and as all of them began to concentrate she felt a warm tingling sensation traveling through her connecting the tree and all the fairies in a powerful energy circle. She looked at Jayda and saw that although her were eyes closed she was smiling. It seemed that the energy was healing her too.

When they finished Jayda opened her eyes and looked up at the group. She thanked them all, "That felt so good. I feel so much stronger now. And my tree is pleased you all came and helped it heal too."

Naida gave her friend a quick hug before she left. "I'm so happy you feel better, Jayda."

When Naida reached her tree her heart sank with disappointment again. There was still no sign of life. She flew around and diligently tried to warm up each place she thought a leaf or flower might appear. But there were still no buds so it seemed to be a thankless task.

Finally, she sat on a branch and sighed. "I just don't understand," she said to her tree. "What do you need me to do so you can wake up?" Of course the tree didn't respond. "Please, I've been trying to wake you up for so long. Everyone else's tree has leaves or flowers or both already!" Still nothing from the tree. "Come on, I'm really trying! I want to believe in you. I want to know what kind of tree you are. I've never seen a real Catalpa tree, so I want to see your leaves and flowers. Please!"

In her frustration Naida was almost going to kick her tree, but she stopped herself just in time. "Oh, dear, that won't help. I'm sorry, tree. I will give you one more hug and good energy and then I'm going home."

Naida put both her hands on the trunk and bent her head to touch it too. She sent all her good energy to the tree for a long time. After a while she began to feel the tree's response. There was an energy there, different from Jayda's Pine tree. It seemed to be coming from deep down in the tree, almost in its roots. Naida felt better and began to smile. "Thank you tree. I believe you're feeling me. I'll wait for you to wake up. I'm sure you know when the right time is for you to make buds. Now I have to go home, but I'll be back tomorrow."

Naida flew home with her heart feeling lighter. She was pleased to see Jayda was already there and went over to see how she was. "Are you feeling better?"

"Yes, Naida. I'm much stronger today. And my tree is definitely healing."

Alicia flew in and joined them. "Oh Jayda, I'm glad you're feeling better. I don't know if I could survive if something like that happened to my tree. You're so much stronger than I am!"

The three of them laughed and hugged each other.

"Oh Alicia, you're strong in your own way," Jayda responded.

"And I can't wait to see your tree tomorrow." Naida added. "Will it talk to us?"

"I hope so," Alicia said. "It only needs a slight breeze, so we'll see. And I'm thrilled you'll all come to see it tomorrow. I hope we can see your tree soon, Naida?"

Naida was about to reply when Merida called them all to the circle. "We'll be visiting Alicia's tree tomorrow. And then we just have Naida's tree left to visit. Naida, can you tell us all something about your tree?"

"Oh, goodness," Naida looked down in embarrassment. "Well, there's not much to tell. It hasn't woken up yet. But I can feel its energy, deep down, like in its roots. I'm sure it will wake up soon."

"What does it look like?" Lara asked. "Does it have big strong branches that can hold everyone like my Oak tree? Or is it tall like Jayda's."

"No," Naida replied uncertainly. "It doesn't look very special. Its branches aren't straight, or especially thick or thin. Some of them are a bit twisted actually. It just looks like it hasn't woken up yet," she finished lamely seeing Sylvia and her friends starting to whisper and chuckle.

"Well," Merida said. "I think we should all visit Naida's tree the day after tomorrow, even if it hasn't woken up yet. That way we'll have all seen each other's trees at least once. Alright, Naida?"

Naida nodded without enthusiasm. "I'd rather everyone came when it has woken up," she muttered.

As they made their way to bed Jayda took Naida's arm comfortingly. "Don't worry, I'm sure everything will work out."

"I don't know about that. But I did talk to my tree today, and I could feel its energy so I'm sure it will wake up eventually." Naida responded. "I just don't know what a Catalpa tree looks like!"

"Well, I didn't know anything about Pine trees either, and I certainly didn't expect it to get struck by lightning!" and the friends laughed as they settled down for the night.

The next morning Alicia was very excited, fluttering around everywhere and getting in the other fairies' way. "Calm down, Alicia!" Merida said sternly. "We're going to see your tree, and we need you to focus and lead the way. Is everyone ready?"

With a chorus of assent the group took off following Alicia. As she had said, her tree was further away than the others, although it still didn't take long to reach it. "Look, my Aspen tree!" Alicia said proudly as it came into view.

The fairies flew up to the tree which was standing by itself on a small mound. It had many of the flat leaves like the one Alicia had brought. As they gathered around to admire it, a bit of a breeze picked up and all the leaves started trembling. "Listen, can you hear my tree talking!" Alicia called out excitedly.

"Goodness, it does sound like its whispering!" Naida was excited too as the leaves continued fluttering the breeze.

"Yes, I hear it!" Jayda and Lara said together, and the other fairies nodded in agreement. Even Sylvia and her friends were laughing and agreeing that Alicia's tree was "talking."

"But can you understand what it says?" Tonya asked.

"Oh, Tonya, you asked me that already," Alicia shook her head. "It just sounds like whispering, like the leaves are talking to each other."

"Maybe they don't want you to know what they're saying!" Sylvia suggested with a laugh. "Oh," Alicia looked sad for a moment. "Merida, do you understand what my tree is saying?"

All the fairies turned to Merida expectantly.

"No, I don't know what your leaves are talking about, just they sound excited to have so many of us visiting them."

Alicia nodded, and then added, "Maybe they're a bit shy, and don't think what they have to say is interesting to us fairies."

"Well, that's a novel idea. But if anyone is going to understand what they are saying it will be you, because this is your tree." Merida was smiling. "Now, Alicia, what is your tree called again?"

Alicia and Tonya listening to Quaking Aspen leaves

"It's an Aspen tree, Merida," Alicia replied, puzzled. "I told everyone that already."

"Yes, but what kind of Aspen?"

"Oh right, it's the Quaking Aspen! Because the leaves quake and shake, and that makes the rustling noise like talking. It is the perfect tree for me, isn't it? I'm always shaking and quaking too!"

43

Everyone laughed so loudly that Alicia became anxious that the Big Ones would hear them. "Oh no, don't laugh too much, I'm shaking more than the leaves on my tree!" she said.

Then it was time for everyone to disperse and take care of their trees. "Thank you, Alicia, for showing us your Quaking Aspen," the other fairies said as they flew away.

Naida spent the day with her tree, trying to encourage it to grow buds before everyone visited tomorrow. But she wasn't really expecting much to happen. She had resigned herself to showing the others her sleeping tree.

That evening, after they had all thanked Alicia again for showing them her "talking tree," Merida suggested they sing some songs. They spent a delightful time singing and laughing together, and Naida was able to relax and almost forget that they would all come to her tree tomorrow.

When she awoke the next morning, though, she remembered and gave a big sigh. "What's wrong, Naida?" Jayda asked. "You're not worried about us visiting your tree are you?"

Naida nodded glumly. "I wish it had woken up like all the other trees."

Jayda gave her a hug. "Don't worry. It will probably wake up when all of us arrive – hard to sleep with all the noise we make!"

When they all reached Naida's tree, however, it was still asleep. She flew over to it and faced the others. "See, my tree is still sleeping. I've been encouraging it to wake up every day, but there's not even a bud yet." She looked up at its branches. "But it's got lots of branches so I'm sure it can have lots of leaves and flowers when it does wake up!"

"What's your tree called, Naida?" Merida asked.

"Oh yes, it's a Catalpa tree."

"A cat-what tree?" Alicia asked looking puzzled.

"A catapult tree?" Sophia questioned. And Sylvia laughed.

"Cat-alpa" replied Naida. "I'd never heard of it either!"

"Why does it have black on these branches?" Sandra asked.

"Hmm, looks dead, doesn't it," Sylvia responded before Naida had a chance to say anything.

"Well, some of its branches might have died," Lara said. "My Oak tree has some branches that don't have any leaves. Doesn't your Maple tree?"

"Not like this!" Sylvia responded loudly. "No, this tree looks dead!"

"No, no, it's not dead," Naida defended her tree. "I can feel its energy; it just isn't ready to wake up yet."

"I think Naida killed it!" Sylvia said, and Sophia and Sandra nodded. "Yes, Naida, you must have done something wrong and killed your tree!"

The other fairies looked worried and turned to Merida. "Is Naida's tree dead?"

Merida looked at the group. "Now, don't assume this tree is dead. Have any of you seen a Catalpa tree? Do you know what it looks like before it wakes up?"

Naida was starting to cry. "You shouldn't have come. My tree isn't ready. Why don't you all just go away and leave me with my tree!"

"With her dead tree!" Sylvia said in a whisper that was loud enough for everyone to hear. Her friends chuckled and got ready to leave.

"Yes, everyone, go to your trees. You all have work to do." Merida told them.

When they had all gone she looked at Naida. "I'm sorry about that. Don't worry, your tree will be fine. Stay and take care of it now."

And Naida was left alone with her tree. "Not dead, not dead!" she said determinedly. But she felt a nagging doubt in the pit of her stomach, and she had almost no energy to share with her tree for the rest of the day.

As Naida flew into the fairies' home she saw Sylvia and her two friends watching her. They were laughing about something, and Naida instinctively felt it was about her and her Catalpa tree. Dejected, she made her way over to her bed and lay down. Jayda came in a moment later and saw her on the bed. "Naida, can I show you something?"

Naida lifted her head without much enthusiasm, "What is it Jayda?"

"Look, my Pine tree has these cone things. Isn't that cool?"

"Oh, yes. Goodness, that's really something different!" Naida was interested in spite of herself. "Are you going to show it to everyone this evening?"

"Yes, I hope so. Come on, let's help get things prepared." Leaving the pine cone by the bed, Jayda took Naida's hand to set up the dinner.

In spite of not feeling hungry Naida was drawn along by her friend, and soon everything was prepared. Jayda spoke to Merida who nodded, and all the fairies sat down.

As soon as it was time for 'show and tell' Merida announced that Jayda had something to show. Jayda went and picked up her pine cone, and lifting it up she explained that her tree now had these cones. "Of course, this is just a small one, some of the others are much bigger but I couldn't carry one of them!" she said with a laugh.

Everyone was fascinated and the room was buzzing as the pine cone was passed around.

"Did your tree have flowers Jayda?" Tonya asked as she turned the cone around. "Or just this ... cone thing?"

Jayda, Pine Tree Fairy with Pine Cone

"No, I didn't see any flowers. I think it just has these cones. Is that right Merida?"

"Quite right, Jayda. Pine trees are a special kind of tree. They don't have flowers. Instead they have cones, like this one."

"Goodness, I thought my tree was special because it's an evergreen, but now it has these special pine cones instead of flowers. I love my Pine tree!" Jayda was thrilled.

Merida smiled. "That's wonderful that you appreciate your tree, Jayda. Now, does anyone else have something to share?" and she looked around the group.

Somehow Naida felt that all eyes turned to her, and she lowered her head hoping that someone else did have something to share. Unfortunately, though, there was a silence. Sylvia broke it by saying loudly, "Well, we should hear from Naida about her tree. If it's come back to life yet!"

As Sophia and Sandra joined her in an unpleasant laugh, Naida shook her head. "No, it's still sleeping. It will wake up when it's ready, not when you want it to."

"Alright, now fairies. Let's be nice to each other." Merida sought to keep the peace. "If there's nothing else to share let's all get ready for bed."

That night Naida couldn't sleep. She tossed and turned until Jayda, who had been sleeping with a smile on her face, gave a groan and kicked her. That made Naida feel even worse. She felt the tears start to well up in her eyes and stuffed the cover in her mouth to avoid making a sound as she began to cry. She must have fallen asleep eventually because it seemed that suddenly the sun was shining and there was activity all around.

"Come on sleepyhead, time to wake up!" Jayda's cheery voice came to her.

"Oh, Jayda. I don't feel well. Can you tell Merida I'm sick?"

"Really, oh dear. Yes, I'll get her right away."

Merida quickly came over to see what was wrong. "Naida, what's the matter?"

"I don't know, Merida," Naida replied weakly. "I couldn't sleep last night for the longest time. And now I feel strange. I think my tree is really sick and it's making me sick. Am I going to die?"

Merida looked at her and frowned. "Alright, Naida, you stay in bed. I'll send the others out to their trees and come back to take care of you."

As she lay there Naida could hear the other fairies talking, and suddenly Jayda came over to the bed. "Naida, don't be sick. You're my friend! You have to get well!"

"Oh Jayda, thanks," Naida smiled.

"I have to go, but please be better when I come home!" and Jayda flew away.

After a few minutes Merida returned carrying a cup of tea. "This is a special tea. I hope it will make you feel better, Naida. Drink it up!"

Naida sat up and started drinking. "Is this what you gave Jayda? It tastes quite nice, I thought hers tasted awful!"

"Actually this is different. You can enjoy drinking this one!" Merida said with a smile. "Now tell me what's the matter. Are you upset because the others said your tree was dead?"

"Yes. I didn't think it was dead, but when they pointed out the black branches and said it looked really dead I got worried. I tried to believe, really I did. I don't want my tree to die! But maybe I did do something wrong, and I've killed it." Naida started to cry.

"Now, now that's not true." Merida patted her arm. "Naida, you felt your tree's energy just the other day. You connected to your tree and have been visiting it every day. You've done nothing wrong. Your tree just wasn't ready to wake up yet. Don't believe what the others say, they don't know your tree like you do. Trust yourself. It's going to be fine."

Naida was nodding as she tried to absorb Merida's advice. She was still crying, though, and a tear fell into her tea cup.

"Oh, Naida, don't cry in your tea. It won't taste so good if you do!" Merida said. And they both laughed. "Come on then, finish your tea and we'll go together to your tree."

Still feeling rather uneasy, Naida followed Merida to her Catalpa tree. When they arrive Merida flew all around the tree while Naida waited on her favorite branch. Although she felt at home here on her tree, she was unable to relax, worrying about what Merida might discover. Her fears were unfounded, though.

"Naida, come here," Merida called from a branch higher up. "Now, can you see these very small bumps on this branch, and here too?"

"Yes, yes, I can see them!" Naida said hopefully.

"These will be buds. You can warm them up today and very soon you'll see them grow!"

"Oh, Merida, thank you!" Naida said gratefully. "You've saved my tree!"

"Nonsense, Naida. You have done everything yourself. I'm just here to guide and encourage you. Now get to work, and I'll see you later."

Naida busied herself giving warming energy to each tiny bump she found, which turned out to be quite a large number. She realized that very soon her tree would have new life. It was so exciting!

When she flew home at the end of the day several of the fairies looked up to see how she was. They were surprised to see Naida's animated expression. Jayda came over immediately to find out what had changed for her friend.

"Naida, you look so much better! What happened?"

"Oh, Jayda, Merida came with me to my tree and she showed me where to give it warmth. I'm sure it's waking up now. I'm so excited to find out what kind of leaves and flowers it will have!"

Everyone, even Sylvia and her friends, seemed relieved that Naida was feeling better and the evening passed very agreeably.

Sure enough, a couple of days later Naida found the first leaves on her tree. They were still small, but a lovely bright green and she proudly brought one home to show the others.

"I know it's not such a special leaf, but it's a leaf from my Catalpa tree, the one everyone thought was dead. So that makes it special to me!" she said as she passed it around after dinner.

"It's a nice little leaf, Naida," Jayda said. "Do you think it will get bigger, or will the leaves stay small like this?"

"Several of the other trees have small leaves, like Catriona's Willow tree and Tonya's Birch tree." Lara commented as she looked carefully at the leaf. "But I think this one looks like it might be going to grow more."

"Well, probably that one won't grow now that I've brought it here," Naida said with a laugh. "But we can wait and see what the other leaves do."

"Your tree needs a lot of patience, doesn't it?" Sylvia commented. "I don't think I could wait so long to find out what my tree's leaves are like!"

Naida, Catalpa Tree Fairy with Leaf

"Well, I needed Merida's encouragement! Thank you Merida!" Naida said.

Merida smiled warmly. "I'm delighted your tree has leaves now, Naida. And everyone is content with their tree, right? But this is still early in the year. Don't forget you have to keep taking care of your trees all the way through the summer. And then we have to prepare them for winter when it starts to get cooler in the fall. But for now we can celebrate new leaves on Naida's tree!"

And everyone raised their glasses to toast Naida's Catalpa tree, the last tree in the group to produce leaves.

Over the next few days Naida was thrilled by the growth on her tree. More and more leaves burst forth from the buds that she carefully warmed each day. And the leaves that had already appeared kept growing, and growing! "Goodness," she thought. "Now I'm beginning to wonder if these leaves will ever stop growing. Some of them are so big!"

The fairies continued to exchange news of their trees, but there was not so much that was changing now. The flowers and catkins on all the trees had finished their job and fallen on the ground to die. Except for Naida and Jayda's trees. Jayda's pine cones were still hanging onto her Pine tree, and Naida's tree still had no flowers or catkins. One evening they all discussed this, trying to get Merida to tell them what Naida's tree would produce.

Naida had told them that the leaves kept growing bigger, but she had to admit there was no sign of flowers or anything like that. Merida kept her silence, only commenting that they should be patient.

Meanwhile Sophia had come home quite excited. "There's an egg! My Robin made an egg!"

Her enthusiasm was infectious and soon all the fairies were clamoring to go see Sophia's egg. They also wanted to know what the egg looked like, but Sophia wouldn't say. She just smiled and said, "It's a secret. You'll have to come and see it for yourselves. Right, Merida?"

So of course Merida had to agree that they could visit Sophia's tree, but she said they had to be careful not to upset the Robins. Everyone laughed at the thought of tiny fairies scaring the big birds!

When they arrived at Sophia's tree the fairies landed in the top branches. Sophia went with Merida to look at the nest, and soon came back with a big smile on her face. "Come on everyone," she whispered. You can see the nest; Merida is waiting for you down there."

They all followed her to where Merida was sitting. "Look, down there. The nest is right there."

"Oh yes, I see it!" Sylvia was thrilled.

"Look, there's a blue egg inside!" Sandra joined in.

Robin eggs in nest with Sophia and Daniela

"Two blue eggs, I can see two blue eggs!" Alicia was squeaking in her excitement. "But where's the Robin bird? I don't want to be eaten by the bird!"

Suddenly there was a rush of wind, and Sylvia almost fell off the branch she was sitting on. But it wasn't wind, it was the Robin returning to the nest and her wings had blown all the leaves just like a gust of wind.

"Ooh, that was a bit scary!" Alicia said and everyone laughed. "Oh no, be quiet, maybe Robin birds can hear us laugh!"

Of course that made everyone laugh even more. Fortunately, the mother Robin had settled down in the nest and seemed to be ignoring them.

"If everyone has seen the eggs, let's move away," Merida said quietly. "We really don't want to disturb the Robin."

Sophia followed them all back to the top of the tree. "Aren't the blue eggs beautiful?" she said proudly. "Now I'm happy the Robin bird chose my tree!"

Naida watched her a bit wistfully as she returned to her tree. "My tree only has leaves, not even any flowers, and Sophia has a bird! Gosh, I shouldn't be jealous, but it seems like my tree is rather boring. It seems that nothing much changes."

Then, one morning as Naida arrived at her tree she saw something different. There were stalks standing up above the leaves. She flew over in anticipation. Could this be the flowers? She looked closely and saw that there were no flowers, but there were buds on these strange stalks. She flew around her tree excitedly, gently warming the buds as she found them. "I wonder what will happen when these open?" she said to herself. "It's so strange, like miniature trees standing up on these twigs where the leaves are growing!"

She told the group that something was happening on her tree, something good she hastened to add. The fairies wanted to know what it was, but Naida just said they should remember what Merida had told them about being patient. "That's right isn't it Merida?" she asked. "I want to see what happens first and then I'll tell everyone. Perhaps we can all visit my tree again when it's ready?"

"Yes, Naida, that's a good plan," Merida agreed. "We only saw your tree before it awakened so let's wait for this development and then we'll all pay it another visit."

The others grumbled a bit but had to agree to wait. Jayda squeezed Naida's arm affectionately. "Now your tree is so interesting to everyone. I'm thrilled for you!"

"Oh Jayda, I think you have the most interesting tree! It has those needles for leaves and cones for flowers. How special!"

"Well, we both have special trees then. Isn't that fun?" and the two friends settled down contentedly.

Naida was disappointed to see that it was raining the next morning. None of the fairies liked to go out in the rain, especially if it was going to rain all day, which is what it looked like. As they all peered out of the tiny cave that was their sanctuary, they shivered slightly not looking forward to getting wet and cold. "Merida, can we stay home today?" Sylvia asked, putting on a pleading face. "It's not nice weather out there, all wet, and our trees probably want to take a rest!"

Merida laughed. "Goodness, Sylvia you do come up with some interesting ideas!"

"Well," Lara said in support, "maybe the trees will just soak up the rain and be ready to grow again tomorrow."

Merida looked at the group of fairies, all wearing hopeful expressions. "Well, my, what a lot you are! And what exactly would you do if you stayed home all day?"

"Oh there's lots to do!"

"We could clean up!"

"We could study more about how to take care of trees in the fall."

"We could fix our clothes!"

"I can make some nice hot tea and you could tell us stories of the great tree fairies of the past. Please Merida!"

"Well," Merida was smiling. "This place could do with some cleaning, and some of your skirts could do with some sewing. And I'll gladly accept some nice hot tea while you all work!"

"And then you'll tell us stories!" Lara persisted, since that was her idea.

"Yes, I'll tell you stories. But only after your work is finished."

"It's a deal!" the fairies agreed, grateful to be given a reprieve from a day out in the rain. And a fun day was had by all. Soon their home was looking spic and span, and everyone's dresses were as pretty as new.

Merida kept her promise and as they all sat drinking their tea she told them stories of the great tree fairies of the past. They were astonished at how hard the fairies had worked to take care of their trees in the old days when the earth was wild. There had been so many other plants that had made it difficult for the trees to grow properly. Merida told the tale of one tree fairy whose tree had been strangled by a big vine that grew up and all around its trunk and branches.

"Oh, no! Did the tree die?"

"And did the fairy die too?"

"Yes," Merida said somberly. "It was a slow and painful death. The fairy couldn't help her tree, and they suffered together for a long time before the end came."

The fairies all looked at each and shivered. "I hope a big vine doesn't kill any of our trees!"

"My Oak tree is strong and has big branches. I think it would be alright if a vine tried to grow on it," Lara said. "If anyone gets a big vine, they can come to my tree to get strength."

"Maybe the Big Ones would help, if a big vine came," Jayda suggested. "I mean that noisy machine that cut my broken branch could easily cut a vine."

"Yes," Merida said. "Now we have good Big Ones to help us with our trees. I'm sure they would save our trees from a vine. But the Big Ones weren't always good. In the past some came and attacked the trees, cutting them down, burning them, and even poisoning them. So you see why we can only take care of trees when we're sure the Big Ones want them to live long, healthy lives. I'm delighted to say that now there are many Big Ones who understand trees and want to help, like our Big Ones."

"I don't know what would have happened if our Big Ones hadn't come after the storm to help my Pine tree," Jayda agreed.

"So the good Big Ones are our friends, even if they can't see us!"

"But they might hear us when we laugh!"

"I still don't think I want a Big One to see me or hear me," said little Alicia, shaking slightly. "I can't help it, I'm scared of them!"

Everyone laughed at that. Lara said, "Alicia, don't worry, I'm sure no Big Ones can hear us laugh with all this rain!" And everyone laughed some more.

Sometime during the night the rain stopped, and in the morning the sun was shining brightly again. The air was quite fresh and clean smelling, and they were all excited to go out and see their trees again.

"Just one day at home and I already miss my tree," said Jayda. And the other fairies all agreed.

"But it was a really nice day too, and we didn't have to get wet in the rain!" Lara added, which made the fairies laugh.

As she flew off to her tree Naida wondered if anything would have changed. Of course she, along with all the fairies, knew that rain was necessary for their trees to grow. But too much rain could be damaging. "I hope those buds didn't get broken off those strange stalks," she worried. But when she reached her tree all was well. In fact, it was beautiful!

"Oh, my!" Naida said in surprise. "My tree is so gorgeous!" Many of the buds had opened up and they were all lovely flowers. Each stalk was standing up like a miniature tree of flowers, and it seemed like so many of the branches had stalks. Of course many of the stalks just had buds, but Naida was confident they would open soon. She flew around her tree delighted, looking for a perfect flower to take back to show the others.

"Well, I should wait till it's time to go home before picking it, or it might get all weak and droopy. Still, I think this one would be a good choice. Oh, my wonderful Catalpa tree, how beautiful you are today, I just love your flowers!" Naida was clapping her hands and dancing around the tree for the longest time.

Eventually she realized she should calm down and take care of her tree. It must have worked hard to produce so many buds and flowers overnight. "I have to give it good energy so it doesn't get weak," she thought. She found her favorite branch beside the trunk and put her hands firmly on her tree, connecting to its life force with her own. The tree's energy was flowing strongly and Naida felt a great happiness being shared between herself and her tree. Then she diligently went around taking care of the leaves, that were still growing bigger, and the buds and flowers on their stalks.

Just as it was about to get dark she returned to the flower she had chosen to take back home with her. It was so beautiful she almost changed her mind, not wanting to take it from the tree. But when she touched it the flower easily came away in her hand, and she could feel the tree giving it to her. "Oh, thank you, Catalpa tree. The other fairies will love your beautiful flower. And they'll all come to see you tomorrow!"

Naida started on her way home with her flower, but she was soon struggling–the flower wasn't heavy but it was delicate and difficult to hold safely when she was flying. "Oh dear, how I am going to get this beautiful flower home without breaking it?"

Just then she heard a voice calling, "Naida, let me help you!" It was Daniela, also on her way home. She quickly flew to join Naida and together they were able to balance the flower carefully between them. "Goodness, Naida, this is such a pretty flower!" Daniela said as they flew home together.

"Just wait till you see my tree!" Naida said as they reached home. "There are so many of these flowers, and they're so pretty."

All the fairies gathered around eagerly to see the flower.

"It's beautiful, Naida!" "Look, it's got colors inside!"

"Is this what you wanted to show us?" Lara asked.

Naida, Catalpa Tree Fairy with Flower

"Well, yes," Naida said. "But you can't guess what the flowers look like on the tree. You all have to come tomorrow and look!"

Merida arrived just then and came over to see the flower. "Beautiful, Naida, very beautiful. But how did you get it here without breaking it?"

"Oh, Daniela came by and helped me. Thank you Daniela. I would never have got it home safely without your help."

"Indeed. And it's such a beautiful flower. Are there many flowers on your tree now, Naida?" Merida was interested.

"Oh yes, and I want everyone to see them tomorrow. Is that alright?"

"Alright indeed!" Merida smiled at Naida's enthusiasm. "Now let's have our dinner and everyone be ready to visit Naida's tree in the morning."

Naida, Catalpa Tree Fairy with Flowers on Tree

Jayda smiled warmly at her friend. "Naida you're thrilled with your tree now, aren't you? Is it really beautiful?"

"Oh yes, Jayda. You'll be surprised when you see it. It's really special. I love my tree!"

In the morning Naida proudly led the way to her tree, feeling so different from the other day when she had dreaded showing everyone her dead-looking tree. Now her tree had green leaves, big green leaves, and was arrayed in all these beautiful flowers. What a change!

As the fairies drew close to her tree they started to get excited. "Naida, your tree looks fantastic!" Jayda was so pleased for her friend.

"Look at those things that look like tiny trees with the flowers on!" Tonya was thrilled. "Oh, goodness, those flowers are so lovely!"

"It looks like it has candles on it, all lit up!" Sylvia was impressed.

"And look at these big leaves, they're like giant hearts!" Sophia said as she flew around.

"We could all sit on one of these leaves, they're so big!" Sandra agreed. "We could have a picnic!"

"I love these flowers! Look, there's room for us all to sit on one of the 'flower trees,' with a flower each!" Daniela was amazed. "I thought the single flower was big and beautiful, but these 'flower trees' are incredible!"

There was so much joy with everyone buzzing around and playing on the leaves and 'flower trees.' Naida just stayed back and watched.

"Oh Naida, your tree is the most beautiful of all." Jayda said. "You just had to be patient!"

"I know, I love my Catalpa tree," Naida agreed. "I never guessed it would look like this when it woke up!"

No-one wanted to leave Naida's tree, but Merida said they must go. "I know you all love Naida's tree now, but you have your own trees to take care of. They're waiting for you, so off you go!"

"Thank you for showing us your tree!" the fairies said as they flew away, and Naida waved cheerfully. "Thank you Catalpa tree for being so amazing!" she said to her tree as she settled down in her favorite spot. She spent the day enjoying her tree. There were so many flowers and leaves, it was fun just flying around and marveling in the beauty of all this life. But

Naida knew she had to keep giving energy to her tree, so she made sure she visited all the branches and tended to them. She felt so elated it was easy to send good energy to her tree.

Naida was still feeling very joyful as she flew home, and hoped that the other fairies also had a good day. Perhaps someone would have something exciting to share, or they would just sing songs, or some other activity. Life as a tree fairy was good indeed!

This time it was Sophia who was excited at home. "What happened?" all the other fairies were clustered around her as Sophia was smiling mysteriously. "I'll tell you after dinner!" was all she would say.

After dinner Merida again thanked Naida for showing them her Catalpa tree. Then, seeing that Sophia was getting impatient, Merida asked her to share her news.

"It's my Robin birds!" Sophia said excitedly. "The eggs have gone and there are funny looking baby birds in the nest! They don't look much like Robin birds, though, they're so small and they don't have feathers. But they open their mouths wide all the time because they're hungry!"

"Ooh, baby birds!" "I want to see them!" "Can we go tomorrow Merida?" The fairies were all excited.

But Alicia looked worried, "I don't want a baby bird to eat me in its big mouth!" she said nervously. "Are you sure it's safe, Merida?"

"Oh, Alicia, you're always worried about something!" Sylvia responded laughing.

"Yes, Alicia, it will be alright if you don't get too close," Merida comforted the little fairy. "Sylvia, she's quite right to be careful. If you got too close to a bird's beak it might think you were food!"

"Oh, well I thought they couldn't see us," Sylvia was chastened. "Sorry, Alicia, I didn't mean to be mean to you."

"It's alright," Alicia said. "I know I'm always afraid. I can't help it. I'm small and I just start shaking whenever something a bit scary comes along. I'm like my Quaking Aspen tree, its leaves quake and shake in the smallest breeze!"

At that everyone was laughing and remembering Alicia's tree with its leaves that "talked" to her.

"But can we all go to see my baby Robin birds tomorrow?" Sophia asked again. "All they want to do is eat so I think they might grow up and fly away soon!"

"Yes, of course we'll go tomorrow!" Merida laughed. "And indeed they will grow up and fly away. But it will take several days before they're ready to fly, especially if they don't have their feathers yet."

The baby Robins were quite a sight. Just as Sophia had said, they had no feathers and huge mouths open to eat. The fairies were fascinated, although some of them, especially Alicia, were careful not to get too close in case they were mistaken for food!

"Look at their big eyes!" Tonya exclaimed when it was her turn to get closer. "Do you think they can see us?"

"I don't know," Merida answered. "Maybe!"

"You're right that they're not much like birds, Sophia," said Sylvia. "Kind of ugly really! But I'm sure they'll look like birds soon," she added quickly not wanting to sound critical.

Sophia just smiled and waited for everyone to have a good look. Then she said, "The big Robin birds come to feed them you know. Maybe it's time to move away."

"Yes, you're right, Sophia," Merida agreed. "We don't want to disturb the Robin parents. Everyone, off to your own trees now. Thank you Sophia for showing us the baby birds."

"Yes, thank you Sophia," they chorused as they quickly left Sophia's Maple tree. Nobody wanted to meet the big Robin again!

Over the next few days everyone asked Sophia about the baby birds when she came home in the evening. She was able to tell them that they started to grow feathers and soon looked just like real birds. One day she was very excited, and it turned out that the young birds had started trying to get out of the nest. They just hopped along the branch but Sophia was sure they would try to fly soon. Hearing about the development of the baby birds was almost as interesting as the growth of their trees!

Finally, the day came when Sophia told them the birds were flying. "I saw them practicing!" she said breathlessly. "One bird flew off bravely but the others were scared to try at first. The big Robin bird had to push the last one off the branch! But they all flew around and came back to the nest. Will they fly away and make their own nests in other trees soon?"

"Well," Merida said thoughtfully. "Yes, they'll all fly away. They only live in the nest when they're young. But I don't know if these birds will make their own nests this year. They might just join the other Robins for a while and sleep with them till they're more grown up."

"I think I'm going to miss my Robin birds," Sophia said wistfully. "I'm so glad they chose my tree for their nest!"

"There's plenty more to do to take care of your tree, you know," Merida reminded her. "All of you. Your trees will have to make seeds that can grow into new trees. That's a very important time. You must make sure they have plenty of good energy to make good seeds. So it's probably a good thing not to be distracted by the birds for much longer!"

"Alright, Merida, don't worry. I'll take care of my tree's seeds," Sophia agreed.

"Yes, we'll all help our trees make good seeds," the fairies promised.

A few days later Daniela came home looking a bit puzzled. "My tree has something, but I don't think they're seeds," she said. "Some of them are red, so that must be why my tree is called Red Mulberry!"

"Yes, Daniela, that's right," said Merida. "And what is the name of your tree?"

"Red Mulberry?"

"Yes, and do you know what a mulberry is? Or something like it?"

"No, it's my tree's name," Daniela looked confused. "Oh, do you mean like a strawberry? It means it has berries! Yes, my tree has berries!" she suddenly understood. "Oh how silly I am!"

Everyone laughed. "Can we see Daniela's berries?"

"Are they good to eat, like strawberries?" Sylvia asked.

"Well," said Daniela, "they don't look like strawberries at all!"

"No, they're not like strawberries. And when they're red they're probably not ripe. They will go black when they're ready to eat," Merida told them.

"Oh, like blackberries!" Tonya said. "I like blackberries, but they have thorns which hurt if you get pricked. Your tree doesn't have thorns does it, Daniela?"

"No, no thorns," Daniela said. "So we can eat my berries when they're black?"

"Yes, I think so," Merida replied. "Do you want to wait until they are ripe before we all visit?"

"That sounds good," Daniela said. "I'll let you know and then we can have a berry eating party at my tree!"

The next day it was raining and the fairies asked for another day inside, and Merida agreed. "Tell us about your tree, Merida." Sylvia asked when they settled down after finishing all their chores. "What kind of tree is it?"

"And where is it? Can we visit it with you?" Catriona was very interested.

"Alright," Merida agreed to share about her tree. "I have an Oak tree."

"Oh, like my Oak tree?" Lara asked immediately.

"Yes, Lara. It's like your Oak tree, but a bit older. It has really big branches that spread out, and it stands on a hill above the other trees. It's a wonderful place to visit."

"So, do you go there every day? Is it far from here?" Sylvia was curious.

"It's a bit far from here, so, no I don't go every day. But I go often. My tree would miss me if I never visited!" Merida smiled.

"But what about the days when you don't go? Doesn't it miss you then?" Lara was concerned.

"Well, I have a friend whose tree is nearby. She visits my tree when I'm not there. So my tree isn't lonely," Merida explained. "When I got the job of taking care of new fairies and assigning them to their trees I introduced my friend to my Oak tree because I knew I might have to travel too far away to visit every day."

"Oh, I'm glad your friend takes care of your tree," Lara was happy to hear that.

"Can we visit your tree with you some day?" Jayda asked.

"Oh yes, Merida, please can we visit your tree?" Naida agreed, and all the other fairies looked at Merida with hopeful expressions.

"Well," Merida looked thoughtful. "I don't see why not. But maybe later on when your trees are prepared to go to sleep we can visit my tree. For now, you still have to take of your trees every day."

Daniela, Red Mulberry Tree Fairy with Mulberries on Tree

"Thank you for telling us about your tree! I'm sure it must be so beautiful. I can't wait to see another Oak tree!" Lara sighed longingly. And all the fairies nodded in agreement, looking forward to the trip to see Merida's Oak tree.

After that there were several days of warm sun which quickly ripened Daniela's berries, and so they all flew together to sample them. Some of the fruits had already fallen on the ground and those that were squashed had made everything purple. The fairies saw a lot of insects enjoying the squashed berries and they flew up to find nice ripe ones still hanging on the tree.

"Delicious!" was the verdict as they started eating them. Of course the juice made them all purple, so soon all the young fairies were quite a sight. Merida sighed, "Goodness, you should all see yourselves! Come on, we need to find some water to wash ourselves clean before we take care of our trees!"

"I know where we can go," said Catriona. "There's a pond beside my Willow tree. Let's go there. It has lovely clear water and it's a really nice place."

So they had a fun time splashing around in the water, all under the pretext of cleaning up! In the end, though, Merida called a halt to the frivolity and the fairies agreed it was time to go to their trees.

"That was fun, Catriona!" they chorused as they flew away. "And thank you for sharing such delicious berries from your tree, Daniela."

Over the next few days all the trees seemed to produce seeds, of one form or another. Sylvia came home one evening with her seeds. "My Maple tree has double seeds and they have wings and can fly!" she said as she landed. "They can fly without me, look."

Sylvia, Silver Maple Tree Fairy with Seeds

And when everyone was watching she tossed the seeds with wings into the air and everyone watched as they spun around and around, twirling as they flew away to land on the forest floor.

"Wow, they really do fly!" "That's so cool!" The fairies were impressed.

Her friends Sophia and Sandra also found similar seeds on their Maple trees. "There are so many!" said Sandra in awe. "I didn't realize there were that many flowers on my tree!"

Tonya's Birch tree also had seeds with wings, but they had just a single seed each with its own set of wings.

Then Jayda came home excited about her Pine cones. "There are seeds coming out of the big Pine cones! I can't bring them, but you can come and see them." So they visited her Pine tree again. Everyone wanted to see the branch that had been broken in the storm, and they touched it reverently, remembering how the Big Ones had come to help it heal.

"Your Pine tree looks so healthy now, with all these cones, and it got lots of new needles. It seems to have recovered from that awful storm," Naida said with a sigh of relief. "I'm so relieved. Otherwise you would have a broken arm forever!"

They found a lot of pine nuts inside the cones, and Merida told them they were good to eat so some of the fairies tried them.

Jayda and Naida agreed they tasted good, but Sylvia pulled a face. "I like Daniela's berries better!" she said. "Of course, these pine seeds do taste better than my Maple seeds would, I'm sure!"

The fairies all enjoyed the acorns from Lara's Oak tree. "They look like they have cute hats on!" Tonya said when she saw the one Lara had brought home.

"They must taste good too, at least to squirrels," Lara said. "I've seen several squirrels carrying these acorns away, and sometimes they just sit in my tree and throw pieces of the shell down. I almost got hit a few times!" That made everyone laugh.

But it was Naida's tree that produced the most surprising seeds. One day she saw long green pods hanging down from the branches. She realized those must be containers for the seeds.

Lara, Oak Tree Fairy with Acorn

"Goodness, my tree never stops surprising me!" she said when she got home. "I can't bring the seeds, but come and see them!"

Everyone agreed that the Catalpa tree had done it again. "What fun these pods are, Naida! We can slide down them, or a whole group of us can hang on one together. You really have a special tree!" Sylvia gave her tree high praise. And as the summer days passed the pods darkened until they were dark brown and hard, even curling up at the ends. Then they opened up and the seeds came out, to Naida's delight.

Soon the days began to be noticeably shorter and when it rained it became quite chilly. The fairies knew that fall had started and soon their trees would have to prepare for the long cold winter season.

To the delight of the Maple tree trio, the leaves on their trees began to change color. There were bright yellows, brilliant oranges, and fiery reds! "How beautiful our trees are," said Sandra as they chatted over dinner. "Yes, I never expected such bright colors to come now. I thought we'd seen all the interesting things, but this is the best yet!" Sylvia was really excited.

Merida suggested that the whole group go on a tour the next morning to see the colorful foliage. The Maples had the brightest colors, but all the other trees had leaves that were changing to yellow or brown, except for Jayda's Pine tree of course! Jayda laughed and said it wasn't necessary to visit her tree, unless they wanted to remember what green leaves looked like. So of course they all said they wanted to see it again. "Your Pine needles are special, Jayda," said Naida. "Your tree is the only one that keeps its leaves in the cold winter. Ours will go to sleep and mine will look like a dead tree again!"

That evening Merida held a special meeting. The fairies sat in their circle and looked expectantly at Merida. They were nervous, wondering what new task was coming. Surely they had done all that Merida had taught them?

Once everyone was ready, Merida sat up very straight and looked at them all quite seriously. "I want to congratulate you, my group of tree fairies," she said. "You have all taken care of your trees throughout the growing season. Each tree is healthy and is well prepared to face the cold winter. Good job everyone!"

And as Merida smiled and clapped all the fairies all joined in, delighted to have done a good job. Then Merida asked the fairies to say what they liked best about their trees. Each one shared something special they had learned from taking care of their tree.

Alicia said that she was delighted her tree was a Quaking Aspen because it shook just like she did when she got nervous. "I feel much better about not being brave when I visit my tree," she said. "Its leaves shake and quake all the time, when there's really nothing to be afraid of!"

Naida, Catalpa Tree Fairy with Seed Pods on Tree

Tonya said that she still liked the paper on her Birch tree trunk. "Even though it has really pretty colored leaves now, I still think the white paper bark is special."

"I love my acorns!" said Lara with a smile. "I thought I would love my Oak tree's strong branches, and I do. But the acorns with their little hats are just so cute!"

"My Red Mulberry fruits were so delicious," Daniela said. "And I was thrilled that we could all have a picnic and eat them. And then of course we had so much fun playing in Catriona's Willow tree pond!"

"My Weeping Willow tree isn't a sad place at all!" Catriona agreed. "Maybe it made the pond with its tears when it was sad, but now it's all joyful. And I'm happy because I like to have fun!"

Sylvia said she was surprised her Maple tree had such bright red flowers and then beautiful colored leaves in the fall. "But still, I like the flying seeds the best!"

"Oh, I like the colors of my leaves," Sandra responded. "The Crimson King is a great name for my tree with dark red leaves!"

"And my tree is so pretty the Robin bird chose it for its nest!" Sophia added. "I think our Maple trees are just perfect for the three of us!"

"I have to say my Pine tree was quite a surprise!" Jayda admitted. "I understood there were evergreen trees, but I didn't know it would have needles instead of regular leaves, and Pine cones instead of flowers. And of course I didn't expect it to get a broken branch from the thunderstorm! My tree was so brave!"

"Well, my Catalpa tree was certainly full of surprises too," Naida responded. "I had to wait so long for it to wake up, you all thought it was dead! But everything was worth waiting for–the beautiful flowers, the big heart-shaped leaves, and the long seed pods. I love my Catalpa tree now! Thank you, Merida, for choosing me to take care of it."

"So everyone is satisfied with their tree?" Merida asked.

"Yes!" they all responded, agreeing that Merida had made the right choice when she assigned them their trees.

"You made good choices for all of us Merida," Sylvia said seriously. "I think Naida's Catalpa tree is amazing, but I would never have had the patience to wait for it to wake up. It takes a lot of patience and strength to be a Catalpa tree fairy."

"Well, I think Jayda was very brave when her Pine tree got struck by the thunderstorm. I don't know what I would have done if my tree was injured like that," Naida said smiling at her friend.

Jayda smiled back, "But Naida, you were brave when we all thought your tree was dead. That took more strength than just having a broken arm.

You had to wait so long for your tree to wake up, and you took care of it every day. I couldn't be a Catalpa tree fairy!"

"Yes," Merida agreed. "You did a very good job, Naida. I'm proud of you! Let's have a toast to Naida, the Catalpa tree fairy!" and all the fairies raised their cups to drink to Naida and her Catalpa tree. Naida smiled appreciatively, grateful that her tree was healthy and content to be in the company of her group of fairy friends.

Beautiful Golden Songbird

The Beautiful Golden Songbird

Paul was quite young when they moved – he celebrated his fifth birthday the day after they arrived – so he didn't remember much about living in New York City. He knew there were lots of people there; plenty of kids his own age to have fun with. He had a vague memory of going to a baseball match with some other boys and their fathers. And they ate hot dogs there.

An only child, he found himself without friends when they moved to this remote place. His parents were concerned about his education. Since the nearest school was quite distant, and apparently not appropriate for him, they hired a tutor. Mr. Black was an older man and kind enough. He and his wife had come from London years ago to start a school and never left. His wife had died shortly before Paul's family arrived, which would have been enough reason to return to England. But he had hesitated, and when the offer to tutor Paul came along he gladly accepted. He was used to living in this village, he told Paul, and it was easier to stay in what had become his home than to return to a country that would probably be as foreign to him as this place had seemed when he first arrived.

Mr. Black was a good teacher, quite fair, but he was a bit of a stickler for having homework completed on time. Paul, who was not really the studious type preferring to spend his time outside, often frustrated him by forgetting to complete his assigned tasks. Mr. Black got around this by encouraging a more active style of learning, where they would go together to study the various flora and fauna and other aspects of their environment. Paul didn't find the study of rocks so exciting, but he enjoyed watching the various creatures – animals, birds, fish, insects and even plants – everything that was alive.

The years passed and Paul grew quite used to his life. He filled his days with outdoor activities and spent most of his time alone. His parents weren't very companionable. His father was always busy, visiting people in other villages and even in the nearest town. Sometimes his mother went with him, but, like Paul who had begged to accompany his father until he had been allowed to go with him one time, she usually preferred to stay behind. Paul often found her sitting on the porch looking vacantly at the garden and beyond, or on a rainy day sitting inside staring out of the window.

Paul wondered if this was normal, but who was there to ask? Mr. Black was hardly "normal." Paul thought of him as quite ancient, beyond the age of adventure or even hard work. Certainly Mr. Black was much less physically fit than he was, so Paul could easily take off on his own, ostensibly to study whatever the lesson was but often to his favorite place – a large tree that grew beside a pond.

He had found the place by accident one day when he was supposed to be studying lizards and their relatives. He had spent the afternoon happily exploring a new part of the forest. The undergrowth was rather thick and he considered turning back, but he thought "just a little further," until he came to the tree. It was a beautiful tree, with thick low-hanging branches covered in mosses and other vegetation. Clearly no-one had climbed it in recent times.

Paul hesitated only a moment and then hoisted himself up onto the lowest branch. He almost banged his head on the next branch, and quickly adjusted his position so that he could look upwards more easily. There were several strong branches that he climbed carefully, aware that the copious vegetation might be hiding something. Reaching a secure fork close to the trunk he sat down and turned around to look out over what he expected to be more forest.

Instead, he saw a pond, and not just any pond, but an almost perfectly circular pond. There were a number of plants that looked like water lilies growing around the side nearest him. Across the water he could see a collection of birds swimming, some kind of moorhen he guessed. And he could hear all kinds of chirps and other sounds of birds and possibly insects calling out to each other.

One bird's voice in particular struck him as especially beautiful. It sounded like someone singing a love song to their special mate, calling them to come and enjoy the afternoon together. Paul looked around but couldn't see which bird was singing so delightfully. He sighed, wishing he had someone who would call out to him in such an attractive way. The only person likely to call out to him was Mr. Black, and that would be to remind him of his task.

That thought made Paul sit up. "I have to find some kind of lizard to bring back, or he'll be upset." He started to look around, wondering where would be the best place to find a suitable specimen. As he raised his head to look upwards at the branch above, an eye met his gaze. The creature's head was cocked a bit to one side, which was why there was only one eye in sight, and Paul wasn't sure if it had seen him or not. He looked closely and realized it was a rather colorful creature, although its bright blues and greens and reds seemed to act more like camouflage than to make it stand out. He could see a leg with several toes that seemed to be stuck to the tree. "Yes, you're definitely a lizard type, a gecko I think." he thought. "Now all I have to do is catch you!"

Paul shifted position to reach into his backpack and take out his specimen jar. Then he reached up and half grabbing half pushing was able to maneuver the reptile into the jar. Closing the lid, he looked at it more attentively. "Yes, you're a beauty. Thank you for being so cooperative! I'll just take you home to show Mr. Black. I'm sure he won't get on my case when he sees you!" Paul put the jar in his backpack and climbed carefully down the tree.

As Paul had predicted, Mr. Black was quite impressed with his catch. He looked at it carefully and agreed it was some type of gecko. Since it was wide awake during the daytime they agreed it must be one of the "day geckos," not the more common nocturnal type. They looked in their book of lizards but couldn't find one that had exactly the same colorful appearance.

Paul's mother, on the other hand, was much less thrilled with his acquisition. She took one look and immediately declared it was not allowed inside. No amount of explaining and efforts to calm her down by Paul and his tutor would change her mind. "Reptiles are not welcome inside!" was her final statement.

Even though Paul had not intended to keep the little fellow, he was quite sad at the thought of returning it so soon. Mr. Black offered to take it to his house for the night and Paul could return it to its natural habitat the next day.

Mr. Black had other commitments so he just dropped off the gecko first thing in the morning and left. His mother was in her usual spot, staring into space, so Paul just gave her an unacknowledged wave and set off with the gecko in his backpack.

This time he had packed some fruit and cookies, as well as his water bottle, hoping to spend more time in his tree. If any interesting creatures came he would have the snacks to share with them. Perhaps that songbird with the beautiful voice would be there, and he could catch sight of it this time. Returning the gecko would be worth it if he could find that bird.

As he made his way through the forest Paul found himself whistling cheerfully. It was quite far, but he remembered the way. For a moment he wondered if the colorful gecko was doing alright in his backpack, but he didn't want to stop and check until he reached his destination.

At last he reached the tree and climbed up to the fork in the branches where he had settled before. He took the specimen jar out of his backpack. "Well, little fellow," he said looking at the gecko, "it's time for you to go home. Easy does it now." He opened the lid and placed the jar on the branch next to him. The gecko looked around, apparently deciding whether or not to venture out of the jar. "Come on, it's quite safe! This is where I found you!" Paul encouraged it.

The gecko stared quite brazenly at Paul, clearly assessing the situation. Then, after looking around a few more times, it cautiously made its way out of the jar. Paul watched it testing the branch and almost reached out to touch it. But with one last look up at him, the gecko seemed to decide which way to go and headed off into the higher reaches of the tree. Paul wondered if there were more geckos in the tree, but "his" gecko had already disappeared into the foliage and he realized it would be hard to see them even if there was a whole family up there.

He checked his backpack and decided it was time for a snack. As soon as he had opened the bag of cookies he heard a rustling sound. Turning around, he half expected to see the gecko coming back to join him. Instead, though, the rustling continued and suddenly a bird emerged. It was the most beautiful bird Paul had ever seen. Its feathers were a bright golden yellow, almost glowing. It settled on a branch and sat there looking straight at him.

Paul hesitated. He was tempted to offer part of his cookie but afraid that any movement would disturb the lovely creature. So he just sat still and watched. The bird continued watching him intently. It shifted position slightly and opened its beak. Paul smiled. "Are you asking for a piece of my cookie?" he thought to himself. "Well, I'd be delighted to share, if you're not afraid." Slowly he lifted the cookie and broke off a small piece. "I'll just put it on the branch here," he thought as he carefully moved his hand towards where the bird was sitting. The bird didn't move. He placed the piece carefully and slowly withdrew his hand, watching the bird all the time. The bird kept its eye on him too.

As Paul leaned back slightly to give the bird more space, the bird shifted its position. Suddenly it leaned forward and grabbed the piece of cookie in its beak and flew off. Paul watched, wondering how far the bird would go, but quickly lost sight of it among the dense foliage. He decided to eat his cookie and wait.

Just as he was finishing the cookie Paul heard a chirp, and then a full blown song started. He was sure it was the golden bird, although he couldn't see it. He listened, enraptured by the bird's beautiful voice. When it finished he murmured softly, "Thank you. That was so beautiful." To his surprise there was a rustling and the bird appeared. Once settled the bird started singing again, this time in clear view. When it finished Paul smiled again and clapped his hands gently, hoping the bird wouldn't be frightened, and to his surprise it stayed watching him.

"Do you want more cookie?" Paul asked softly, carefully taking another cookie out of his bag. As if in response the bird moved closer. Paul broke off a couple of small pieces and gently placed them on the branch in front of the bird. This time the bird came forward and picked up a piece and didn't fly away. Instead, it just took a couple of steps backward and proceeded to eat the piece of cookie. Paul realized he was holding his breath watching the bird so close to him. He gently exhaled and wondered what would happen next. As if in answer to his unspoken question, the bird gave a quiet chirp and moved to take the second piece. Once the piece was in its beak the bird paused, as if deciding whether to stay or fly away to a safer location. Paul didn't move. The bird started eating.

Paul realized he was smiling again. "Goodness," he thought, "what a treat to see this bird so close. I hope it sings again." And sure enough, when the cookie was finished the bird started its song. This time it kept singing for a long time. At the end, it gave Paul a look. Paul laughed and clapped his hands gently saying, "You want applause, is that it?" The bird chirped a few times and then flew away. Paul leaned back against the tree trunk and laughed some more. "Bye bird, hope to see you again!" he called out.

Paul saw the bird again many times. In fact, meeting this bird at the tree became an almost daily occurrence. Paul would arrive at the tree as early as his schedule allowed, which was usually right after lunch when Mr. Black seemed to need to take a nap. Since Paul was able to complete all his school work either during the morning sessions or in the evening, it was never a problem to just take off in the afternoon. To assuage Mr. Black's concerns about his student, which did surface on occasion, Paul provided accounts and samples of the interesting flora and fauna he had investigated on his trips. Fortunately, the pond was well stocked and he was able to come up with new specimens on a regular basis.

He mentioned the golden songbird on one occasion. Mr. Black seemed interested but was unable to identify the bird in his books and so Paul didn't bother to talk about it again. Yet it was really the bird that Paul went to visit. Even before he arrived at the tree Paul would start to listen, trying to hear the bird's song. Usually he heard nothing until after he arrived at the tree, or had climbed up to his usual spot. He began to think the bird was waiting for him, waiting to sing that special song just for him. Of course, Paul realized the bird also came for the cookies. He had discovered that the bird liked peanut butter cookies as well as oatmeal raisin; the chocolate chip cookies he had brought one day had been rejected.

He had thought it might be silly to talk to the bird, so he had tried to develop an appropriate whistle, but without success. It sounded like he was calling a dog and the bird would have none of it. When he called out, "Bird, are you there?" he was usually met with chirps and then a song, so he decided talking was the way to go. He had decided to think of her as "she" on account of the beautiful colors of her feathers as well as the sweetness of her singing voice, but hadn't been able to come up with a suitable name, so she was still "Bird."

As the days went on, Paul began to share more and more with the bird. He told her about his parents, how his father was always gone to work and how his mother seemed to care about nothing, just stared into space. He talked about Mr. Black, and often asked the bird what he should bring back for him that day. Although the bird didn't exactly make suggestions, when Paul climbed down from the tree and said he needed something to bring home the bird would fly towards a tree or bush that had beautiful flowers, or was hosting some interesting insect, or was even home to a bird's nest. Paul always thanked the bird and told her all about Mr. Black's reaction the next day.

Paul enjoyed his talks with the bird, but the most special times were when she sang for him. She had such a beautiful voice, and seemed to be able to put together the notes in a variety of ways that Paul found enchanting. He always found himself smiling as she sang, and feeling warm and contented inside.

He wondered if there was only one of these songbirds. He had never seen another golden bird at the pond, and there never seemed to be an answering song when his bird sang. "I hope you're not lonely, Bird," he told her one day as she perched on the branch beside him eating pieces of cookie. "Don't you have a bird family?" The bird just looked at him with her black beady eyes, cocking her head to one side as if thinking about it. Then with another chirp she hopped closed to Paul, landing on his finger.

"Oh, my!" Paul was surprised, but tried not to move his hand. "Well, hello, Bird, you are friendly today! Are you telling me you don't have a bird family? That I'm like your family?" Paul looked at her closely, with a tender look in his eyes. "I have to say, you're my best friend, Bird." The bird responded with a gentle chirp and a short but very sweet song before flying away.

Paul treasured those moments. He knew that it was silly to believe that the bird understood his words, yet it felt like real communication. Even if the bird didn't say anything in reply, she always sang to him. Those songs were far more meaningful than the boring conversations with his father, if his father talked to him at all, or the vacant stares of his mother, or even discussions with Mr. Black, which usually ended with him saying he would research that matter and get back to him.

One day Paul's world came crashing down. His father announced that they were moving to the city. He explained that his job had changed, that he no longer needed to travel to all the different villages to see his clients, that he would be meeting people in the city. So it made sense to move to there. Paul would be able to finish his studies at a good school, and his mother would have more opportunities to do things with other women. Then he paused and looked at Paul and his mother, expecting them to be excited, or at least interested in the news. But both of them just stared at him blankly.

Paul was in shock, he had lived in this remote place for so long, hadn't been in touch with other kids his age for years, and his bird lived here. This news meant his whole world would change. His mother recovered first, or at least was able to say something. It was basically just along the lines of "that sounds nice, dear." Paul thought that she was accepting it too easily. He wanted to question, to argue against the move, but his father started talking again, mentioning how Mr. Black was really too old to continue to tutor Paul so he would have to go to the school in the city anyway. Paul looked at him and managed a nod. "Um, when will we go?" he said weakly.

"We should go as soon as possible," his father responded enthusiastically. "There's a house we can move into at the end of the month. Would you both like to come and see it so we can decide if it's suitable?" He looked at his wife hopefully.

"A house in the city? Yes, I'd like to see it," Paul's mother was actually showing interest. "Can we go tomorrow, or the next day might be better, I suppose," she wondered.

His father smiled and said that the next day would be better. He had to arrange for someone to show them the house. Paul was relieved, at least one day to prepare himself to go to the city, so he nodded his agreement and quickly escaped to his room. Sitting on his bed he wondered what to do. How could he leave this place, and his bird?

As he thought about it more he had to admit that going to school with others his own age did sound quite exciting. And even though it wasn't New York City, the only city he could even vaguely remember, still there might be fun things to see and do. Yet the thought of leaving his bird weighed heavily on him. At least I can go and visit her today he decided, and quickly picked up his backpack and went towards the kitchen. His parents looked up and nodded when he said he was going for a walk. He took some cookies for the bird and quickly left.

When he reached the tree he climbed up and called out to the bird. There was no answer. Paul called out again, and brought out the cookie hoping to tempt her. "Come on Bird, your favorite cookie!" he called. Still no answer; and Paul started to feel a sense of despair. "Please come, Bird," he said. "I have to see you today." He started to eat the cookie, and suddenly he heard a familiar chirp and rustling sound and the bird appeared.

"Oh Bird, you're here!" Paul was so excited he wanted to reach out to the bird. But he remembered to give her a piece of cookie first. She quickly ate it and hopped towards him looking for more. "Come on my finger, Bird," Paul said softly. "I'll share my cookie with you." The bird looked at him with interest, as if sensing something different. Then she hopped closer and perched on his finger, chirping softly. "Alright, here's your cookie," Paul held a small piece out to her. "I won't see you tomorrow; I have to go to the city. But I'll come back and tell you all about it!" The bird looked at him and started to sing, softly at first and then building up to her full song voice. Paul was smiling when she finished, and happily gave her another piece of cookie.

The next day they set off early in their old car. Paul and his mother were both more excited than they had expected to be. His father seemed in high spirits and talked about the city and how different it would be for them all to live there. As they drew closer he started to point out different buildings and places of interest, explaining that their house was in the center but that the road went around the outskirts because of the river. After what seemed like an endless tour, they pulled up on a street outside a nice looking house. "This is it!" he said. "And there's the person with the key to let us in. Let's go!"

Paul and his mother exchanged glances and obediently got out of the car. As they made their way to the house Paul was looking around, noticing that there were trees lining the street and it looked like some kind of park at the end of the road. They went inside and Paul's mother began to examine each room, starting with the kitchen. She seemed excited and upbeat, and Paul wandered off to explore the rest of the house. He hoped there would be a back yard, and indeed there was. It was small, but quite well kept, with fruit trees as well as a colorful flower bed.

As he made his way through the rooms, which had a few pieces of furniture here and there, something caught his eye. There was a stand with something hanging on it, something covered in a cloth. He removed the cloth and to his surprise there was a beautiful birdcage. It was empty, and very clean, with places to put water and food and several perches. Paul looked at it in disbelief; it was perfect for his bird. Taking it off the stand he carried it over to where his mother was admiring the back yard. "Mother, look, it's a lovely birdcage. I want to bring a bird from where we live, to remind me, you know, of all the good things there."

His mother turned to look and seemed to hesitate. Paul's father came over and smiled, "Yes, that's a good idea Paul. A bird would be a fine thing. I think this house will do very well don't you?" He looked at them hopefully.

Paul was nodding, thinking that he had no choice so he must just make the best of it, and if he could bring his bird it might be alright. His mother was nodding too. She said that the kitchen was fine, and the rooms seemed to be a good size. Paul's father was looking relieved. "So I can tell them we'll take it," he said. "There's a lot to organize to bring all our belongings but you can take care of that, right dear?" He looked at his wife who was smiling. "Yes, dear, it's going to be quite an adventure!"

And an adventure it was. Paul's mother seemed to have come to life as she coordinated the move. She quickly sorted out their furniture into two groups: one to go to the city and one to be left behind. Then she started packing things in boxes. Paul helped when she asked him to do something but most days he was able to escape, suggesting that he was just in the way. He had gone to visit his bird as promised, and told her that big changes were coming. He hadn't brought the birdcage yet, although his mother had almost packed it in a box one day.

That decided him and he took the cage the next day on his visit to the bird's tree. Of course he had brought cookies too. He settled himself down and started to eat the first cookie, putting a piece out for the bird. As soon as the bird appeared she looked at the cage, but took the piece of cookie, and then perched on his finger as if to say, "well, what's that thing for?"

Paul moved his other hand towards the cage, putting a piece of cookie inside. "Would you like to check it out?" he suggested. The bird looked at him and then hopped over to the door of the cage. As Paul held his breath she looked in at the piece of cookie, and then hopped in, chirping. Paul closed the door quietly and sat there eating his cookie. "Well, Bird, now you're in the birdcage! What do you think of it?" The bird was busy exploring, and had found the other piece of cookie so she gave an answering chirp and seemed quite content.

"We're going to the city in a couple of days, and I really want you to come with me," Paul said. "So I think I'll bring you to our house now, and then you'll be all ready for the big move. Don't be afraid." Picking up the cage he started to move down the tree, trying to balance it so that the bird wouldn't be too disturbed. When he reached the ground he looked at the bird, and she was looking back at him. "It's okay, Bird. I'll take care of you, and we can be together in my new house."

Paul carried the cage carefully back home and into his room. The bird was quiet, but seemed fine. She even gave a gentle chirp when Paul placed the cage on a table next to the window. He put the dish of water he'd prepared into the cage and also some food in case she got hungry, and went downstairs to see if there was any dinner. When he came back he put the cover on the birdcage to let the bird sleep. As he lay in bed that night he thought to himself that now he was ready for his new adventure in the city.

A few days later Paul and his parents had moved into their new house in the city. Although there was still a lot of unpacking to do, Paul could tell that his mother already felt at home. He had installed the birdcage by the window that faced out onto the back yard so that the bird could see trees and greenery, in case she was afraid of the cars on the street. She had been very quiet so far, but Paul wasn't worried, at least not yet. It was all strange to him too, and he hoped things would settle down into a routine soon.

His new school was on vacation so he didn't have to go to classes for another couple of weeks, although his mother was anxious to take him shopping to buy supplies and appropriate clothes. It seemed that there was a dress code but not an actual uniform.

His father went to work every day as usual, but came home at a more reasonable time since he didn't have to travel so far. His mother had been talking about inviting people over for a house warming once everything was unpacked, but Paul didn't know anyone yet so he wasn't sure how that would work out.

Basically life was rather dull. He tried to explore a bit. He went to the park at the end of the street, but found it to be occupied mostly by mothers with young children. Paul tried to talk to the bird every day, bringing her food, especially her favorite cookies, but the bird remained quiet. At first she had chirped when he spoke, and when he gave her a piece of cookie, but she never sang. Paul tried to encourage her to sing, but to no avail. In fact, she didn't even chirp much now. Paul was beginning to worry. "Don't you like it here, Bird?" he asked her sadly one morning. "I thought we could be happy together, even if it's far from the pond and our tree. Won't you sing your beautiful song for me?"

The bird just looked at him and then turned away, hanging her head. Paul's mother came over just then. "Paul, I don't know about that bird. It doesn't look right."

"I know, Mother. I think she misses her home in the forest. I haven't heard her sing once since we came to the city, and she has the most beautiful voice. What should I do?"

His mother looked at him intently. "Well, Paul, when you take someone away from what they love in life they kind of fade away, like they're not really living. Do you know what I mean?"

"I think so. Her feathers used to be the most beautiful golden color, and now they look faded. And her beautiful voice is gone. I guess I'll have to take her back to the forest." Paul's voice shook slightly as he said that, but he squared his shoulders and looked at his mother. "I can take her back tomorrow. There's a bus that goes twice a day. I'll be back before dark."

His mother just nodded. "I'll give you money for bus fare," she said. "And then we'll go shopping to get you some new clothes for school, and whatever else you need," she said brightly, turning to go back to the kitchen leaving Paul with his bird.

"Did you hear that, Bird?" Paul said. "We're going back to the forest tomorrow. I can't keep you here if you're unhappy. I don't want you to fade away. I want you to be free to sing!"

The next day Paul set out with the birdcage, keeping the cover on so that the bird wouldn't be frightened. It was a bit of a walk from where the bus dropped him, but he didn't mind. It was nice to be out of the city and breathing the fresh air of the forest again.

All too soon they arrived at the pond and he climbed the tree, holding the birdcage carefully. Opening the cover, he looked in at the bird. He took the cover off and the bird blinked several times, as if unaccustomed to the bright sunlight. She looked around and chirped and looked at Paul, chirping again.

"Yes, this is your home, Bird," he said, opening the door of the cage. "Come on out."

The bird looked at Paul and hopped out of the cage onto the branch. She shook herself and hopped along it, and then began fluttering her wings, chirping. Suddenly she took off into the air and flew around chirping loudly. As she reached the next tree she burst into song. Paul was watching in excitement and he clapped and shouted out. "Yes, Bird, you're home. Oh, you can sing all you want now!"

Suddenly Paul realized there was an echo. And then he saw a second bird fly out of the tree. The two golden birds circled around each other and disappeared into the branches. Paul couldn't believe it. His bird had a friend.

Then he heard the familiar rustling and chirping that signaled her arrival. Instead of just his bird, both birds appeared and landed on the branch not far from him. One approached him chirping. "Bird, is that you?" Paul asked. "And this is your friend? I'm so glad. You can stay here together and sing to each other." He realized the cage was still there and he quickly closed its door and put the cover back on. "No more cage for you!" he said.

His bird cocked her head and looked at him. She gave a loud chirp and burst into song. And then the other bird joined in. They finished their duet and Paul softly clapped his hands, not wanting to scare them. His bird chirped and Paul nodded in response, and then the two birds flew off together. As he climbed back down from the tree Paul heard them singing together again. "Goodbye beautiful golden songbird; I did the right thing bringing you back."

As he waited for the bus to take him back to the city he wondered if he should bother bringing the birdcage. There didn't seem to be anywhere to leave it, so he just put it on the seat beside him when he got on the bus. A couple of villages later more people got on and he heard a voice asking if they could sit in the seat next to him. "Oh yes, I'll just move this," he said picking up the birdcage.

"Is there something in it?" the voice asked. Paul turned to answer and saw a young girl about his age had sat down beside him. "Is there a bird in there?" she asked.

"Um, no. There was a bird, but I had to let her go." Paul managed to respond. He saw the girl's quizzical expression and continued, "I took her from the forest to our new home in the city, but she didn't like being stuck in the cage so I brought her back. She's fine now."

"But you're a bit sad?" the girl said.

"Well, yes, I guess so. I'll be okay though. I expect I'll make new friends when school starts."

"Oh, are you going to the Christian High School? That's where I go."

"Yes, I think that's what it's called." Paul looked at her. "Is it really like a church? I mean, my family doesn't go to church."

"Oh, no," she laughed. "I think it's just called that because some missionaries started it long ago. We don't have to go to Bible classes or anything! You'll be fine." She was smiling and Paul smiled back. "I'm Anna, by the way," she said.

"Paul," he responded.

"Well, Paul, it's nice to meet you. You should come over to my house on Saturday. We're having a barbecue before school starts. There will be a bunch of kids there. Your parents can come too, if they like."

"Oh, that sounds great!" Paul was surprised. "My mother was talking about having a house warming party once we get to know some people. Maybe she'd like to come and we can make new friends. Thanks."

"Alright then." Anna took a pen and piece of paper out of her pocket and started writing. "Here's my address, and phone number, and my parents' names. My parents would be pleased to meet your parents I'm sure."

Paul took the paper and nodded. They continued to chat as the bus took them back to the city. At least Anna kept talking, her voice rising and falling almost like a song. Paul wasn't really paying attention to the conversation, just listening to her voice. He was also fascinated by the way her long hair was shining in the sun; it looked almost like gold. Then it was her stop and she got up to leave. "See you on Saturday, Paul," and she was gone.

Paul looked out the window and watched her walk away, her golden hair blowing slightly in the breeze. She turned and waved, and he waved back, smiling hopefully.

The Math Professor

"Wake up, you'll be late!" Someone was pulling at the covers on my bed.

I groaned and pulled the comforter over my head. But the voice and pulling were persistent. My mind slowly remembered that Erin, my roommate, had promised to wake me in time for my math class. She had even agreed to get up and walk with me as far as the coffee shop to make sure I made it on time.

"Come on, let's go!"

"Yes, yes, I'm coming," I opened my eyes and sat up in bed. Fortunately, my backpack was beside my bed, or had Erin just put it there for me? Anyway, I assumed it had all I needed inside. I just had time to brush my teeth, and my hair, and put on the clothes I'd tossed on the floor yesterday, and follow her out the door.

As I struggled to keep up with Erin, who was unbelievably full of energy, I couldn't believe I had thought it was a good idea to sign up for a math class that started at 8:00 am. I mean, who can do math at 8 in the morning!

Erin had thought I was crazy too when I told her my schedule over lunch after our first classes. "You mean you have to be in class every day at 8 am!" she said in shock.

"Yep, every day, not just Monday," I told her, sighing heavily. "My parents thought it would be fine since I had to be at my high school by 7:30 every morning, and the dorm is so much closer to the lecture hall."

"Well, I guess your only hope is for me to get up and go with you every morning then," Erin had replied.

"But why, you don't have class till 10, or 11 some days?"

Erin had smiled and said she had her reasons, which seemed to involve being a good roommate, among other things. Of course, it wasn't totally altruistic on her part. She had eventually admitted there was a cute guy who worked in the coffee shop in the mornings.

"So is the cute guy here?" I asked as we walked in.

"Yes," she whispered, "see over there by the espresso machine."

"Oh, him with all the red hair?" He did look kind of cute so I let her do the talking. My order was to go of course, a small coffee with lots of cream to cool it off so I could gulp it down as I made my way quickly to class. We weren't supposed to bring food or drinks into the lecture hall, and I had a feeling the professor was the type to stick by such rules.

As I made my way to my seat I noticed there were fewer students in the lecture hall than yesterday. I wasn't really surprised, since I was thinking of dropping the class myself. I had been sort of forced into taking this Math 140 calculus class when my advisor questioned my understanding of what an astronomy degree entailed. "You'll need a lot of math for that you know," she said when I had suggested I might be better taking the pre-calculus course this semester. "No, better get started on the real thing now. If you can't do it you need time to think about a new major," she stated, not unkindly though. "Your math grades are fine; you'll have no trouble," she had added. So here I was.

I pulled my textbook and notebook from my backpack and got settled just in time. A door opened and Dr. Nott walked in. He was wearing the same slightly rumpled suit that he had worn yesterday, and which surely had a covering of chalk dust over most of it. In one hand was an ancient looking briefcase which he placed on the table before turning to pick up a piece of chalk. No power point slides or computerized anything for him, just your basic chalkboard! With his unruly white hair and old fashioned clothes this guy really looked like a caricature of an old math professor. I heard a few snickers from students sitting near me as he started writing on the board. He paused for a moment, as if deciding whether to tell them to be quiet, and then continued writing.

His teaching style wasn't exactly enthusiastic, yet there was something about him that kept my attention. I realized that this guy actually loved the equations he was writing on the board. But his methods of problem solving were so long and complicated, I soon found myself getting frustrated. By the end of the class I was determined; I was going to my advisor and dropping the class!

Since I had free time for the rest of the morning I headed to her office, 'Dr. Maggie Wainright' it said on the door. I knocked and walked in. "And what can I do for you?" she asked.

"I've come to drop Math 140," I said. "I'll take Math 115 instead."

"Ah, Zoe Callahan, yes the astronomy major. I remember you. Sit down." Dr. Wainright was clicking on her keyboard and looking at her screen. "Nope, not a good idea. I told you that already. And anyway Math 115 is all full."

"Oh," I fidgeted in my seat. "Alright then, can I switch to a different section of the 140?"

She looked up and stared at me. "May I ask why?"

"Well, um, it's just Dr. Nott's lectures don't make sense to me."

"But he shows up on time?" she was looking at me closely.

"Oh yes, of course. I'm sure he's a good teacher. He seems to really like math, but I just don't get it, the way he wants us to do things."

She sat back in her chair. "Well, if you think he's a good teacher you should give him the chance to explain it to you. Go and see him in his office, it's room 412. He has office hours every morning after class." She stood up.

I got up too, realizing the conversation was over. "So is he there now?" I asked on my way out.

"Yes, I believe so," she picked up her phone and clearly dismissed me.

After a few wrong turns I found the correct hallway and made my way to room 412. It was right at the end, and the door was ajar. I knocked and called out, "Dr. Nott?" Not hearing a response, I peeked around the door and saw a rather messy office, the desk covered in papers and a chalkboard covered in math equations. Then a door opened at the side and Dr. Nott emerged.

"Ah, and to what do I owe this pleasure, young lady?" he asked.

"Well, um, Dr. Nott," I stumbled over my words. "I'm in your Math 140 Calculus class, and, well, I have some questions."

"Questions, yes, a questioning mind is all important!" he beamed at me and made his way to behind his desk. "Sit, young lady, and tell me your name."

"I'm Zoe Callahan. I'm a freshman and my major is astronomy."

"Excellent. Of course you need a lot of math for that. You can take several of my classes!" he leaned forward in his chair, his eyes bright and focused on me.

"Um, well, I don't know about that," I said hesitantly. "You see, I don't understand why you're teaching it the way you do. It doesn't make sense to me. It's not like how we learned it in high school."

"Well, you have to study hard to understand math you know, it's not all fun and games."

"I know that," I said a bit defensively. "But I just don't understand why you're teaching it the way you are."

He looked at me intently. "You'll have to explain yourself better than that."

"Alright," I leaned forward in my chair. "It's like remembering the colors of the rainbow. The way I do it is ROY G BIV. Then it's easy – Red, Orange, Yellow, Green, Blue, Indigo, Violet. The way you teach it seems like you are making us memorize the wavelength of each color and then having us figure out the order from the sizes of the wavelengths. Remembering the order of the colors as ROY G BIV works much better." I sat back and looked at him.

"Well, my goodness. That's a fascinating argument, ROY G BIV, yes that tells you the order, but only if you know what the letters stand for. You still need to know all the colors. That's why I'm teaching you about the colors, so you can really understand how the rainbow works."

We looked at each other. Without meaning to I rolled my eyes and sighed. Shocked at my rudeness, I felt myself go red and shifted uncomfortably in my chair expecting Dr. Nott to be angry. Instead, I heard a sudden sound, a cackle. Looking up I saw him shaking with laughter. Surprised, I found myself joining in.

"Well, Miss Zoe Callahan, you've got quite a good brain I can tell. Go and apply it to understanding calculus and we can meet again."

"I have to do it your way?" I asked.

"Yes. Learn to do it my way. Come back when you've understood it. Then we can talk more," he stood up and ushered me out the door. "See you in class tomorrow!" he called after me as I made my way back down the hallway.

There was still half an hour before my next class so I made my way to the cafeteria to grab something to eat and another cup of coffee. As I carried my tray to the tables I heard a voice call out to me and saw Dr. Wainright sitting by the window. "Come and join me, Zoe," she said.

I walked over to her table reluctantly. "Hi, Dr. Wainright," I said and sat down.

"Oh call me Maggie," she smiled. "I'm not really a scary ogre you know, I'm here to help."

I nodded and started on my muffin.

"Did you see Dr. Nott?" she asked.

"Yes, I did. What an interesting person he is," I took a drink of my coffee.

"Indeed," she agreed. "He really loves teaching math."

"Yes, he said I could take lots of his classes!" I chuckled. "I suppose I can't escape from him after all."

Maggie was smiling. "It seems not, and I'm glad. He's semi-retired you know, but he enjoys new students so much we keep him on."

"It's funny though," I said. "He seems kind of set in his ways. I'm sure lots of students drop his class. There are certainly fewer people now than in the first class. That's why I thought you'd let me drop it," I looked at her pointedly.

She just smiled back. "Well, Zoe, some of those students complained about him, said he didn't show up for class, so I had to let them change to a different section. But you said you thought he was a good teacher so I hoped you would stick with him, for his sake," she added thoughtfully.

"Well, I did have an interesting talk with him in his office, and he told me to come back again, so I guess I will." I finished my muffin and stood up. "I have to go to my next class now. Thanks for, well, thanks for encouraging me to go see him."

When I met Erin at lunchtime I told her about my encounter with Dr. Nott. She looked at me a bit strangely and commented that she knew a few people who had been assigned to his class but then switched to a different professor. I nodded and agreed that there were fewer students now, but he was such an interesting guy I was going to stick with it. She shook her head and carried on eating her lunch. Finally, she looked at me and said quietly,

"Some people say he lives in the closet in the lecture hall! They think he was evicted from university housing."

I stared at her, wondering how people could be that mean. "You just don't want to have to keep waking me up for that 8 o'clock class!" I said at last with a grin.

Erin shrugged, but she kept her word and I didn't miss a class. I was even beginning to enjoy math as taught by Dr. Nott. He didn't have much interest in astronomy or any of the sciences it seemed, although he was convinced that a real understanding of math was essential for any true scientist. In the end he did stimulate a new appreciation of math in me. First, though, we had a few arguments.

By the end of the second week of class I was struggling again with his methods and I marched into his office ready to do battle. "We did some calculus in high school and the way we did it was much better," I began as soon as I walked in his door.

"Better! Come, come, are you sure you don't mean easier!" Dr. Nott was sitting at his desk and he looked up at me with a rather amused expression.

"No, see this example you gave us in class today," and I opened my notebook, "I can do it in fewer steps that make more sense."

Dr. Nott jumped up out of his chair and went to the chalkboard. "Here," he said, cleaning it off with rapid movements. "Let's see your method. Take a piece of chalk and show me how you would do it."

"Alright," I was nervous, but determined. I wrote the first line of the problem on the board as he stood beside me.

"Go ahead Miss Zoe Callahan, and we'll see whose method is better," and he started writing the equations the way he had shown us in class.

I quickly worked on my side of the board and reached the solution in only five lines. I turned and looked at Dr. Nott who had also finished, but I could see there were eight lines of math on his side of the board.

"See, my way is shorter. And I don't think there's anything wrong with it." I stood back and he joined me, both of us looking at the board.

"Well, see here, you made an assumption that these two are equal and so cancel out," he said, pointing to my equation. "That assumption might not be valid in all cases."

"I see that," I frowned looking at the board, comparing his work with mine. "But in high school we were taught to cancel them out."

"Yes, but can you prove they are always equal," Dr. Nott's eyes were shining and he was quite animated. "In high school you can get away with such an assumption because the teachers only use examples where it is true. But in the real world that might not always hold true, like in astronomy," he added pointedly.

"Well, how do we prove it?" I asked. "Or show it to be false, might be easier I suppose."

"That's right, good. Prove it false," he was smiling and nodding. "Can you do that?"

"I don't know," I shook my head. "It works in all the examples I've encountered so far. Maybe you should prove it false, since you're the one who doesn't believe it works!"

He looked at me and started laughing. "Well, Miss Zoe Callahan, what a little spitfire you are! I'll certainly take up the challenge."

"So, can I use my method until you prove it false?" I pressed my advantage.

"At your own risk, at your own risk," he was still laughing. "I might find an example that proves it false and then you'd be in trouble, wouldn't you!"

I started laughing then. "Well we'll have to see, won't we? I have to go now. I have class."

"Come back soon," he said, turning to write on his chalkboard.

So at least once a week I made my way to Dr. Nott's office. I noticed in passing that there never seemed to be anyone in the other offices in his hallway, but he was always there and seemed to enjoy our meetings so I just kept visiting him. And we still hadn't found an example that falsified my method.

When mid-terms came around the schedule was different and Erin and I didn't have to walk to the coffee shop in the early morning. Instead, we sat in our room trying to study.

"How's it going with the cute guy with the red hair in the coffee shop?" I asked.

"Well, I found out his name is Tim and he's studying anthropology. We don't have any classes together this semester but maybe next semester," Erin was smiling dreamily. "I told him about the party on Saturday in our dorm and he said he'd try to come. Maybe he has a friend for you!"

I just laughed, but I was glad Erin was happy. She was certainly attractive with her long blond hair and bright smile, and she seemed to find it easy to talk to guys she liked. I wasn't so confident. No-one had ever called me attractive in high school. I suppose wearing braces hadn't helped. And anyway all the popular guys thought me too much of a nerd since I was always busy doing my school work or more interested in using my telescope to watch the stars than hanging out. And now I had become friends with the oldest math professor in the school, how hopeless was that!

Tim did attend our party, and after that he and Erin started dating. I didn't mind as I had found a group of people who enjoyed the stars as much as I did and we hung out at the observatory on our free evenings. I had to study hard too. As well as the calculus class I had to take physics, and astronomy of course, and a boring history class. It didn't sound much compared to all the courses I took in high school, but with the labs and all the assignments and readings for history I found myself quite stressed.

Sometimes I went to see Dr. Nott, more for the general support and encouragement he gave me than for a specifically math-related question. Even though he was old-fashioned in his teaching methods he had a real love of learning and somehow that helped me stay interested in my studies.

One day as I made my way to his office I smelled paint and saw a collection of materials lying in the stairwell. I asked Dr. Nott what was going on and he just shrugged in that absent minded way he sometimes had. "I didn't notice anything. I'm sure they won't bother me," and he started writing some new equations on his chalkboard.

The next time I was going up the stairs I encountered two painters. When I asked them if they were painting the offices or just the stairs and hallways they looked at me a bit strangely. "We're doing all the stairs and hallways and some of the offices, yes," one of them said. "But we don't do the ones on the fourth floor. We don't go in there. There's no need." It seemed Dr. Nott was right; they weren't going to bother him.

When it was time to sign up for the next semester's courses I went to see Maggie in her office. She seemed pleased to see me, and agreed with my choices. "And you'll be taking Dr. Nott's math class won't you," she said firmly.

"I will indeed," I replied. "I really like him, even though he's quite unusual!"

"Good, good," she nodded typing on her keyboard. "I'm glad. And you're enjoying your astronomy class too?"

"Yes, and I go to the observatory whenever possible. There's a group of us and we have a lot of fun, well in a nerdy kind of way!" I laughed slightly embarrassed.

"That's all good," Maggie laughed with me. "Good you have made friends. And there's nothing wrong with being nerdy."

I was grateful for that support. Somehow Erin didn't rate my friends so highly, and she certainly didn't think much of my spending time with Dr. Nott. But she was involved with Tim and mostly left me to my own devices.

Time flew by and before I knew it I taken two years of classes with Dr. Nott. There were fewer students in each class I took, which allowed him to give more personal attention to those of us who stuck with him. I never was able to get him to come and visit the observatory with me to look at the stars, but he did enjoy my excited accounts of new observations I had made. In the first semester of my junior year I took my last math class and visited him in his office quite regularly, but by the spring semester I was too busy with my own studies and rather neglected him until finals were over.

I went to his office to see him before leaving for the summer. The door was ajar as usual but he was nowhere in sight. "Dr. Nott," I called out and knocked on the door again. "It's me, Zoe Callahan, are you there?" I hesitated and then decided I could go in and leave him a note. The office was just as it always was, with equations on the chalkboard and papers all over the desk. I was just starting to write him a note when the door at the side opened and he stepped out of what seemed to be a closet, a big smile on his face. "Miss Zoe Callahan! How lovely to see you!"

"Oh, Dr. Nott, I thought you weren't here. I was just going to leave you a note." I explained. "Were you hiding in the closet?"

"Hiding, oh no, of course not!" he looked back at the closet a little confused. "I was just, well, I was doing something and then I heard your voice. It's great to see you! How are you?"

"I'm fine," I replied truthfully, for my classes had gone well and I felt confident about my finals. "I'm sorry I didn't come and see you this semester. I do rather miss having you as my teacher."

"Well, well. And you were such a critic at first!" Dr. Nott's eyes were sparkling again. "I think I've taught you all you need to know, though. You need to apply yourself to your astronomy studies now."

"Thanks, Dr. Nott," I said quietly. "Well, I'm off for the summer now. I just wanted to see you before I left. I'll be a senior next year when I come back, you know."

He looked at me closely, and then sighed. "Yes, my dear. And you'll do very well I'm sure. Now run along, and have a wonderful summer."

I let him usher me out of his office. Although I didn't see him again the next year, I remembered his enthusiasm whenever I struggled with a problem, especially if it involved anything mathematical.

As Erin and I hugged each other in the morning of our graduation I felt a pang of regret that I had apparently forgotten my old professor friend. To my surprise, though, as we milled around at the end of the ceremony greeting friends and looking for parents, I suddenly found him by my side. "Miss Zoe Callahan, congratulations!" he said.

"Oh, Dr. Nott, you're here!" I gave him a big smile. "I'm so pleased to see you. Thank you for all your encouragement, I'd never have made it without your help."

"Nor without my advice, I reckon," Maggie Wainright, my advisor, joined in.

"Oh, my two favorite people!" I said happily. "I must introduce you both to my parents." I turned to look for them, and saw them on the far side of the rows of chairs. I waved and turned back to Maggie and Dr. Nott, but only Maggie was standing there. Out of the corner of my eye I saw a movement, like a glimpse of the old professor waving to me in the distance and then he was gone. "Maggie, where did Dr. Nott go?" I asked.

"Oh he couldn't stay. He hasn't been teaching here since last fall, did you know?"

"No, I was so busy I just didn't take time to look for him. Oh, now I feel bad. Do you have his address? I'd like to visit him before I leave here altogether."

Maggie looked a bit disconcerted. Then she smiled and said, "Are these your parents, Zoe?"

"Yes, Mom, Dad, this is Dr. Maggie Wainwright, my advisor. She's been such a great help to me."

They all said the usual complimentary things and there were smiles all round, culminating in a round of photos, and then another round when Erin and Tim, now engaged, showed up to join us. But in the back of my mind I was still thinking about Dr. Nott, and I determined to go and see Maggie to ask for his address before I left.

We didn't have to leave till the next day so I hurried over to Maggie's office first thing in the morning. She smiled when she saw me. "Come in, Zoe. I thought you might show up today."

"Yes, I want to see Dr. Nott before I leave. Where does he live?"

"Zoe, please sit down. It's not so simple."

I sat down, a sinking feeling in my stomach. Maybe Erin's friends were right in thinking he had been evicted from campus housing, maybe there was some kind of scandal.

"Oh, I heard some bad things, and ...." My voice trailed off as I saw Maggie's face.

She quickly reassured me, "Zoe, he didn't do anything wrong. Let's take a walk." Maggie stood up. "It's not far."

I was puzzled but followed her out the door. "Are we going to see him?"

"I'll explain in a minute. Just come with me."

We walked along the path that led to the edge of the campus, where there was a large church. I had never been inside, and somehow it never occurred to me that Dr. Nott was religious so I was even more puzzled. But we didn't go into the church; we went around the back towards the graveyard.

She led the way towards a large oak tree. There was a headstone just under its branches and she stopped and motioned me forward. I read the name and stepped back in shock. "No! It can't be him," I protested. "This must be some other Dr. Nott. This person has been dead for ten years!"

"I'm sorry, Zoe. That is our Dr. Nott," Maggie had a strange look on her face. "He was my favorite professor too," she added.

After a few minutes we walked back towards the center of campus so I could meet up with my parents. Maggie left me sitting on a bench, still thinking about Dr. Nott.

"Hello, dear, are you ready for breakfast?" my mother's voice startled me. "What's the matter?" she was looking at me with concern. "Are you alright? You look like you've seen a ghost!"

"I'm fine," I managed to say. "I was just saying goodbye to my favorite teacher. Let's go." And with that I got up and walked off the campus and into the next stage of my life.

The Mermaid and the Dolphin

Astrid was enjoying the waves moving gently across the rocks. Some of them made it across her tail into the tidal pool she was watching; others just lapped at the rocks surrounding it, splashing her slightly. She couldn't stay out of the water for too long, so this was the perfect place. Every now and then she would dive back into the water, submerging her whole body to reinvigorate herself. It was a joy to feel the strength of the ocean pushing and pulling at her with its endless power.

The rocks could be dangerous of course. Her parents had warned her many times not to get too close when the tide was coming in and the waves were pounding towards their jagged edges. She had almost injured herself one time, misjudging her distance from a large rock. But she had changed direction just in time and had escaped with only a small scrape on her tail. She hadn't told her parents how it happened; only her sister Adrienne knew. She had told her to be more careful and given her a hug. "I couldn't bear to lose you," she said, and Astrid had determined to be more careful in the future.

These rocks were usually safe, with the ocean being remarkably calm around them. When a big storm arose her parents always told her to stay home. But it was after a storm that she found the most interesting sea creatures in the pool, and so she always made a point of coming here as soon as possible it had passed. There were always some starfish and seahorses and even actual fish that had washed over and been trapped there, hiding among the strands of seaweed. She would rescue them and return them to the ocean. Amazingly the limpets that clung to the rocks never seemed to be washed away. They were always still there after a storm. Astrid thought they had a rather boring life, just clinging on to a rock. But she had noticed that they actually moved, "walking" along the rock as they ate the algae from its surface.

Suddenly she heard her mother's voice, her beautiful tones carried on the wind, calling her family home for dinner. With a quick flip of her tail Astrid plunged into the water and rode a wave out into the deeper ocean. She swam down into the depths and she joined her sisters as they gathered at their underwater home. Father was there already, waiting for his daughters to arrive. Astrid was rather in awe of the handsome merman. He was much taller than her mother, with the strongest tail she had ever seen. She glided past him into the cave where Mother was waiting to greet them. Mother was beautiful, and Astrid never tired of admiring the beautiful locks of hair that flowed effortlessly behind her head, and the ever changing shimmers of color on her tail. Astrid's hair always seemed to be tangled, and her tail seemed plain compared to her mother's. Still, she was young and had seen her older sister Amelina's tail change color as she reached her full size and hoped the same would happen to hers.

As they gathered at the table to eat she noticed her Father looking at her. "Is something wrong, Father?" she asked nervously.

He just smiled and shook his head, leaning back contentedly. "I'm just pleased to see all my beautiful daughters home on time to enjoy this feast. Let's thank Mother for preparing such a wonderful meal for us!"

Mother blushed with pride as they all joined in clapping and then raised their glasses in gratitude. "Thank Agneska too, then, she helped me arrange everything," Mother smiled at her second oldest daughter. The other sisters clapped enthusiastically, for it was well known that Agneska was the best at helping to prepare the meals and, truth be told, they all wanted her to stay home and help as often as possible.

After dinner they gathered together before getting ready to sleep. "How were your singing voices today?" Father asked. "I heard some lovely tunes from you Amelina, but what about the rest of you?"

Astrid felt herself shrinking as she tried to appear invisible; she hadn't been singing at all. Fortunately, Adrienne started talking about how she had been singing and a dolphin had appeared beside her. Astrid was immediately interested. "Really, Adrienne, a dolphin? That's wonderful. Can I come with you to try and find more dolphins tomorrow?" Her sister smiled at her and nodded in agreement. She knew Astrid hated to sing. "Is that alright, Father?"

Father looked at them, and seeing his daughters' enthusiasm he was unable to suppress a smile towards Mother. "Why not," he replied. "Singing for dolphins is better than not singing."

Mother nodded in agreement, glad her husband was content with their daughters this evening. "Let's sleep now," she said gently, and Astrid smiled at the musical tone of her voice.

"Mother, even when you just talk down here it sounds like music!"

Mother patted her youngest daughter's head and smiled. "When you're older, Astrid, your voice will be beautiful too." Encouraged, Astrid went to sleep easily, despite her excitement at the possibility of meeting a dolphin tomorrow.

In the morning she and Adrienne waved goodbye to their sisters and swam together in the direction where the dolphin had appeared. As they approached an island Adrienne slowed and looked around. "See that island? I was on a reef on the other side and a dolphin came."

Astrid was so excited she rose up out of the water looking for the dolphin. "Come on, let's go and can you sing?" The two sisters made their way around the island to the reef. They found a comfortable spot where they could see the waves rolling across a wide expanse of ocean on one side, while on the other was a calm lagoon between the reef and the island proper.

Adrienne started singing and Astrid sat beside her impatiently. "You could sing too, you know," Adrienne said when she stopped for a minute. "Two singers are more powerful than one."

Astrid sighed. "Yes, but my voice is so, well, ugly. I might scare the dolphins away!"

Adrienne laughed. "Come on, try it. We can sing together, that's easier."

Adrienne started singing again, her clear voice soaring above the sounds of the waves. Astrid tried, but she was unable to reach the high notes and her song ended up more like the cries of an injured creature. "I really don't think I'm going to attract anything except maybe a shark looking for something to eat!" Astrid said shaking her head.

Adrienne laughed and then looked at her more seriously. "I have an idea. You can sing lower notes much better than the high ones. Why don't you sing harmony with me?"

Astrid looked puzzled.

"You know how Father and Mother sing together? She sings high notes and his deep voice sings the low notes. That's harmony. You can try to sing like Father!"

Now it was Astrid's turn to laugh. "Goodness, I could never sing like him! But I think I understand the idea. Let's try." As Adrienne started singing again Astrid tried to pitch her notes lower, in the range more comfortable for her voice.

They were so engrossed in their song, which was sounding rather good, that they hardly noticed the three dolphins until one had almost reached their rock. Startled, Astrid grabbed her sister's hand and pointed. "They've come!"

Adrienne smiled and continued singing as the first dolphin circled closer. Astrid joined in for a minute, and then broke off and slid into the water close to the beautiful creature. She swam up to the dolphin, who turned to look at her and then swam away a short distance before turning back as if to invite her to follow. With a huge grin on her face Astrid swam with the dolphin, following its moves and turns and even trying to leap in the air with it. The dolphin suddenly turned and dove under her, rising up quickly so she shot up in the air with it. "I'm flying!" Astrid shouted as she and the dolphin arced through the air together before landing with a big splash. The other dolphins also came to join the fun to Astrid's delight. "Come on Adrienne!" she called out. "Come and play with the dolphins!" Shaking her head in disbelief at what she was doing, Adrienne also abandoned her rock and her singing and joined them in the water.

The two mermaids and the three dolphins frolicked together for the rest of the morning. Astrid was quite oblivious to her surroundings and was horrified when Adrienne suddenly grabbed her and pointed to the shore. Without realizing it, they had made their way through a gap in the reef and into the lagoon. They were now in clear sight of the beach, and a group of people had sat down on the sand and were watching them!

"Oh no, we have to leave!" Adrienne cried. "Keep behind the dolphins and hopefully they won't see us." The dolphins seemed to understand the need to leave the lagoon, and the group quickly retreated to the far side of the reef and then further out to sea. "I hope they didn't see us," Adrienne was worried.

"I'm sure it's alright," Astrid said with greater confidence than she felt. "They would just have thought we were dolphins anyway. It will be fine." Both sisters knew it was important that humans never saw them.

"I'm not coming back here," Adrienne decided. "At least not in good weather," and she turned away.

Astrid sighed. "It was such fun playing with the dolphins though. I hope we can find them again somewhere else."

Astrid didn't want to tell Father about the humans, but Adrienne said they must be honest. So over dinner the two girls told their story. Adrienne started with a description of the island and the reef. Astrid then became excited telling how they had found a way to sing together and Mother smiled approvingly. Then she told about the dolphins, and how they had played in the water with them. Father had nodded, his face interested but not angry. Astrid was relieved, because she knew Father had strict ideas about how mermaids should behave. Then Adrienne took over the story, explaining how the people had come to the beach. She saw Father's face and explained that they had quickly swum out to sea together with the dolphins, so no-one saw them.

"This time," Father said sternly. "You must be more careful in the future. Playing with dolphins is no good if it's going to distract you from seeing danger."

Astrid was quick to come to the defense of the dolphins, explaining that they had hidden among them so the people saw only dolphins. "It's like the dolphins knew we had to hide from the people," she said.

"Yes," agreed Adrienne. "If the dolphins hadn't helped we would have been in trouble alright."

Mother smiled and said she was glad it all turned out alright, and she returned the conversation to their singing. "How clever of you both to sing together in harmony. We'd like to hear it some time, wouldn't we Father?"

Father nodded and Adrienne squeezed Astrid's hand, pleased that her little sister was going to be able to sing nicely for their parents at last.

The next morning the whole family set off together. Astrid was nervous, knowing that soon she would have to sing in front of everyone. Then she remembered how the beautiful dolphins had come when she and Adrienne sang together, and soon she was swimming enthusiastically, enjoying the waves. They all gathered at a rocky outcrop surrounded by deep water. Astrid knew her parents came here often; in fact, it was the place where they first met. Father liked to tell the story of how he had been attracted by a beautiful voice and had risen out of the ocean to see Mother singing. He had boldly joined her on the rock and begun singing with her, creating harmonies that sounded more amazing even than Mother's solo voice.

Now the family was ready to sing and Father began with his deep bass. After a while Mother joined in, while their daughters sat enjoying the music. Soon, though, Father stopped singing and turned to Amelina: "Right, Amelina, let's hear your song."

Amelina smiled and settled herself on the rock and started to sing. Her voice was not as strong as Mother's, but it had its own beauty. Astrid found herself smiling and waving her tail in time to the melody. Mother saw her and smiled. When she finished Astrid and her other sisters clapped enthusiastically. Father looked slightly disapproving, but when Mother joined in he smiled. "Well, you've won over your audience, Amelina. Well done!"

Next up was Agneska. She had a pretty, lilting style and her melody seemed to be carried easily on the wind. Astrid listened entranced, her thoughts traveling on the wind along with her sister's song.

After Agneska finished it was Adrienne's turn. She began quietly, singing the song she and Astrid had sung together the previous day. Astrid listened enviously, wishing she could sing so easily. Then, as Agneska reached the end of a phrase she turned to her and said, "Join me Astrid, like we did yesterday!"

Although this had been planned, Astrid felt very nervous. At first she couldn't find her note and her voice came out all wrong. She tried not to look at her sisters but she heard a muffled snort of laughter. Agneska stopped and patted her arm. "Sing like we did yesterday, with the dolphins!"

The image of the dolphins flooded Astrid's mind and she started singing to them, her eyes closed. Her voice gained strength and she found the perfect harmony to Agneska's melody. As they sang together she kept her eyes closed and was unaware of the effect she was having on her sisters and her parents. When the song ended she was shocked to hear their applause! Opening her eyes, she saw her whole family with broad smiles on their faces.

"Astrid, that was excellent!" Father said. "Excellent!"

Mother gave Astrid a warm hug, and her sisters all joined in.

"What a great day!" Father exclaimed. "All my daughters have found their voices! Now off you go to your places to practice singing, and we'll celebrate tonight over dinner."

Mother saw Astrid hesitate and asked her where she would like to go. "Well, Mother," Astrid began. "I'm not sure. I have a favorite place with a little pool in the rocks. I love it there."

"But?" Mother asked.

"Well, I've never been able to sing there. I'd really like to go back to the island Adrienne showed me, where the dolphins are. I think I can sing for dolphins."

"But there are people on that island, aren't there?" Mother remembered the story.

"Yes, but there's a lagoon separated by the reef, and that's where we were singing. It was only when we went in the lagoon that they could possibly see us. If I stay on the rocks and don't go in the lagoon it will be fine. Please can I try?" Astrid looked at her mother with a hopeful smile.

"I suppose so. But leave immediately if people can see you. Promise!"

"Yes, yes, I promise! I'll sit on the edge of the reef and stay far from the lagoon. Thank you Mother." Astrid swam away full of excitement.

She quickly reached the reef that protected the island and settled herself on a nice rock. "I wish Adrienne was here with me," she thought as she prepared to start singing. She forced herself to focus on the idea that the dolphins would come if she sang, and she started to sing. As she sang her confidence grew and at the same time her voice grew stronger. Soon she found her voice was carrying a beautiful tune, different from the lovely melody Adrienne had sung, but she realized she could make her own music in her voice. She was so focused on singing that she didn't see the dolphin until it came close to her rock and splashed her!

Astrid and Dolphin

105

Laughing, Astrid splashed the dolphin back and soon the two of them were playing in the waves. She found that the dolphin was willing to let her hold onto its neck and half carry her for a short distance. After a while though, the dolphin always leaped up into the air and Astrid would let go to plunge back into the water laughing happily. All too soon Astrid heard her mother's song and turned to the dolphin to say goodbye. "I'll be back tomorrow!" she said as she swam away.

That evening as they all gathered for dinner Astrid was excited to tell how she had been able to sing. "I sang so well the dolphin came to play with me!" she said proudly.

Her sisters laughed but Father looked rather stern. "Astrid, you have to focus on singing, not just playing!"

"But Father," Astrid asked, "why is it so important for us to sing? I mean, there are so many things to do, why is singing so special?"

Her parents exchanged glances and Astrid looked at her sisters. "What? Do you all know what the big deal is about singing?"

"Well, since you have learned to sing now I will tell you," Father said. "We mermaids have a responsibility to take care of the ocean and all that lives in it. Our voices are special; they calm the waves that storms bring. When we sing, the waves are drawn towards us and around us instead of going deep into the lower levels of the ocean, so the lower levels stay calm enough for all the fish and other sea creatures to survive. But it's dangerous for us to stay above the water during the storm if we can't sing strongly. We might be swept away by the strong waves and injured or even killed. So we have to learn to sing with a strong voice and keep singing while the winds blow. Can you do that, Astrid?"

"Oh, I don't know!" Astrid was surprised and a bit afraid. "You mean if we keep singing the waves won't hurt us?"

"That's right," Mother said. "The wind and the waves are drawn by our song, but they just circle around you and you can stay safely on your rock."

"But what about the dolphins? When I sing dolphins come. Will they be alright if they come during a storm?" Astrid was worried.

"I don't know about that," Father shook his head. "I never heard of dolphins being attracted by our songs. Boats are often swept onto the rocks when we sing, but I never heard of any sea creatures being harmed."

"Well I hope the dolphins are alright," Astrid said. "I don't want to sing if it gets the dolphins into trouble."

Adrienne gave Astrid's arm a squeeze. "I'm sure the dolphins will be fine. They know how to be safe in a storm."

Astrid smiled at her sister. "Thanks. I hope you're right. Maybe I could tell them to go into the lagoon if a bad storm is coming." The sisters hugged and everyone seemed cheerful again.

Every day Astrid went to the island reef and sang and played with the dolphins. She was careful to spend a good amount of time practicing her singing in case a storm came. But she always found one dolphin tempting her to play. She also returned to her favorite rock pool to check on the sea creatures there. Life was good for the young mermaid!

Eventually, though, the day came when Father announced that a storm was on its way. He looked around at his daughters and asked if they were all ready to sing during the storm. His eyes rested the longest on Astrid, as this would be her first experience. She looked at her sisters and her mother and finally looked up at Father. "Yes, Father, I'm ready."

Father nodded and they all swam up to the surface together. The sky was already overcast and Astrid could see large dark clouds on the horizon. She shivered slightly. Everyone held hands in a circle and Father spoke some special words that Astrid had not heard before. When he finished Mother began to sing, her voice gentle and calming. "Now go to your places, and do well," Father said.

As Astrid let go of her sisters' hands and began to swim away she felt excited and proud to carry out this special responsibility of protecting the sea creatures. She quickly reached the island and positioned herself on a rock on the ocean side of the reef. The waves were already beginning to swell and she looked around nervously. "No, I don't need to be afraid," she thought to herself. "I can sing!" Cautiously at first, but with mounting confidence, she began her song. Soon her voice was soaring above the sound of the wind, which had increased greatly. She watched the waves changing direction and coming towards her, but as Father had directed she kept singing and found that they only washed gently over her tail and she was in no danger of being hurt.

Once she thought she caught a glimpse of a dolphin, but as the waves continued to grow she had to focus on singing. Suddenly she saw something in the water. It was a small boat, and inside was a man and a small child! Astrid knew that people should never see her, but she couldn't stop singing. To her horror, as she sang, the boat was caught in the current and dashed on the rocks just near her. She saw the man and the child fall in the water! Without thinking she plunged into the water to help.

The child, a girl, had some kind of floating device but was unable to swim against the current and was in danger of being crushed against the rocks. She grabbed hold of the little girl and began to swim around the reef to get into the lagoon. Looking back, she saw the man was struggling. She quickly pulled the girl to shore and swam back towards the reef to help him. The man was still in trouble and Astrid wasn't strong enough to pull him to safety. Then, to her amazement she saw a dolphin! The dolphin swam right up to the man and was clearly trying to help him. Astrid grabbed the man's hand and placed it on the dolphin's neck as she had done herself in play. His hand slipped and he went under, but Astrid used all her strength to grab both of his hands. This time she got them around the dolphin's neck and together the three of them were able to make it into the lagoon. In the calm water of the lagoon the man seemed able to hold on better and by the time they reached the shallow water his daughter was able to help him reach the shore.

Astrid quickly swam back towards the reef with the dolphin, hoping they hadn't seen her. The worst of the storm had already passed, but she decided she had better resume singing for a while longer. As she sang on her rock she looked towards the shore and to her relief saw that other people had come to help the man and the girl. The dolphin was still swimming at the edge of the lagoon and she saw the man pointing towards it. As she was about to turn away, she thought she saw the girl looking towards the rocks, as if to see the mermaid who had saved her.

Astrid returned many times to that reef to sing during storms. Happily, no more boats foundered on the rocks. Perhaps the close call of the man and his daughter persuaded the people on the island to be more careful during bad weather. Astrid confidently told her family that no-one had seen her; that they thought the dolphin had saved them. Indeed, the people of the island told tales of dolphins that would help people who got into trouble in the ocean.

But there was one girl who believed it was a mermaid who had saved her life, a mermaid who had been singing when their boat hit the rocks, and this mermaid had used a dolphin to help save her father. This girl often walked along the beach by herself, looking out towards the reef. Astrid saw her several times, and smiled to herself as she plunged into the water to play with the dolphin.

The Cat

No-one was quite sure when they first saw the cat, but it was in the summer soon after Joey's 10th birthday. He had been asking for a dog for ages, and really hoping for one for his birthday. Mom had been supportive, to some extent, although she had warned that training a dog was a lot of work. Then she had mentioned that the dog shelter had many older, fully trained dogs that just needed a new home. Joey was excited about the idea and agreed it wasn't necessary to get a puppy. However, his father was less supportive, and had said no on several occasions to the idea of a dog. Joey and Mom had continued to talk about how it was good to have a pet, but Dad appeared to remain unconvinced.

Joey's birthday arrived and he tried to eat his breakfast but was struggling to eat more than one pancake. "So," he said after a while, his anticipation winning. "About my present?"

Dad looked at him and smiled. "Well, I got you something. It's in the living room. Not a dog, mind," he warned his son who had jumped up from the table excitedly.

Joey slowed a bit and turned to his mother. "Mom, do you know what it is?"

"No, I don't," she replied. "Let's find out, shall we?"

When they got opened the living room door there was a big box on the floor. Joey rushed over and then stopped in front of it. There were several small holes in it. He pushed at it with his foot and turned to Dad who had followed them into the room. "Can I open it?"

"Yes, of course. Hurry up now."

Joey found the tape holding the top closed and ripped it off. As the box opened he peered inside and saw a cage. "Oh, it's a cage!"

"Careful with it," Dad warned. "You don't want to …."

"Do what? Is something in the cage?" Joey was excited now. He struggled to get the cage out of the box and in the end accepted Mom's help. They couldn't see anything alive in it, just a food dish and a water bottle, a round thing that looked like a miniature igloo, and a big wheel. "What is it? I don't see anything."

"It's probably scared and hiding in its house, which I suppose is that igloo thing," Mom said. "Let's put it on the coffee table for now and wait and see if something comes out." She looked at her husband. "Of course, it might be sleeping now."

"I wouldn't be sleeping if someone made all that noise opening the box and taking my cage out!" Joey exclaimed. "Come on whatever you are, come out so I can see you!" He was trying to see inside the house, and when he couldn't he stuck his finger in the cage and poked at the house. "Can I open the cage? Will it bite me?" he asked impatiently.

His parents looked at each other. "Well, you got it, dear. Can he open the cage?" Mom said.

Dad looked at her and shrugged. "Actually, I don't know much about these creatures. They said they make good pets, that's all. I guess it's OK to open the top of the cage and move the house to see what it's doing."

Mom sighed. "Alright, Joey. Here I'll help you open the top of the cage, like this. Now you can reach in, carefully, and pick up his house."

Joey did as Mom said and when he lifted the igloo he saw something curled up in a bed of what looked like wood shavings. As he looked closer the creature opened its eyes and looked at him. "Ooh, it's a funny little mouse, and it's looking at me!"

"It's a hamster, isn't it?" Mom said peering over his shoulder.

"Yes, a hamster," Dad confirmed.

"Can I take it out and play with it?" Joey was already reaching in to pick up his new pet.

"Gently," Mom warned. "If you scare him he might bite."

"Come on little guy," Joey picked up the hamster carefully and brought him out of the cage. "Let's see, I'm going to call you .... What should I call him?" he looked up at his father. "Is it a boy?" he added.

"Yes, they said it's a boy," Dad confirmed.

"Okay, that's good," Joey was looking at the hamster closely. "He looks like a mini teddy bear, doesn't he?" His parents nodded, smiling. "I'll call him Teddy. Hi, Teddy. Do you like your new home?" Joey looked into the hamster's eyes as if expecting a response. "Maybe he's hungry. What do you have to eat, Teddy?" and he put the hamster back in his cage beside the food dish. "Oh, that doesn't look very delicious! Can he have something more interesting? Like, I dunno, do hamsters eat fruit?"

"Yes, I think he could have a little piece of apple or carrot or maybe some other vegetable. But perhaps we should let him get used to his new home first. Tomorrow you can try a small piece."

"The people at the store said this is the best kind of hamster food," Dad said. "So I've got a bag of it, not just what's in his bowl. See it's got different things like seeds and nuts and dried fruits as well as those boring looking pellets."

"Yeah, those pellet things look awful!" Joey pulled a face. "But maybe Teddy likes them, they might taste good to him, right?"

"He's stored a bunch in his house," Mom said. "Look, you can see he has a collection of food in his bed!"

"Oh, no, bad Teddy!" Joey was ready to take the bed apart.

"No, wait. Hamsters like to store their food," Mom stopped him. "He has special pouches to put all the food in and take back to his home. You'll see when he goes to eat. His cheeks will get all fat."

"Oh, how weird!" Joey shook his head. "I like to eat my food not store it in my bed! Anyway, I'm hungry. Can I have more pancakes?" And he ran back to the kitchen leaving Mom to close up the cage.

"Wash your hands now, Joey, before you eat. You've been touching the hamster, remember," she called out.

"Okay!" Joey responded.

"Good thing you know about hamsters. You can teach him how to take care of it," Dad said as he followed his son back to the kitchen to finish off the pancakes.

"Indeed," Mom said with a sigh. "And I'm sure I'm going to get a lot more practice taking care of this hamster!"

She was right. Although Joey was interested in the hamster, it was a nocturnal creature so it slept most of the day and then stayed awake at night running in the wheel, which meant it wasn't available to play with most of the time. At first Joey kept the cage in his room, but after a few nights he asked Mom if it could be moved to the living room. "That wheel squeaks and wakes me up!" he complained.

So Teddy and his cage moved to the living room. Mom tried to generate more interest by buying a hamster ball – a hollow plastic ball that opened up so the hamster could go inside. After Teddy had rolled the ball all around the house and there had been no problems, she told Joey he could take it outside in the yard as long as he made sure the ball was properly closed and didn't leave it alone. That proved to be quite successful. Joey's friends came over to play and they all chased the ball around on the grass for a while until Mom rescued the hamster. "Alright," she said. "Let's give Teddy a rest now. You can all have some lemonade if you like," and the group of boys were satisfied, and Teddy survived.

The next day, though, Joey was back to asking if they could get a dog soon, like maybe for Christmas. His father looked at him ready to say no again, but changed his mind and just commented that he'd better show he could take good care of the hamster first. Joey sighed and agreed to help Mom clean the cage, but she could see he was disappointed with the whole deal.

Soon after that Joey told his parents that he had seen some kind of monster outside his window the previous evening, or maybe it was a ghost! When asked for more details he just said he could see a pair of eyes shining in the darkness, looking in his window. Mom went with him to his bedroom to close the curtains when it was getting dark, and they both saw the eyes. "See, Mom! There's eyes looking in at me!"

When she reached the window to close the curtains though, the eyes had already disappeared. Joey was waiting by the door. "What is it, Mom?"

"I don't know," she replied. "But I definitely saw something. I'll get your father to go outside and check, shall I?"

"Ooh, yes! Dad, you have to go outside and find the monster!" Joey ran back to the living room excitedly.

"Yes, I saw something too. Can you go outside and check? Here, take the flashlight."

His father sighed, but since his wife was holding out the flashlight he had no choice. "Alright, but I don't believe in monsters you know!" And sure enough he came back a few minutes later announcing that there was nothing there.

"Maybe it's a ghost and it escaped when you went outside!" Joey was determined that there was something there. "Mom saw it too, right Mom?"

"Yes, I saw something. Maybe it will come back in the day time and we can get a proper look at it. Go to bed now."

The next day Joey went outside early and looked at his bedroom window. He came running back inside all excited, "There's footprints on the window ledge! Come and see!"

Although his father had to go to work he went with him to check quickly. "See Dad, footprints! What is it?"

His father shook his head, "I'm not sure. It looks like paw prints, from a smallish animal, maybe a cat?"

"Ooh, a cat! That would be fun!" Joey ran around the house looking for the cat. "Hey cat, come here!"

"Can you deal with this, dear?" his father asked his wife, getting into the car to leave. "It might not be a cat, and even if it is it could be diseased. Don't let him bring it into the house, if he does find it!"

"Don't worry dear, we'll be careful," she smiled and waved to her husband. Then, hearing Joey still calling for the cat, she suggested "Joey, you're probably scaring him. I think we might be able to get him to come to us if we put out some food."

Joey ran over. "Oh, that's a great idea, Mom! What kind of food would he like?"

"Let's see. We have some canned tuna. I'm sure a cat would eat that." She got a can out of the cabinet and began to open it.

"Yeah, cats like fish don't they," Joey agreed. "What can we put it in?"

Mom hunted around and came up with a small plastic dish. "This would work, don't you think?"

"Sure. Do we put it on the window ledge? Or how 'bout we put it on the deck. He might feel safe here. Don't you think?"

"Good idea, Joey. We can put it out now and have our own breakfast."

Joey put the dish on the porch, in a corner where he thought the cat would find it. "Okay, I'm hungry now. What's for breakfast?"

Mom laughed and got out some bacon and started cooking it. Joey sat down to wait, but kept looking towards the deck hoping the cat would come. "Do cats like bacon? It smells so good, if we open the door maybe he'll smell it and come to check it out."

"Well, yes, that might work. Go ahead. But don't make too much noise or you'll scare him away." She made some toast and quickly scrambled some eggs to go with the bacon and they sat down to eat, both of them with their chairs positioned so they could see the deck. Just as they were almost finished eating, Joey saw a movement in the bushes. His eyes opened wide and he almost dropped his fork. "Mom," he whispered. "I see him!"

Sure enough, a creature was slowly walking towards the house. They watched as it climbed the steps and looked around, sniffing the air. After a while, it made its way to the dish and began eating the tuna. Joey let out a big breath and leaned forward to see better. It was certainly a cat. He wanted to go and pet it but he could see his mother motioning him to wait. The cat finished eating and looked around. Then it sat down and began cleaning itself!

"Mom, he's not scared!" Joey whispered. The cat stopped for a moment and then carried on cleaning. "Can I go out?"

Before his mother could answer, the cat finished and stood up again. It looked around and its gaze landed on the chairs. Without looking into the house it jumped up on the closer chair, which happened to be in the sun, and settled down looking quite at home.

"Mom! It's on the chair!" Joey was beside himself with excitement. "I'm going to pet it," and he got up from his chair and walked to the door.

"Offer him your hand first to sniff," Mom said quietly behind him. "And move slowly so you don't scare him."

Joey tried with all the patience of a ten-year-old boy to move slowly and quietly towards the cat. Fortunately, the cat seemed quite unfazed by the intrusion and just looked up at Joey as he approached. Mom watched in amusement as her son introduced himself to the cat. "Hi cat," he said holding out his hand. "Did you like the tuna?" The cat sniffed his hand and then looked at him, slowly blinking his eyes. Joey moved his hand closer and the cat leaned in so he could scratch his ear. Joey responded and soon sat down on the deck while still stroking the cat, who had begun purring loudly.

His mother came out to join them, and sat carefully in one of the other chairs. "Mom, he's so friendly. Can we keep him?" Joey was beaming.

"Well, I don't know yet. Maybe he belongs to someone. But it's fine if you play with him out here on the deck."

"But if he doesn't have a home, can he live with us?" Joey was looking at the cat wistfully. "He's a good cat, see. And he likes me. You can stroke him too, Mom, come on."

His mother smiled and stood up and moved over towards them. The cat looked up at her expectantly, his big green eyes wide open. "Hello," she said, extending her hand slowly. "You are a handsome one, aren't you?" The cat sniffed her hand and then licked her fingers, before turning back to Joey.

"See, Mom, he wants to be my cat!"

"Well, like I said, you can play with him out here on the deck. I'm going in to wash the dishes and do some laundry. I'll come back out with my coffee in a bit," and she went back inside smiling, leaving Joey with his new friend.

She put a load of laundry in the washing machine and quickly washed the dishes, and then looked out the window to see how Joey and the cat were doing. They were obviously having a good time. Joey had found a piece of string and was swinging it in front of the cat, who was batting at it with his paw. She watched for a few minutes, observing how the cat looked healthy. His coat was quite glossy, and although he was still young he had quite well developed shoulders and big paws. "A strong one," she thought to herself. It had the typical coloring of an American short hair cat, black tiger stripes which were very noticeable on the front legs, and black stripes with grey and brown colors on its body and face. As it stood up to reach for the string that Joey was holding higher above its head, she saw its belly was lighter with dark spots, and as it twisted around she saw a black stripe down its back. "You'll do," she said quietly, nodding.

Joey turned and saw her at the window. "Mom, he likes playing! Come on out and see."

"I'll be right there," she replied. "Just putting another load of laundry in and making my coffee." In a couple of minutes she joined her son on the deck.

"Look, Mom, he lets me pick him up!" Joey demonstrated, grabbing the cat around its middle and lifting him up with outstretched arms. Surprisingly, the cat didn't struggle, but just hung quite limply in his arms with all four legs dangling.

"What a good cat," Mom said and reached over to give him a stroke. The cat purred loudly in response.

"We can keep him, can't we?" Joey said, looking at her with hopeful eyes as he put the cat back on the chair.

"Well, he can't come inside until we're sure he doesn't have any diseases. But he can certainly stay here on the deck as long as he likes."

"You'll stay, won't you Cat?" Joey spoke to the cat. And the cat calmly sat there cleaning his fur. They spent the rest of the morning together, playing happily. When it was time for lunch Joey told his mother he wanted his lunch outside with the cat and she obliged by bringing out some sandwiches. Joey had moved another chair over and he and the cat sat there together like best friends. The cat was sniffing at his sandwich and Joey checked to see what was inside. "Mom, can Cat have some of my sandwich?"

"No, wait a minute, I'll get him a piece of turkey." She came out with a small slice of turkey cut into little pieces on a separate plate. "You can see if he likes this. It's not good to give cats people food, so don't let him eat your sandwich. This is just smoked turkey so a bit should be okay."

The cat was licking his lips as Joey took the plate, and nudged against him in his excitement to get to the turkey. "Hey, you'll make me drop it!" Joey exclaimed, and he put the plate down on the chair beside the cat. "Here you go. That's for you." The cat ate the pieces of turkey quickly and sniffed at the plate, checking to see if there was any more. "Mom, he ate it all!"

His mother smiled. "So I see. Well, well. Just don't let him eat your sandwich!"

Joey had been waving his sandwich rather close to the cat, and now he pulled it back and took another bite. The cat stared at him. "This is my lunch, Cat," he said. "Mom, is there any lemonade? I'm thirsty. Oh, and maybe Cat is thirsty too."

His mother laughed and brought out a glass of lemonade and a dish of water. "I'll put the water dish beside the dish where we put tuna. He can drink it if he wants." She sat down and started eating one of the sandwiches. "Joey, aren't you supposed to meet your friend Mike this afternoon, and go swimming together?"

"Oh, yeah, I forgot." Joey nodded and then looked at the cat. "Well, I guess cats don't like to go swimming, so he can just stay here till I get back, right?"

His mother nodded and the cat settled down on the chair, ready for a nap.

"Mom, what if he gets hungry again? Can we get him some more food?"

"I'll go to the store on my way back from Mike's house and buy some cat food. That will be better for him than just eating our food."

Joey smiled and took another sandwich. The cat was stretched out on the chair, looking quite content.

After lunch it was time to get ready to go swimming and Joey gave the cat a last stroke and told him he'd be back soon. As he got his stuff together he asked his mother how they can find out if the cat had any diseases. "Does he have to go to the doctor?"

"Yes, an animal doctor, a vet," his mother replied. "There's an animal hospital not far from here I've heard good things about."

"Can we take him tomorrow?"

"Well, let's see if he really wants to stay first. And then I can call and make an appointment."

Joey seemed satisfied with that plan and his attention shifted to going swimming with Mike. The boys were going to the nearby pond with Mike's mother, who would then bring Joey home after dinner. His mother was glad this was the plan, since it would give her time to discuss the cat with her husband, and hopefully have him agree to consider letting the cat stay. In the meantime, she picked up a bag of dry cat food and a pack of treats from the store. The cat was still on the chair when she returned and she washed the dish that had held the tuna and put some of the cat food in it. When she put the dish back outside, the cat watched with interest, but declined to get off the chair to eat.

Joey's father came home not long after and she offered him some iced tea. He accepted a glass and headed for the deck. She stopped him, and explained there was a cat on one of the chairs. "We think it's the cat that was looking in Joey's window the past few nights," she added.

"We?" he asked suspiciously.

"Yes, he arrived this morning and Joey played with him for a while."

"And he wants to keep him I suppose?" He moved over to the door and looked out. "Aha, I see him. Got the best chair of course!" and he walked outside looking straight at the cat. "So you think you can just move in here do you?"

The cat stared at him and lazily stretched out one of his front legs. Dad sat down and drank his iced tea. "No coming in the house, mind!" he told the cat.

Mom smiled and poured herself a glass of iced tea. "If he's still here I'll take him to the vet next week to have him checked out. He looks healthy but he might have fleas or need a rabies shot or something."

Dad nodded. "Yeah, even if he just stays out here on the deck, we don't want fleas!"

After a while the cat got up and walked over to the dish of food, brushing past Dad's leg as he went. He ate some food and then slowly walked down the steps and across the lawn, disappearing in the bushes.

"Think he'll be back?" Dad asked.

"Oh yes, why wouldn't he be? Food, a comfortable chair, and nice people, what more would a cat want?" Mom laughed. "Talking of food, I'll make dinner. Joey's at Mike's so we're eating by ourselves this evening."

Soon after they finished dinner Joey arrived with Mike in tow. "Is Cat still here?" he asked. "Mike wants to meet him."

"Well, he went for a walk after he ate his dinner," Mom replied. "I didn't see if he came back yet or not."

They went to the porch and she could hear their disappointment that no cat was to be seen. "But he'll be back," Joey said confidently. "See, this is the chair he likes. And here is his food dish, and there's water too."

"If you whistle will he come?" Mike suggested.

"Nah, he's not a dog. Cats don't come when you whistle," Joey rejected the idea. "But he'll come back tonight. Look, I'll show you his paw prints on my window ledge," and the two of them hurried around the house to look. Their mothers found them there, examining the paw prints on the window ledge.

"Good luck with your new acquisition," Mike's mother said. "Come on Mike, we have to go! You can come and visit another day."

With promises that Joey would tell him when the cat came back, Mike reluctantly went off with his mother. Joey wanted to stay out on the deck and wait for the cat, but Dad told him to come inside when it got dark. Seeing Joey was unhappy with that direction, Mom reminded him that the cat had looked in his window around bedtime so maybe he would come back then. That had the added benefit of Joey being excited to get ready for bed on time, which pleased both his parents. Joey's idea, however, was to sit up by the window until the cat came, rather than actually get into bed. Mom just smiled and shook her head. "The cat will come whether you sit up or go to bed!"

"I know, but I want to see him!" Joey pleaded.

"Well, a watched kettle never boils you know. So maybe if you get into bed and read your book he'll show up."

"Alright, I'll read for a bit," Joey agreed. He was on the second 'Harry Potter' book and was enjoying it, even though he had seen all the movies already. "I think I like this book even better than the movie," Joey had confided to his mother. "I mean the movies are really cool, but it's fun to read the story and imagine it all happening in my mind. J.K. Rowling is such a great writer. I wish I could write like her."

Later when she checked in on him he was still reading and there was no sign of the cat at the window. "He'll come, I'm sure," Joey said. "Maybe he met some friends tonight."

"Well, I hope he doesn't invite them all to visit!" Mom replied. "One cat is quite enough."

The next morning Joey was still asleep when she got up. She put the coffee on and looked out at the deck. The dish of cat food was empty! "And where are you now, cat?" she muttered opening the door. "You're not going to just eat all the food and disappear I hope!" Still, she refilled the dish and sat down with her coffee. A minute later she heard a meow and the cat came up the steps towards her. "Well, good morning to you too," she said and reached down to stroke him as he walked past. "Come for breakfast have you?" He went over to the dish and sniffed, and then turned to look at her. "What, not good enough?" she said. The cat sat down and stared at her.

Just then Joey came out, still in his pajamas. "Ooh, Cat you're back!" He bent down and picked up the cat. "Good Cat, you've come for breakfast." He put the cat back down beside the food dish, but the cat backed away and sat down staring at Mom. "What's the matter? Mom, what does he want?"

"I think he wants tuna," she said. "He probably remembers it from yesterday."

Joey laughed. "Tuna for breakfast, that's funny! Mom, can we give him some then?"

Sighing, she got up and went inside. "Sure, but we'll have to get a different dish. I just refilled the other one with cat food. Let's see, this will work. Go on, give it to him," and she handed the dish of tuna to Joey who gladly took it out to the cat.

"Here you go, Cat," she heard as Joey put it down beside the other dishes. "You can have tuna for breakfast if you want." A moment later Joey called out, "can I have breakfast too?"

Joey spent most of the day outside on the deck with the cat. He called Mike and told him the cat was back and his mother brought him over for a short visit. Mike was suitably impressed and Joey was very proud of what he clearly thought of as his cat.

They brought Teddy out in his ball to roll around the deck while the cat watched with interest. At one point the ball rolled close to the cat and he put out his paw to pat it. The boys thought this was a great game! "Come on Cat, can you see Teddy inside the ball?" The cat was looking fixedly at the ball and Teddy was standing up to look right back at him. After a while Teddy started the ball moving again and Cat jumped back in surprise. He recovered quickly and soon was chasing the ball around the deck, patting it every so often to keep it moving.

Mom came out when she heard the boys cheering him on, and immediately rescued Teddy. "That's enough excitement for one little hamster," she said sternly, and she took the ball back inside. The boys smiled at each other, planning to get the cat and the hamster together again in the near future. Before they could do that though, Mike's mother showed up to take him home.

Joey went back to the kitchen after seeing Mike off and Mom showed him the pack of treats she had bought for the cat. She warned him that cats don't really learn tricks like dogs, but still you can reward them with a treat when they're good. Joey immediately took some treats over to the cat, who had taken up residence on the chair again. "Come on, Cat. If you get off the chair and come down here I'll give you a treat," Joey said. The cat looked at him disdainfully. Then Joey waved the treat in front of his nose and then took it away. The cat looked at him. "Off the chair and you get a treat," Joey repeated. The cat slowly got up and jumped off the chair onto the deck and sat looking at him. "Come here, Cat," Joey commanded, still not giving him a treat. The cat didn't move, but then he raised one front leg and waved it in the air. Still holding the leg in the air he looked at Joey. "Oh, Mom, look he's begging!" Joey was so excited he gave him two treats. "Mom, Dad, come and see him beg!" Joey called out. When his parents came out he waved another treat in front of the cat's nose. "Beg, cat!" he said, and the cat lifted his paw up again in a good imitation of a one-armed beg. "Well, I'll be," Dad said in surprise. "That cat is a beggar!"

Joey didn't understand right away why both his parents started laughing. "Hey," he said. "Don't laugh at Cat, he doesn't like it!" But that only made them laugh harder. Joey looked worried as the cat looked back and forth between his laughing parents.

"Beggars can't be choosers," Dad said. But Mom just smiled. "I think this cat has chosen very wisely, actually. He's done pretty well for himself here so far."

At that the cat walked around her, rubbing against her legs, and then jumped back on "his" chair and settled down to clean himself. Joey breathed a sigh of relief and sat down on the chair next to him. "He's a smart cat alright, knows a good thing when he finds it," said Dad before turning to go back inside.

Joey stroked the cat affectionately. "Yeah, Cat, we're going to have lots of good times aren't we?"

The cat stayed around all weekend, leaving to go off on his own at times, but always coming back, especially in time for the next meal. Mom arranged for him to get a checkup. When the vet asked what they were calling him, Joey replied "Cat." His mother shrugged and the vet laughed. "Well, it's better than calling him "Begger" like Dad said, isn't it," Joey defended the name.

"You're right about that, young man," the vet said with a smile. "Let's check out Cat then, shall we?" Examining the cat, she said he seemed very healthy, around a year old, and he had been neutered so probably he had been someone's pet until recently. Then she explained he would be given shots to prevent various cat diseases, and advised using a monthly flea control treatment. She went to get the vaccines and came back with a sample of flea treatment which they were to apply to the back of his neck. She also suggested they buy a proper cat carrier, not just the cardboard box they had used to transport him. For today, though, she suggested they could take one of their cardboard carriers, which was sturdier and closed properly with handles for carrying it safely.

Joey was thrilled with all the attention, and money, being lavished on the cat, knowing this meant he was staying. Dad was less thrilled, but agreed that since the cat appeared to have chosen them that he should be allowed to stay. "And he can come in the house, right?" Joey asked. "I mean, if it rains or something, he needs to come in to keep warm and dry."

Dad sighed and admitted defeat. "In the house is alright, but not in the bedroom, mind!"

"But he can come in the living room, can't he?"

Dad nodded and Joey gave his father a hug and went to tell Cat the good news. "Come on Cat," he said. "I'm leaving the door open so you can come inside if you like." When the cat didn't move Joey came back into the kitchen. "Mom, can we put his food dish inside, in the kitchen? It might rain soon and his food will get all wet if we leave it outside."

Mom smiled, knowing that her son was trying to get the cat inside. But she played along, suggesting a space in the corner that wouldn't be in the way. They carefully brought the food and water dishes inside. Joey made a point of showing the cat what he was doing and telling him to come in and eat. The cat slowly made his way to the open door and looked inside. He sat in the opening, surveying the scene inside. After a while, he got up and walked inside towards the food dishes which he sniffed with great interest. Then he started to explore the kitchen.

Mom scolded him when he got too near the stove where she was making dinner. "Watch out or you'll get cooked!" she said. The cat backed off immediately and headed for the door, stopping when he reached it. He sat down and looked at her, apparently contemplating the situation. "It's alright, you can come back inside," she said in a friendly tone.

"Yes, please come back inside Cat," Joey added.

The cat sat there watching. Finally, he walked back inside and went over to his food dish to eat. After sitting on the floor cleaning himself, he got up and quite deliberately walked back to the door and went outside. Joey had been watching and got up immediately to follow him. "Where are you going Cat?" The cat continued across the deck and down the steps, stopping at the bottom to give Joey a quick glance, and then continued off across the grass.

"Dinner time, Joey," his mother called him back inside. "Don't worry about the cat, he'll do things at his own pace."

"Okay, Mom," Joey sat down to eat. "Anyway he came inside!"

"Yes, we'll not be able to get rid of him now!" Dad said with a smile.

Sure enough, the next morning the cat was back on the deck waiting for the door to be opened so he could get his food. He still liked to eat tuna for breakfast so that become part of Mom's morning routine, as soon as she had the coffee brewing. "Come on in, then. I'll get your tuna," she said as she opened the door for the cat. Aware that the cat might be nervous she left the door open wide enough for him to get out if he wanted. This time, though, after eating the tuna he headed into the living room and started exploring there. He jumped up on the couch and was checking it out for comfort when Joey arrived.

"Where's Cat, Mom?" he asked walking straight into the kitchen without seeing him on the couch, but noting the partially open door. "Did he come for breakfast?"

"Yes, he did. And I think he's making himself at home in the living room now if I'm not mistaken."

"Oh, he's on the couch!" Joey saw him and ran over. "Hi, Cat! You found the couch. Do you like it?" In answer the cat gave a big sigh and stretched out looking entirely comfortable.

Having the cat on the couch seemed to be fine with everyone, including Dad who just muttered about keeping him away from his chair. However, there was a problem. During the morning they left the door open and the cat was free to come and go. In the afternoon, though, it started to rain and Mom closed the door. Joey and the cat were in the living room and didn't notice. The cat had found a spot on the back of the couch which allowed him to look out the window, and he was focused on some squirrels running around just in front of the house. Suddenly a garbage truck came along the street making a lot of noise and the cat jumped off the couch and ran towards the door, clearly afraid. Seeing the door closed obviously made him more upset and he ran around meowing loudly, even knocking his food dish over in his panic. "Mom, what's the matter with him?" Joey asked, worried about his pet.

"He was scared by the noise I think. Now he wants to get outside and hide. I'd better open the door," and she went over and opened the door. The cat saw the opening and shot outside, ran across the deck and disappeared into a bush.

"Poor cat," Joey said. "He got scared and now he'll get wet in the rain! Can we leave the door open so he can get back inside?"

"Yes, let's leave it like this so he can push it open. And don't worry, he won't get very wet. He has a very thick fur coat."

"But he was scared!" Joey was still worried. "He will come back, won't he?"

Mom smiled at her son. "Yes, I'm sure he will. Come on, I was going to make cookies. Do you want to help?"

"I can help eat them!" Joey cheered up. "I'll just read my 'Harry Potter' book till they're ready," and he went to get his book.

When Dad came home they explained about the cat wanting to get out and getting upset when it was closed. "I suppose we'll be getting a cat door for him next," he said in response.

"A cat door? Can we?" Joey asked immediately. "How does that work anyway?"

"Well, we have to cut a hole in a door or a wall and put a little door so he can get in and out. Let's see, we could fit it here," Dad was looking at the door that led out to the deck.

"Can we get it now?" Joey asked impatiently. "Cat hasn't come back yet and I don't know if he'll be scared to stay inside if we close the door again. But he'll know how to work a cat door, won't he?"

His parents looked at each other. "Well, you do have time to go to the store before dinner," Mom suggested.

Dad looked reluctant, but Joey was so excited he gave in and the two of them went off to buy the cat door. After suggesting they check out the carriers too, Mom stayed behind. Looking out at the back yard in the direction of the bush where the cat had taken refuge, she said, "You'd better appreciate all that's being done for you!"

Although the cat didn't exactly express appreciation, he made himself at home. The cat door was a great success. Joey showed him how it worked and the cat got the hang of it very quickly. He seemed to enjoy being able to go in and out whenever he wanted and Joey's parents were glad not to have to keep opening the door for him. He also found Teddy's cage and spent a while sitting watching the small creature run in his wheel. Mom found him there and told him in no uncertain terms that Teddy was their pet and not food for the cat, and he shouldn't even think of hurting him if he wanted to stay in their house. Cat sat and listened, and then deliberately spent time cleaning himself and ignoring the cage. It seemed he accepted the hamster as another member of the family.

Cat on couch

The cat had clearly decided this was a good place to live. He enjoyed the couch, whether he was up on the back looking out the window or stretched out on a cushion enjoying the comfort. The first time Joey saw him lying on his back with his paws in the air he had to laugh. "Oh Cat, you do look a bit silly like that!"

Mom came over and agreed. "But it means he's very comfortable here, he feels safe. Look at his belly with those spots – makes me want to rub it!" she reached over to stroke his belly but the cat quickly turned over and his back legs kicked her hand. "Oh, you don't like that! Alright, I'll just stroke your head then." The cat purred and stretched out again, but not on his back. "Better watch out when he's on his back," she said to Joey. "He doesn't seem to like his belly being rubbed."

"But he likes his head and ears stroked, doesn't he?" Joey reached over and gave him a stroke too. The cat purred contentedly and Joey smiled. "I'd like to be able to purr like that, wouldn't you Mom?"

"Indeed, it's a lovely sound. Makes me feel happy too."

"Aren't you glad Cat came to stay?"

"Yes, I am."

"Dad too?"

"Well, now I don't know if he'd admit it, but yes I think he likes having Cat here with us. But make sure he doesn't come in our bedroom will you? Dad isn't quite ready for that!"

Joey looked at his mother, realizing that she knew that the cat had begun sneaking into his bedroom at night, and sleeping with him on his bed. So he just nodded.

Soon summer was over and Joey was back in school every day. The cat was scared of the noisy school bus when it first came along the street and stopped outside their house, and retreated to his bush in the back. After a while, though, he learned that the school bus in the afternoon meant that Joey was coming home and he would come trotting round to the front door as soon as it had passed.

As winter approached the cat still went outside a lot, but clearly enjoyed the comfort of the house. Joey was thrilled he came to sleep on his bed at night. "Keeps us both warm," he told Mike when they were hanging out after school one day. Mike was a bit jealous, knowing his parents wouldn't allow him to have a cat because his sister was allergic. "But I'll get my own cat, and a dog, when I'm all grown up and have my own place," he told Joey. They discussed whether Cat would be friends with his cat and dog. Joey was of the opinion that although Cat might want to be friends with a cat he didn't like dogs: "He growls and the fur on his back stands up and his tail gets all fat when a dog goes past the house. I don't think he likes dogs." They agreed that it was probably wise not to have a dog.

As Thanksgiving approached Mom bought a big turkey and lots of other food for them to eat. Joey's cousins were coming to share the meal and he was looking forward to the holiday. What they didn't expect was that the cat would become extremely excited when Mom brought home the food. He ran around sniffing all the bags and trying to climb into the one that held the turkey. Mom grabbed it just in time. "Well, you're a turkey fan alright!" and she patted him on the head.

On the big day the turkey was in the oven and Cat was prowling around the kitchen sniffing everywhere. Joey and his father were in the living room when they heard a crash. "Everything alright out there?" Dad called out.

"That cat has tipped over the trash can!" Mom called back.

Joey went running to the kitchen to see what was going on. The cat had indeed knocked over the trash can and was pawing at the contents. "What are you doing Cat?" Joey said leaning over to see what he was trying to get. "Oh, Mom, it's the turkey! Look, he's trying to get the wrapper that was on the turkey! No, Cat you can't have that. Wait till it's cooked!" Joey picked up the cat and took him away.

Mom gathered up the trash and tied the bag tightly. "Dad, can you take this outside to the garbage can, and make sure the lid is on securely so the cat doesn't get at it."

When the turkey was cooked the cat's interest increased and he almost tripped up Dad as he took it out of the oven. "Keep that cat away!" he yelled to Joey.

"Come on Cat, we'll give you a piece when it's all carved up," Joey took his cat to the living room. But the cat was nearly frantic with excitement and escaped again to go back to the kitchen. This time, though, he sat a bit away from Dad and watched in anticipation as the bird was cut into pieces. Unable to control his eagerness completely he let out a few meows and kept shifting position. Dad turned to him with what he intended to be a warning glare, but he was unable to avoid it turning into a smile. That encouraged the cat to edge closer and give a louder meow, lifting his front leg in his begging pose at the same time.

"Alright, then," Dad sighed and looked at the plate of turkey. "Joey, come and give that cat some turkey. He's even begging for it now!"

Joey gladly complied and gave the cat several small pieces of turkey, which he devoured instantly. He sat down licking his lips and staring at Joey. "You can't have more until we all get to eat!" Joey said sternly. The cat just stared at him.

Mom kept a keen eye on the turkey, just in case, while everyone enjoyed the delicious feast. Cat even got several more pieces of turkey, as Joey told his cousins how he was crazy for turkey so they each gave him a bit. And the cat ate every one and licked his lips appreciatively. When Mom packed up the leftovers and put them in the refrigerator the cat watched her every move. She gave him one last piece, with a promise that he could have more the next day. The cat accepted and settled into his place on the couch, refusing to move when the cousins came to sit and watch the football game on TV. Joey explained that was the cat's place, and they all squashed together leaving the cat a whole cushion to himself. All in all, it was a very satisfying day.

Soon after that a big snowstorm came and blanketed the area in two feet of snow overnight. School was canceled for the day and Joey wanted to make a snowman. Mom said they had to shovel the snow from the driveway first. Dad happened to be out of town for a business meeting and wouldn't be able to get back to help until the snow had been cleared. As Joey went outside to help, he realized that Cat was nowhere to be seen. "Mom, did you see Cat this morning?" He tried to go around the house looking for paw prints but the deep snow slowed his progress too much. "Mom, we have to shovel the snow so Cat can get in!"

They both grabbed their shovels and soon made a path all around from the driveway to the deck, up the steps and then cleared the deck over to the cat door. But where was Cat? "He might be in his bush over there," Mom suggested. They went back down and Mom made her way across the lawn to what had become known as "Cat's bush." There was a lot of snow all around it and no paw prints. She managed to get close and could see that the ground under the bush was clear. "Cat?" she called out, peering into the branches. "Oh, I see him!"

"Can you get him?" Joey called out to her, still struggling to get across the snow to them.

"Yes, come on Cat, let me help you," Mom reached in and grabbed Cat. He didn't struggle, but let her pick him up and carry him across the snow to her son.

"Silly Cat, you got stuck outside in the snowstorm!" Joey said as he took him from his mother. "Let's go inside and you can have your tuna!"

The cat readily complied and ate all the tuna in one go. He seemed none the worse for his time outside and soon curled up on the couch in his usual spot.

Mom poked her head inside and said that if the cat was fine could Joey come back out and help shovel the snow. Joey sighed and slowly got his coat and boots on again. Then he cheered up, remembering the plan to make a snowman after the driveway was clear. Mom was getting tired shoveling but with Joey's help it was soon done and she joined in the snowman making. "Can you get a carrot for his nose and something for his eyes, and a scarf?" Joey said as they had it nearly done. "I'll get a stick for him to hold, here in his arm. Does he need a hat too?"

His mother went inside to gather the various items and noted that cat was sleeping on the couch. "Well, you're a lucky one for sure," she said. "But I'm glad you're all right." The cat stretched and went back to sleep.

They finished the snowman and agreed he was the best they'd ever made. "Dad will be impressed, right?" Joey said as they went back inside to have mugs of hot chocolate. "Do you think Cat will be impressed too?"

"Somehow I don't think he's too impressed about anything to do with snow right now," Mom said and they laughed.

After that experience of being trapped outside in the snow the cat was expected to be more inclined to stay inside. They discussed getting a litter box for him so he wouldn't need to go outside at all. But the cat had other ideas. He still went outside almost every day, avoiding only those with the very worst weather. Even then he would go out of the cat door onto the deck and look around for a short time before coming back inside. Then he would go to his spot at the window and look out as if hoping that it was better weather at the front of the house. Of course it never was, and after a while he would settle back down to sleep.

The cat faithfully went outside every afternoon in time to meet Joey off the school bus. On days when Joey didn't come home by bus the cat would sit outside waiting hopefully, sometimes staying out until Joey did come back from his after school activity. In those cases, though, if Joey came in a friend's car the cat would run around the back of the house when the car arrived, and then peek around the corner to see if Joey was coming.

When Joey caught a bad cold and had to stay home from school for a couple of days the cat joined him on the couch, sleeping beside him all day. Of course he slept on his bed at night too, which Dad had to accept. "I suppose he's taking care of the boy, so that's a good thing," he said. "I'm sure the cat likes this responsibility!"

As the weather warmed Joey spent more afternoons at sports practice after school, and the cat got used to having to wait longer for him to come home. He found a nice warm spot by the front driveway that got the afternoon sun and would stretch out there if the bus failed to produce Joey. And once Joey arrived he knew there would be a lot of attention, usually including a treat or two. Not a bad life for a cat!

In the summer there was less of a clear schedule, no school bus for one thing. After a couple of weeks of spending lazy days at home Joey went to a soccer camp for two weeks. It was just a day camp so he came home every evening in time for dinner. The cat quickly learned this new schedule and lay out in the sun in his spot by the front driveway to wait for him. The second week of the camp though the cat was absent when Joey returned. "Mom, where's Cat?" he called out after he looked around for him.

"Haven't seen him since this morning," she replied. "But then I wasn't looking for him. He did eat his breakfast, that I can say."

Joey went out on the deck with a snack and his 'Harry Potter' book, now the fifth in the series and longer than any book he had ever expected to read. His mother was impressed that Joey invested in reading all the books, knowing that many of his friends had just watched the movies. He repeatedly told her that he loved the books and that he wanted to be able to write books when he got older. But right now he was distracted by the absence of his cat. "Where can he be, Mom?" he asked when she called him in for dinner. "He's never late to greet me when I come home."

Although his parents reassured him that the cat would be fine, just off on an adventure as is typical of cats, Joey continued to worry. When the cat didn't come home all night and hadn't appeared to eat his breakfast by the time Joey was due to leave for soccer camp he was almost in tears. "Mom, I can't leave without finding Cat!" he cried. Only when his mother promised to go around the neighborhood looking for him did Joey agree to go, reluctantly.

Mom was true to her word and walked all around the neighborhood calling out for the cat, but to no avail. She asked a couple of the neighbors she met but they said no, they hadn't seen him. By the time Joey got home and there was still no cat she was beginning to worry. Joey was quite distraught when the cat didn't come to greet him, and even more so when Mom told him the bad news that she hadn't seen him all day despite looking. "Well I want to go and look," Joey said determinedly. "We can ask all the neighbors to look for him."

Dad came home just then and the trio set off to look for the cat. They started with their own back yard, checking every bush and under the deck and any other place they could think of. But no cat. Then they walked up and down the street, calling on each neighbor's house to ask if they had seen him. No one had, but they all promised to look out for him. They met everyone except the Palmers, who lived two doors down, and who Mom said had gone away on vacation yesterday. Joey wanted to check their backyard in case the cat was somewhere back there and wouldn't take no for an answer. His parents figured it wasn't really trespassing since they kind of knew them. Although Joey called out and went all around, he found no sign of the cat. Tired and discouraged he agreed they should go home and eat dinner.

Dad promised to take one more look after dinner, saying that cats often sleep during the day and he might be awake again in the evening. In fact, as Mom knew, Dad thought that most probably the cat had been run over and he was going to check along beside the main road for his body. Joey agreed to stay home, believing that the cat was going to come back whenever he finished his adventure. Dad stayed out for about half an hour and when he returned he shook his head, "no sign of him." Joey and his mother both sighed, although his mother's was a sigh of relief that he hadn't found the cat dead.

The next few days Joey was very quiet, and went off to soccer camp each day with a sad face. His mother continued to put fresh tuna in the cat's dish each morning, hoping the cat would return. Joey noticed and was happy to see that his mother hadn't given up on the cat, but he was seriously worried. The weekend arrived and Joey sat on the deck with his still unfinished 'Harry Potter' book.

"Shall we go swimming this afternoon?" Mom asked. "We can bring Mike if you like, do you want to ask him?" Although Joey wasn't very excited he agreed to the plan. It did pass the time instead of just worrying about Cat. They had ice cream on the way home and picked up a pizza to eat for dinner.

As they gathered on the deck to eat, Mike, who was always ready to stay for food, sat in the cat's chair. "I'll move if Cat comes, okay?" he said quickly seeing Joey's face.

"Yeah sure, but I don't think he'll come," Joey said.

"Well, he might," Mike insisted. "My Dad said when he was a boy his friend's cat used to go off for days, hunting he said. And he always came back."

"Cat's been gone six days now," Joey replied. "That's almost a week. Right Mom?"

"Well, we saw him on Monday morning so yes, that's getting close to a week. Must be quite an adventure!" she said trying to make Joey smile.

"Yeah, I bet he's having lots of fun!" Mike added. "This is good pizza; can I have another slice?"

"Oh, I want more too!" Joey chimed in, not having lost his appetite despite his concern over Cat. And the two friends finished off the pizza quite cheerfully.

The next day Joey went over to Mike's house to play video games since it was raining. As Mom returned home she noticed the Palmers pulling into their driveway and opening their garage door. Even though it was raining she stopped and ran over to greet them and tell them about their missing cat. They were busy unpacking the car and bringing suitcases inside but they agreed to look out for him. They remembered seeing the cat with Joey many times so they knew what he looked like.

When Joey came back from Mike's in the evening she told him the neighbors were home and she'd asked them to look out for his cat. He nodded and said he had decided to finish his 'Harry Potter' book, and maybe then Cat would come home. "I know it's silly, but 'Harry Potter' is all about magic so maybe it will work," he said looking at his mother earnestly. She gave him a smile and agreed that was a good idea. "I'm going to finish it tonight, even if I have to stay up all night. There's no more soccer camp or anything so I can sleep late tomorrow, okay?" Mom laughed and gave him a quick hug.

When she checked on him later she saw he was still sitting in bed reading, determined to finish the book. She smiled and went to bed proud of her son for following through on his idea of a way to bring back his beloved cat.

In the morning she made a fresh dish of tuna as usual and sat down with her mug of coffee. Joey was still sleeping, having apparently finished the book, since he had closed it and put it on his nightstand. She sat on the couch and looked out, thinking about the cat. She saw Mr. Palmer in his car pulling out of the driveway and driving off up the street. At that moment her arm gave an involuntary shudder, almost spilling her coffee. And then she heard the sound of the cat door. Again almost spilling her coffee, she turned around quickly and jumped up to see what was going on. It was Cat! He had gone over to the dish of tuna and was gobbling down the food.

She ran over to him and petted his head. "Cat, is it really you?" He looked up at her and opened his mouth to give a very faint meow and then continued eating. "Oh, you look so thin!" she said stroking him. "But you're back!"

"Joey!" she called out and ran to his room. "Joey wake up! Cat's here!"

"What, what?" Joey was still sleepy.

"Cat's here! Come on, wake up!"

"Cat!" he jumped out of bed and ran to the kitchen. "Cat, you're back! I knew you'd come back!" and he grabbed the cat around the middle and hugged him. "Mom he's back! But he's so skinny. Where have you been Cat?"

The cat didn't answer but struggled to get down so he could continue eating. Then he moved over to the water dish and drank thirstily. Mom got out the bag of cat food and put some in his dish, and the cat eagerly started eating that too.

"Mom, he's starving! Where has he been?"

At that moment there was a knock at the front door. Mom went to answer it and saw Mrs. Palmer standing there. "Did your cat come back?" she asked. "Because we think he was stuck in our garage while we were away on vacation!"

"Yes, he's here!" Mom started laughing. "He's a bit skinny but he seems fine. He's busy eating now."

"Well, I'm glad to hear it. He must have gone in when we were getting ready to leave last week and hidden behind something so we didn't see him when we closed the door. And we didn't see him yesterday when we got home."

"He was probably scared of the noise and stayed in hiding, and then you closed the door on him again!" Mom suggested.

"Yes, I think so. And then this morning my husband opened the door to take the car to go to work and he must have taken the chance to escape. I hope he's alright, there wouldn't have been much to eat in there, unless he found a mouse!"

Joey came over just then. "A mouse! Would Cat eat a mouse?"

"If there was nothing else to eat I'm sure he would," Mom answered.

"Well I'm just happy he's okay and home safe," Mrs. Palmer said. "I'll be off now."

"Thank you," Mom said with a big smile. "And hopefully he's learned his lesson not to get trapped in a garage!" They all laughed, except the cat who was pacing around the kitchen looking a bit confused.

"Are you alright, Cat?" Joey asked, picking him up. "You're so skinny. I bet that mouse didn't taste so good. Mom, can he have extra tuna, and some treats?"

"Yes, he can. We're very glad you're home safe, Cat," she said getting a new can of tuna from the shelf.

"And don't do that again," Joey said waving his finger at the cat's face. "You made us so worried!" He put the cat down again. "But here's a treat for coming home safe. We have to fatten you up again!"

Joey spent the rest of the day with his cat. He brought him into his room when he went to get dressed and then took him out on the deck with his breakfast. "Here, Cat, you can have your chair. It's in the sun so you'll be nice and warm. I bet you were scared stuck in that garage! Now you can lie out in the sun again."

Later on Mike came over. "Told you he'd be back, didn't I?" he said, pleased his friend was back to his old carefree self. "He is kind of skinny though. Guess there wasn't much to eat in that garage."

They decided that if there was a mouse and Cat caught it, any other mice would have been scared away. "One mouse isn't much for a big cat like you," Joey told his pet.

When Dad came home they told him the story. "Well, I have to say I'm happy he's back," he commented. "And if he did enjoy eating the mouse I hope he catches any that try and live in our house!"

"Yeah, Cat, you can be our mouse catcher now," Joey responded. "See, having a cat's really a good thing!"

Judging by his parents' big smiles it seemed that they agreed. "Just as long as he remembers Teddy is a hamster not a mouse," Mom added. That made them all laugh.

After all that excitement the rest of the summer passed rather uneventfully. Cat regained his weight and his misadventure seemed to have no permanent ill effects. When he was taken back to the vet for his annual checkup they told her the story. She had nodded when Joey said they thought he ate a mouse during his time stuck in the garage. "Well, mice have all the nutrients cats need to be healthy, so that would have been good for him. I can see he's healthy and seems to be a bit heavier than last year. That's good, since he's still young. But don't let him get too heavy!"

Joey laughed and told Cat he couldn't have too many treats. The cat just stared back at him.

School started again and the cat resumed his schedule of waiting for Joey to come home. He had moved on to middle school now, so he had to go earlier on a different bus that didn't stop outside their house. Cat soon learned that when he came home Joey didn't get off the bus that came past the house but instead walked up the street from where the bus dropped him at the corner. Cat decided that he would just stay in their yard and never ventured close to the intersection where the bus came. Joey had been worried about that at first, but soon realized the cat was afraid of the bigger road with the noisy traffic and so stayed away. "Good Cat," he told him. "You wait at home for me, where it's safe."

Of course it wasn't completely safe at home. There were several occasions when they heard cat fights at night, and one Saturday morning Mom found Cat lying in the corner by the couch instead of sleeping on it. His ear was torn and bleeding and when Mom went to pick him up he snarled at her and she realized he must be in pain. She called Joey and they examined him carefully, finding a wound on his shoulder and it looked like one of his front paws was injured too. "Goodness, Cat. You were in a fight alright!" Joey was impressed despite his concern. "I wonder what the other cat looks like!"

Mom called the vet and got an appointment for that afternoon. "We're lucky they can see him today," she said. "I was afraid they'd close early since it's Saturday."

The cat didn't move all morning. After lunch they collected the cat carrier and prepared to put him inside. "Maybe we need a blanket for him, or something?" Joey asked concerned about his cat's injuries.

"Good idea," Mom replied. "I'll get a big towel and we can use it to pick him up so he doesn't scratch us." That was a good plan since Cat was not interested in being picked up, let alone pushed into the carrier. He snarled and growled as they carefully wrapped the towel around him, and yelped in pain when Mom picked him up.

"It's alright, Cat," Joey said. "The doctor will fix you up." He was holding the door open and quickly closed it as soon as Mom was able to shove the towel surrounding the cat into the carrier. "Watch your tail!" Joey said, and Mom pushed the tail inside just in time.

When they arrived at the animal hospital Cat was still clearly upset with the situation but had stopped meowing. The vet examined him and said she would take him in the back to clean his wounds and give him an antibiotic shot. After quite a while she came back with him, and Joey started to laugh. "Oh Cat, look at you!"

"Yes, he's quite the wounded soldier isn't he," the vet said, putting him on the table. "We put a bandage on his paw, and hopefully it will stay on for long enough for that wound to heal."

Joey looked at the striped bandage that covered the bottom section of Cat's front leg. "Nice bandage!" he commented. "But what's this big collar thing round his neck for?"

"Ah, yes, that's to stop him from licking the wound on his shoulder," she explained. "It's quite soft, not like the old lampshades we used to put on cats. He still won't like it, but keep it on for three days and then bring him back to see me. You'll be good, won't you?" she said stroking the cat's head. He looked at her and shook his head, trying to get the big collar off. He then tried to lick the bandage on his paw, but again the collar got in the way. So he sat down with his back to her and looked at Joey.

"No, I'm not going to take it off!" Joey said, reaching down to pat him on the head. "You have to keep it on for three days, the bandage too," he added as the cat lifted his paw up and started shaking it.

"Oh, and keep him inside. We want that bandage to stay clean if possible," she said, ready to leave.

They took the cat home after making an appointment to return on Tuesday. By the time they got home Cat was getting sleepy, and he settled on the couch as soon as he got out of the carrier. Mom said the antibiotic had probably made him drowsy, and it would be good for him to rest. Joey got his book, the final one in the 'Harry Potter' series. "My turn to take care of you now, Cat," he said as he settled down beside him. The cat managed a quiet purr, and then fell asleep.

The cat remained very quiet and docile through the evening, and Joey picked him up and brought him to bed with him. His parents agreed this was a good plan. They had closed the cat door to prevent him from getting out if he did wake up in the night.

In the morning Mom checked on them, and saw Cat still lying on the bed but he opened his eyes when she looked in. She went to the kitchen and prepared his tuna dish and was just pouring her coffee when she heard a shuffling noise. Cat was limping along headed for the tuna, stopping every few steps to shake the bandaged paw. He reached the tuna dish but the collar prevented him from eating it! He looked up at Mom, who was unable to suppress her laughter as she bent down to adjust the collar for him. Just then Joey came in, still sleepy. He saw Cat trying to eat and joined in the laughter. Cat turned and glared at them, but quickly returned to the dish to continue eating.

Mom made some breakfast while Joey sat and watched his cat. Soon they were all eating together. Cat finished first, and sat there, apparently trying to decide what course of action to take. He stretched his bandaged paw out and started licking the part he could reach around the collar. Then he shook it, obviously disturbed by it. Joey could see the collar was still preventing him from licking the patch on his shoulder which had been shaved to clean the injury. After a minute he got up and walked towards the cat door, still stopping to shake his bandaged paw every few steps. Joey was laughing again as he watched Cat's progress.

When he reached the door the cat tried to push his way out, but it was locked. He tried again, as best he could with the collar in his way. Frustrated he turned to Mom with a pleading look. She shook her head. "You can't go out with that bandage on!" Cat sat down by the door and stared at it. "And you look ridiculous wearing that collar. You shouldn't go outside like that!"

"Maybe he needs to go to the bathroom," Joey suggested. "Can we take him out and then bring him back after? I don't think he can run away with his paw all bandaged up."

His mother considered it. "Alright, but let's finish breakfast and get dressed first. Then if he's still by the door we'll try that."

The cat didn't move, except to give his paw another shake, and so once Joey was dressed they approached him cautiously. "Maybe we should open the real door. That collar thing might get stuck if he tries to go through the cat door," Mom suggested. Joey nodded and they stood beside the door and Mom slowly opened it. "Do you think we need to carry him?" Joey asked as the cat hesitated. Before they could pick him up though, the cat set off out the door and across the deck. He stopped again at the stairs and looked across towards his bush. "I can carry you down the stairs," Joey offered and bent down to pick him up.

"Gently, now," Mom said coming up behind him.

Joey put him down at the foot of the stairs and Cat shook himself and headed under the deck to a patch of earth. "We shouldn't watch," Mom said. "Cats like to be private when they're doing their business." So they both turned away and waited.

After a while Joey turned back to look and saw Cat was scraping at the earth. He finished and limped back towards Joey. "Alright, Cat, are you done?" Joey asked, bending down to pick him up. "Oh, you made your bandage dirty! Come on, back inside now." The cat didn't resist and they all trooped back inside. Joey put him down on the kitchen floor, and the cat tried to clean his bandage.

Mom shrugged and commented, "Well, he's trying to keep it clean! Just as long as it stays on till Tuesday he'll be fine."

The bandage did stay on until Tuesday, but that very morning he finally got it off. Joey was already at school and Mom saw the bandage roll across the floor. "Cat, have you taken that bandage off?" she asked accusingly. The cat looked up at her all innocent, and then licked his now uncovered paw.

She took him to his appointment and explained that the bandage had been on until that morning. The vet laughed and agreed it was fine. "Saved us from taking it off, didn't you?" she said to the cat. "Well it's healing well, the shoulder too. I think he can take the collar off too. Just keep an eye on him and if there's any problem bring him back. Otherwise he's good to go."

Joey was thrilled when he got home and saw Cat looking more normal. He still had the shaved area on his shoulder and his paw, but Mom said his hair would grow back soon. It did grow back, with the same color markings as before, which Joey found fascinating. "That's so cool, the hairs know what color to be!" he told Mike, who was also duly impressed. "His ear doesn't grow back, though, does it?" he asked. "Oh no, that's like his scar from battle now. Cat's a real fighter!" Joey said proudly.

After that incident life went back to normal. The cat never did catch a mouse inside their house, although he did bring a few creatures in from outside. The first time Mom found a dead mouse on the mat beside the front door she thought Cat had caught it inside the house and praised him lavishly and gave him several treats. The next morning there was another dead mouse in the same place. And Cat was sitting in the kitchen waiting for his treat! On the third morning she was becoming suspicious. Were all these mice really living in their house? She found Cat sitting beside the food dish looking pleased with himself and gave him a hard look. In response he lifted his front leg in his beg pose and waited. Mom just laughed and gave him a treat. "But I'm on to you, Cat," she told him. "You're bringing in these mice from outside. That's enough now!"

The next morning she looked at the mat expecting another mouse but there wasn't one, just the cat watching her beside his food dish. She served his tuna as usual and he went outside. Later, when Joey came back from school he went into his room to do his homework. A short while later he came running out. "Mom, there's something under my bed!" She followed

138

him back into his room and sure enough they could both hear noises coming from under the bed. Mom picked up a flashlight and they peered underneath. At first they saw nothing, but then suddenly something jumped in Joey's direction and he fell back in surprise. It was a small frog! They spent the next ten minutes chasing the frog around the room until Mom was able to trap it under a plastic container. They could see the tiny creature trying to get out and Joey felt sorry for it. "Can we take it outside and set it free?"

They were able to slide a piece of cardboard under the container and Joey carefully carried it outside. When he got to the deck he found Cat sitting on his chair watching him with interest. "It's a frog, Cat," Joey told him. "Now, leave it alone when I let it go." He took the container to the other side of the yard, away from Cat's bush, and opened it up. The frog hopped away, apparently unharmed. The cat had followed Joey and sat down, obviously interested but pretending not to be. As Joey looked at him Cat focused his attention on cleaning his tail. "Let's go inside now," Joey said and started walking back to the house. He turned and looked at the cat, who got up and slowly walked towards him, stopping to throw a glance back towards the place where the frog had disappeared before continuing to the house.

"The frog is fine, Mom," Joey said when they got back inside. "And Cat was very interested but I told him to come inside and leave the frog alone."

Mom looked at the cat keenly. "I wonder if Cat brought that frog inside?" she said thoughtfully. "I told him yesterday I'd had enough dead mice placed on the door mat, so maybe today he tried a live frog!"

Joey laughed. "Cat! Did you bring the frog inside?" The cat rubbed himself against Joey's legs and then sat down and did his beg.

"Well I think that means he did," Mom laughed. "Alright, you can have a treat. But no more creatures, alive or dead, you hear. We have plenty of food here, thank you very much!"

After that she found no more "gifts" in the morning, although one summer morning she found a bird flapping around in the kitchen and wondered if it had really flown in the open window by itself or if the cat had brought it in.

The cat never hurt Teddy. He seemed to enjoy watching him run around in his ball in the living room, watching him to make sure he didn't get stuck behind a piece of furniture. And he was often found sitting beside the cage in the morning, watching Teddy run in his wheel. It was Cat who alerted them to Teddy's demise. No one else had noticed that Teddy had been very quiet. He did usually sleep during the day after all. But he hadn't come out to take any food after Joey filled the dish and the cat started pacing around beside the cage, obviously agitated.

"What's wrong, Cat?" Joey asked when he got home from school. "Do you want to play with Teddy?" Joey went over to the hamster's cage and then he realized the food dish was full. Cat was sitting beside him and put a paw on Joey's leg. Joey looked down. "Is Teddy sick?" he asked. "I'd better check on him." Joey carefully opened the cage and lifted up the igloo house. Teddy was curled up in a ball in his bedding. When Joey touched him he didn't move. "Mom, something's wrong with Teddy!" He picked up the little creature who lay quite still in his hand. "Oh, he's cold, Mom. Is he dead?"

Mom took a look and gently reached out to touch the hamster. "I'm afraid so."

At that moment the cat stood up on his hind legs and tried to reach the hamster in Joey's hand. "Meow," he said. Joey lowered his hand and let the cat sniff the dead creature. "Yes, your friend is dead, Cat," Joey said softly. Then looking up at his mother, "Can we bury him, Mom?"

"Let's wait for your Dad and do it together," Mom said, turning away so Joey wouldn't see the tears in her eyes. "Poor Teddy, I hope he enjoyed his life."

"I bet he did. It was kind of short, but I guess hamsters don't live so long?"

"Right, I think two or three years is normal," Mom responded.

"So he did alright," Joey was nodding. "He's like two and three quarters." He put the body back in the cage. "Can I have snack now and then I'll do my homework?"

Joey was busy doing his homework when his father came home and Mom told him what had happened. Dad went and got a shovel and they all trooped outside to make a grave for Teddy. Mom had found a box to serve as a coffin and Joey put a tissue in it to make Teddy comfortable. When the burial was done Dad put a stone over the grave to mark the spot. Cat sniffed all around the new grave and seemed to approve. Then they all went back inside for dinner.

The years passed and Cat and Joey remained constant companions, almost inseparable when both were at home. Just as the cat accepted that Joey had other activities that took him away from home some days, so Joey accepted the cat's need to go outside on his own adventures.

His parents had always expected that Joey would go to college after high school, and when he was a sophomore they began talking about where he might go and what he would study. Dad expected him to be interested in something scientific, being an engineer himself. Mom knew that Joey's interests were not the same as her husband's but even she was surprised when Joey declared one day that he wanted to be a writer.

"What kind of writer?" Dad asked, puzzled.

"Do you mean a journalist?" Mom suggested. "I know you've written a lot of good articles for the student newspaper."

"No, I want to write novels, or maybe screenplays. But I think I'd rather write novels," Joey answered.

"Well, is there any money in that?" Dad asked. "And you do plan to go to college, don't you?"

"Yes, of course! I found this great course in Creative Writing at Stanford University," Joey responded. "They have a fiction into film track too, so I could try it and see if I like it. I do love movies and I'd love to learn how to turn a book into a great movie, like 'Harry Potter' that I loved when I was a little kid." He looked at his parents who were in shock.

"Stanford's in California, isn't it?" his mother asked tentatively.

"And it's really expensive," Dad added. "I think it's hard to get accepted there too."

"Well, you asked what I wanted and that's it," Joey got defensive. "I'll apply to other places too, of course, safety schools, and the state school here as well just to be really safe," he added hoping to make Mom feel better. "But I'd love to go to California, you know," he concluded. "Except for Cat," and he looked around but the cat was out on his own adventure. "But wherever I go I won't be able to bring him, so that doesn't really matter."

Joey had spoken to his guidance counselor at school and already knew what he needed to do in high school to be accepted into such a program. His parents were delighted to see him focused on his goal, instead of spending all his time playing video games or worse. Not that he didn't have friends and know how to have a good time with them, but Joey wanted more out of life. He wanted to travel and meet people, more interesting people than those in this small mid-western town, and he spent time dreaming of such adventures while sitting on the deck accompanied by Cat.

The day came when Joey was to leave for college. Accepted into Stanford as well as the other schools he'd applied to, he had persuaded his parents that California was calling him. They decided that Dad would fly out with him, it being too far to drive comfortably, and two people could take his luggage more easily. Mom said she'd stay home, not really wanting to make the trip. "I'll visit you later after you're all settled in," she declared and Joey agreed. He promised to take photos of the campus, especially his dorm, as soon as they got there, so she would know what it was like.

As Joey and Dad left for the airport Mom held Cat in her arms so they could get a final look at him as he waved from the car. "Well, Cat, he's off on his big adventure now." The cat looked at her and she put him down and he ran off to his bush. Later in the day she found him on Joey's bed. He looked up when she came in, and she went over to stroke him. "Yes, I miss him too," she said. Cat purred and snuggled up to her.

The next day she got a phone call from Joey. "Mom, it's so great here! I love it. The campus is amazing, and well the dorm is fine. I've met my roommate and we're getting on great. His father is here too, and they're staying at the same motel. It's all really cool. How's Cat?"

Mom laughed. "Well you do sound cheerful, that's good. Cat is fine. He slept on your bed last night. I think he misses you."

"I miss Cat too. Say hi to him from me? Is he there?"

"No, he had his breakfast tuna and went outside. I'll tell him though."

They chatted a bit longer and then Joey said he had to go. There were some orientation meetings for new students and their parents so he had to be ready to go with Dad. They said goodbye, but not after Mom reminded him to send photos.

That evening she got a text with a photo of Joey standing in front of his dorm. "Look Cat," she showed the photo to him. "This is where Joey is now." Cat was on the couch and he jumped up to look out the window. "No, Cat, here on the phone. See in the photo. That's Joey. He's in California." Cat looked at her questioningly. "Joey went to college in California, Stanford. It's far away from here, Cat. But it's a really nice place and he's enjoying it there. See, he looks happy." Cat stared at the phone, and then lifted his front leg in a beg. "Meow," he said.

"I know, you miss him. He misses you too."

"Meow, meow," Cat said, begging again.

"You want to see him, don't you," Mom stroked his head. "It'll be alright, Cat."

Cat got down off the couch and headed towards the kitchen and the cat door. He stopped at the cat door and gave another look at her. "Meow," he said and went outside. "Be safe, Cat," she said.

The phone rang and it was Dad. He said Joey was really excited and thrilled to be there, and he could see why. The place was great, and he had enjoyed spending time with his roommate's father. Mom went to bed feeling content, although somewhat lonely.

In the morning she noticed that Cat didn't come to eat his tuna for breakfast, and his dish was still full of the dry food that she had put out at dinner time. She had a busy morning planned so she put it out of her mind. In the afternoon she got an excited phone call from Joey. "Mom, you won't believe this. Rob, he's the RA in my dorm, he has a cat. And it looks just like Cat, you know, my cat?"

Mom smiled. "But can he have a cat in the dorm, dear?" she asked.

"Well, no, but he's the RA so who's going to report him!" Joey laughed. "Anyway, he said this cat just showed up at his window last night and wouldn't leave. So he let him in and he's going to keep him. He's just so much like Cat, I can't believe it! I'm going to buy him all the food Cat likes and Rob says I can visit any time and help take care of him. And maybe we can get an apartment together later and the cat can live with us. Mom, it's so great!"

Before Mom could say any more Joey had to go. She ended the call and said with a smile, "Well done, Cat!"

The Bird Lady

No more school,
Summer sun is shining.
No more school,
All the birds are singing.
No more school,
Lots of flowers blooming.
No more school,
Something, something, something.

Maria sang cheerfully to herself as she skipped along the path through the forest, her backpack bouncing on her back. There wasn't much in her pack today, as she had brought all her books home earlier in the week; just a few papers and things from today's classes had remained. And now it was summer. Endless days and weeks of freedom! Maria danced around in a circle laughing. How good it felt.

As she made her way along the path she started singing again. It was just a little song she had made up in the moment, and it made her feel even happier. Until she reached that pesky last line again. What else was cheerful? Oh, maybe:

No more school,
The little stream is running.

Maria hesitated. That line was alright, but she thought she had heard laughter. She stood still for a moment listening. But all she heard was the birds and the stream.

No more school,
Summer sun is shining.
No more school,
All the birds are singing.

"Yes, they are singing!"

This time it was words, and so clear that Maria knew she wasn't imagining it. She stopped again and looked around. Suddenly she shivered. "Oh no!" She had remembered that there was a cabin in the forest which was said to house an old witch. "I hope it isn't the witch!" she muttered under her breath.

"Come on child, don't be shy!" the voice called out to her. "I'm over here. Come on over and join me for a minute. Some of those birds you are singing about are here with me. You can feed them some bread if you like."

Maria knew she shouldn't talk to strangers. But she was already in the forest, and the voice didn't sound dangerous. And feeding bread to birds was certainly a nice thing to do! So she walked cautiously in the direction of the voice, following a not very well trodden path.

The path led towards a small cabin, nestled among the trees. Maria looked at it suspiciously. It did look rather like a witch's house from the fairy tales! Then she saw an old woman sitting at a table in what would be the front yard, if there was a fence. The woman saw her and waved. "Come on dear, there's nothing to fear," and she smiled a friendly smile.

"I don't know," Maria said reluctantly. "My mother taught me not to speak to strangers."

"Well, let's introduce ourselves and then we won't be strangers!" the woman stood up holding out her hand. "I'm Mrs. Bird, and I'm very pleased to meet you. And this is my cat, Callie. Do you like cats?"

"Oh, yes, I love cats!" Maria stepped forward in spite of her fears. "My name is Maria," she said holding out her hand.

Mrs. Bird took it in hers and they stood there for a moment. Her hand was rough and the fingers were rather brittle, almost like claws, Maria thought. And her nose was rather long, and pointed at the end. Maria wondered if she should just run away. Then she felt something touch her leg and she jerked backwards letting go of the woman's hand.

"It's only Callie. She wants to say hello too," Mrs. Bird said, leaning down to pet her cat.

Maria looked down. It was the cat's tail she had felt brushing against her legs. She put her hand out and the cat nuzzled against it, and then walked away a short distance before sitting down to clean herself.

"That's a cat for you. She likes you though, or she wouldn't have come to say hello." Mrs. Bird smiled as they both watched the cat busy licking a patch of fur.

"Her name's Callie?" Maria asked, still nervous.

"Yes, short for Calico. She's a calico cat you see. With those patches of color and a lot of white," Mrs. Bird explained. "She thinks she's beautiful of course."

"She is beautiful!" Maria was quick to defend the cat. "If I had a cat I'd want one just like her."

"You would, would you?" Mrs. Bird was smiling. "What would your parents say about that?"

"It's just me and my Momma," Maria replied quickly, looking down. "But I'm sure she'd love Callie and let me have a cat like her. Can I bring my Momma to visit you?"

"Well, of course, dear. That would be very nice. Then she won't worry about you visiting a stranger. Why don't you bring her over tomorrow?"

"Oh yes, I will," Maria was excited. "It's Saturday and she doesn't have to work in the afternoon. We can come after lunch."

"Excellent, that's our plan then," Mrs. Bird picked up a piece of bread from the table and gave it to Maria. "I said you could feed the birds. Why don't you break this bread into small pieces and throw it over there under that tree and see who comes to eat it?"

"Alright, but won't Callie frighten the birds?" Maria was still watching the cat. "I mean, don't cats eat birds?"

"Well, yes, they can do. But Callie knows I don't allow that. She only catches mice and little animals, never birds. So it's quite safe."

Maria was surprised but she obediently broke the bread up into small pieces and threw them in the direction Mrs. Bird had pointed. Before all the pieces had landed, she heard the rustling of wings and a bird swooped down to grab one. "Oh, that was quick!" Maria was so startled she let out a squawk of surprise. Callie stopped her cleaning and gave her a look as if to say, control yourself girl; that's what the bread is for!

As they continued watching, many other birds of different sizes and colors flew towards them. Some landed on the ground and started eating immediately; others landed in the tree or a bush nearby and then flew closer to the bread. Within a few minutes all the bread was gone. One of the birds was still on the ground and it turned to face them, cocking its head. It made a couple of chirping sounds and Mrs. Bird said firmly, "That's all for now." The bird made what Maria thought was a rather disapproving noise and flew away.

"He's a brave one, that blue jay. Thinks he's the boss, he does." Mrs. Bird chuckled.

"You understand what the birds say?" Maria asked, looking at her in admiration.

"Oh, it's not so hard. They all have their different voices and behaviors. I see them every day, when I'm sitting out here, so we get to know each other quite well."

"Could you teach me about the birds? So I could understand them too?"

"Well, you'd have to come here often, not just one day," Mrs. Bird was looking at her intently.

"I know. We'll ask my Momma tomorrow!" Maria grabbed her pack that had dropped to the ground earlier. "I have to go now or I'll be late. See you tomorrow!" and she ran off excitedly, stopping suddenly to turn and say "Bye Callie, I'll see you tomorrow too!"

Mrs. Bird laughed. "Well, Callie. It looks like we made a new friend. Isn't that nice?"

Callie's ears twitched but she carried on cleaning herself.

Maria's mother was skeptical, but since it was the beginning of the summer vacation she decided to humor her daughter by going for a walk with her into the forest. She didn't really believe there was a witch living in a cabin there, so there was no need to be afraid. Still, she felt protective of her young daughter and hoped this wouldn't lead to some great disappointment.

"Come on Momma," Maria called out as she skipped ahead along the path. "Mrs. Bird will be waiting for us."

"Yes, dear, I'm coming. There are a lot of branches on the path, be careful not to trip."

Maria looked back and saw her mother was cautiously navigating a fallen tree trunk. She sighed and tried to be patient. But it was impossible not to be excited. This was going to be the best summer ever!

"Mrs. Bird!" she called out as soon as she saw the cabin. "Mrs. Bird, it's me Maria, and my mother. We're here!" And she ran the rest of the way, arriving all out of breath at the table where Mrs. Bird had been sitting yesterday. "Mrs. Bird? Callie? Are you there?" Maria called out.

Before she heard anything she felt Callie rub against her legs. "Oh, Callie, here you are! You remember me, don't you?" and Maria leaned down to stroke the cat. "Momma, look this is the cat I told you about. Her name's Callie. Callie, this is my mother."

Callie looked up at her mother and then turned to go towards the cabin.

"Isn't she beautiful?" Maria was excited. "Can I go to the cabin and see if Mrs. Bird is home?"

"No dear, we should wait here."

There was no need to wait, though, because at that moment the door of the cabin opened and Mrs. Bird appeared. "Hello, Maria! And this must be your mother. Welcome to my humble home."

"Mrs. Bird! Callie was out here and she remembered me!"

"Of course she did, Maria. I told you she likes you." Mrs. Bird made her way towards them. "Hello, you must be Maria's mother. I'm Mrs. Bird, and I'm very glad to meet you." She held out her hand.

"I'm glad to meet you too. I'm Enid Rossi, Maria's mother."

"Please sit down," Mrs. Bird gestured towards the table.

"We brought some bread, can I feed the birds?" Maria asked taking a small bag out of her backpack.

"Yes, indeed. They are waiting for you to feed them."

As Maria broke up the pieces of bread and threw them towards the tree where the birds had eaten yesterday, her mother was watching Mrs. Bird.

"So, you live here alone?" she asked.

"Yes, just me and my cat."

"No family?"

"No, I'm a widow. Like you, is that right?" and Mrs. Bird smiled gently at Enid.

"Yes, that's right. My husband died three years ago. It's just me and Maria now. Do you have any children?"

"Yes, but they live far away. They have their own lives, and I have my cat." Mrs. Bird smiled again and turned to look at Maria who was watching the ground, waiting for the birds to come. "Don't worry, Maria, the birds will come in a minute. See, there's the blue jay. He'll tell the others the bread is here."

Sure enough the blue jay had landed on a branch in the tree and was looking down at the bread. He let out a few squawks and flew down to start eating. Within a minute there was a fluttering of wings and several other birds joined him. Maria almost clapped her hands in delight, but stopped just in time, realizing she would frighten the birds away.

"See, Momma, there are so many birds here, and Mrs. Bird knows all about them. I want to come here and feed them every day!"

"Well, now that might be too much," Enid started to say when Mrs. Bird interrupted.

"I can teach her all about the birds. It's no trouble, and I'd enjoy the company."

"Like a summer camp, Momma! I can come here when you go to work, it's perfect!"

"Well," Enid looked at her daughter's shining face and hesitated. "I'd have to pay you," she turned to Mrs. Bird.

"No, no. No money. Just make sure she brings some bread or cookies for the birds, something with nuts or seeds. Oh, and she could bring her own lunch too."

"Yes, I can come for the whole day, just like school, only better!" Maria was dancing with excitement.

"We can make it a serious summer project," Mrs. Bird suggested. "She could make a scrapbook with pictures of all the birds and write something she learns about each one."

"Yes, yes! I can take photos of the birds with my new phone, the phone I'm getting for my 10th birthday. I could get the phone now and use it for this bird project. My teacher next year will love it!"

"Well," her mother was still wavering.

"Please, please Momma! If I have my phone you can call me or text me to make sure I'm OK any time. So you won't have to worry about me, right Mrs. Bird?"

Mrs. Bird was nodding and watching them both carefully, waiting.

"Well, I don't know. Do you have good cell service out here?" Maria's mother was looking around at the forest.

"Oh, I don't have a phone," Mrs. Bird answered.

"Try yours, Momma," Maria was determined to have the plan work out.

"Alright, let's see. Hmm, yes. I can see 3, no 4, bars. There does seem to be good reception here."

"Yes! I knew it! Momma, let's get my phone today so I can come on Monday. This will be so amazing. And I'll work very hard to learn all about the birds, and make a scrapbook and everything. Please, Momma!"

Mrs. Bird was smiling at the girl's enthusiasm, but still waiting for her mother to make the final decision. In the end it was Callie who swayed her. She had been sitting watching the exchange, aloof from the proceedings but her ears twitched with each rise and fall in the conversation. Now she stood up and purposefully walked over to the table where Maria was standing beside her mother's chair. The cat almost pushed Maria aside and went right up to her mother. She reached out her front paw and laid it firmly on Enid's knee. When Enid looked down in surprise, Callie gave a meow and prodded her knee gently.

"Well, I do believe this cat wants me to say yes!"

"Ooh, yes, please say yes! Callie is already my friend, isn't she special?" Maria put on her best pleading voice.

"Well, if it's really alright with you Mrs. Bird ..."

"Yes! Yes!" Maria interrupted.

"I suppose we could try it for a week and see how it works out," her mother continued.

Mrs. Bird smiled and nodded. "Yes, of course. I'll be very pleased to see Maria on Monday morning, with her new phone!"

"Oh thank you, Momma, thank you!" Maria was already dancing her way back to the path. "Let's go and get my phone!"

"Well, that's settled then," her mother looked less certain, but got up from the table. "She'll come on Monday then."

"Bye Mrs. Bird, bye Callie. I'll see you on Monday!" and Maria was skipping along the path back home. "Come on Momma!"

Her mother followed more slowly, turning once to wave to Mrs. Bird who waved back, smiling.

"Good job, Callie," she said to her cat, who had sat down and begun cleaning herself. "This promises to be a good summer."

On Monday morning Mrs. Bird was already sitting outside at her table when Maria arrived, even more excited than before.

"Mrs. Bird, Mrs. Bird, I'm here! And I've got my phone, and food for the birds, and for me too!" she announced as she ran up the path. "Oh, where's Callie?" she asked looking around.

"She's over there watching you, dear," Mrs. Bird was smiling. "She knows you didn't bring her anything so she's keeping her distance."

"Oh Callie! But I brought my phone and I want to take a photo of you." Maria dropped her backpack on the table and ran over in Callie's direction.

As she got her phone out of her pocket Callie looked at her somewhat suspiciously. Maria fiddled around for a moment, muttering, and then lifted the phone and pointed it in Callie's direction. Unfortunately, the cat had chosen that moment to raise her hind leg and clean herself.

"Oh, she's cleaning her butt!" Maria exclaimed with a giggle, and turned to Mrs. Bird who was laughing quietly.

"Perhaps she doesn't want her photo taken just now," she said gently.

"But I need to practice before the birds come. Please Callie, I want to take a photo of your pretty face." Maria moved closer but the cat kept on with her cleaning. "Well, I'll just take a photo of you with your leg stuck up in the air then," Maria announced and she started taking photos. Callie continued to ignore her.

Soon she had several photos on her phone, and had figured out how to get the focus in the right place. Callie kept her head down, but Maria was satisfied, for now. She walked back to Mrs. Bird at the table. "I'll get a better shot another time," Maria told her. "But look, see how my phone takes nice photos?"

"Goodness," Mrs. Bird exclaimed. "I never saw a phone take such photos before. That's wonderful, Maria."

"I can take your photo too," Maria said and reached out to take the phone back. At that moment it started buzzing and vibrating, much to Mrs. Bird's surprise.

"Oh, what's happening?" she almost dropped the phone.

"Someone's calling me!" Maria grabbed the phone. "It's Momma." She quickly righted the phone and answered the call. "Hi Momma, it's me Maria." She nodded vigorously while listening to her mother. "Yes, Momma, everything's fine. Mrs. Bird is here and Callie, but she didn't want her photo taken. But I took some anyway. I'll show you when I get home." She shook her head. "No, no, Callie didn't want her photo taken! She started cleaning herself and wouldn't look at the camera." She nodded again and then held the phone to Mrs. Bird. "Momma wants to talk to you."

"Hello Mrs. Rossi. Yes, Maria is here. Everything is fine." Mrs. Bird was nodding now. "Of course. It's no trouble." She was looking a bit puzzled. "Well, if Maria knows how to set the alarm on her phone. I'm afraid I'm no good with these technical things." Then she nodded and gave the phone back to Maria.

"Yes, Momma. Don't worry. I'll be home by 3. Bye!" Maria was smiling. "She wants us to set the alarm on the phone to remind me to leave in time. Hmm. I think this is how it works. Oh, that's loud!" They both started laughing as the alarm went off.

"That will certainly scare all the birds away," Mrs. Bird was still laughing.

"I don't think Callie liked it much either." Callie was staring at them with a most disapproving look. "Sorry, Callie. I'll make it quieter." Maria fiddled with her phone some more. "OK, I think that's it," and she put her phone on the table and sat back. "That was hard work! Now I'm thirsty. I hope Momma packed a juice box for me." She rummaged in her pack. "Nope." She looked at Mrs. Bird hopefully. "Can I have a drink? I'm thirsty."

"Yes, of course, dear. Do you like lemonade?"

"Ooh, yes, that's a good idea. Shall I help you?" Maria offered without standing up.

"No, no you sit there. I'll just be a minute," and Mrs. Bird quickly got up and started towards her front door.

"Is it pink?"

"What, the lemonade?" Mrs. Bird turned back. "No, I just have the regular yellow lemonade. Is that alright?"

"Oh yes. Sometimes I like pink lemonade but yellow is good too. Can I have ice?"

"Yes, dear. I'll be right back with it." And sure enough Mrs. Bird took only a few minutes before returning with a tray carrying a pitcher full of lemonade and two glasses each half full of ice. There was also a plate of cookies. "Here we go. I brought some cookies too in case you felt hungry watching the birds eat."

"Oh thank you. Are they peanut butter?"

"Yes, they are," Mrs. Bird poured lemonade into both glasses.

"Do birds eat peanut butter?" Maria asked as she bit into her cookie.

"Indeed they do. Many birds like nuts, including peanuts. Some birds will take a whole peanut in its shell but others like them taken out of the shell. They enjoy peanut butter too. Did you bring something for the birds to eat today?"

"Momma gave me some stale bread. It was good bread with whole grains, that must be nice for birds, right?" Maria asked hopefully, and she picked up her glass and took a drink of lemonade.

"Oh, yes, that sounds excellent. All kinds of seeds and nuts are good, and dried fruits as well."

"Like trail mix?"

"I suppose so. You can buy bird food at the store you know, much cheaper. Maybe your mother would buy some?"

"Yes, I'm sure she will." Maria drank some more of her lemonade and smiled contentedly. "Oh this is going to be such a fun summer. I'm so glad I met you Mrs. Bird!"

"I'm glad we met too, Maria."

Finishing her cookie Maria picked up her phone and was just about to point it in Mrs. Bird's direction, when Mrs. Bird saw her and quickly moved aside. "Oh no, please don't take my photo. I look worse than Callie!"

Maria sighed. "Alright. As long as I can take photos of the birds, that's the important thing. But I do want a nice photo of Callie, and you, some day."

Just then they heard a loud squawking sound. As they turned to look, a bird flew down and landed on a small table under the tree. It sat there and stared at Maria.

"Oh, is that the blue jay?" Maria asked.

"Yes, he's impatient isn't he?" Mrs. Bird chuckled. "I put that small table there for you to put food on. Some birds don't like to eat on the ground and it's easier to see them up on the table. He's waiting for you to put your bread there!"

Maria laughed excitedly and grabbed her pieces of bread. "Alright, Mister Blue Jay, I'll bring you some bread!" and she ran towards the tree.

Of course the bird squawked and flew up into the tree. Brave though he was, her sudden movement had unnerved him. He didn't leave, however, but sat on a high branch and watched her.

"I'm sorry, Mister Blue Jay. I didn't mean to scare you," Maria had reached the table and looked up into the tree. "Here, I've got some bread for you. I'll break it up into pieces, so maybe you can tell the other birds to come too?" She broke the bread into several small pieces and scattered them on the table. Then she backed away, moving more slowly this time hoping not to upset the bird again.

By the time she had reached Mrs. Bird, the blue jay had worked his way down to the lowest branch just above the table. He cocked his head, looking at Maria and then at the bread. Suddenly he made up his mind and flew down to land on the table. Maria held her breath as he pecked at a piece of bread. Then he opened his beak and cried out a few times before picking up a piece and flying off to land in another tree.

"Oh, he took a piece of bread!" Maria whispered to Mrs. Bird. "Will he come back?"

"Maybe not for a while. But he told the other birds the food is here so you'll have plenty more customers."

Sure enough there were other birds already appearing. Several landed in the tree and seemed to be chattering to each other.

"What are they saying?" Maria asked, fascinated.

"Well, listen to them. One of them knows his name. Can you hear it?"

Maria listened carefully. It sounded like a collection of chirps and tweets all mixed up. After a few moments one little bird landed on the edge of the table and looked at the bread and then looked around. "Chickadee-dee-dee!" he said and hopped onto the table to peck at one the closest piece of bread. "Chickadee-dee!"

"Oh, is that a chickadee?" Maria said excitedly. "He sounds like he's saying Chickadee."

"Yes, indeed," Mrs. Bird nodded.

"Oh, there's another one, on the other side of the table. Are they friends?" Maria was reaching for her camera, realizing she was supposed to take photos not just marvel at the birds.

"That's his wife, I believe," Mrs. Bird replied. "She came because he said it was safe enough."

Black capped Chickadee

"But they look the same!" Maria was puzzled.

"Yes, in many species of birds the males and females look the same to humans. But birds can tell the difference."

"Oh, how funny," Maria was taking photos now. The first chickadee was watching her with interest, but stayed on the table while the second one ate.

"They are so cute," Maria said. "They have black caps on their heads!"

"Chickadee-dee-dee!" the first chickadee responded.

"Yes, I know!" Maria laughed.

Then the two chickadees each grabbed a piece of bread in their beaks and flew off.

"Bye, chickadees," Maria called out after them. "Oh, they were fun!"

"Hmm," Mrs. Bird said thoughtfully. "They are quite the little acrobats you know. If we had a hanging feeder they would show you how clever they are at balancing."

"Ooh, yes. That would make great photos too!" Maria looked around. "But how can we have a hanging feeder?"

"Well, I'm thinking. Let's see. If we had a small log, we could make holes in it and hang it from a branch. We can put peanut butter in the holes. Woodpeckers would love that too."

"I can find a log, there's so many trees here, and lots of branches fell down. Momma almost tripped on one when we came here." Maria stood up and started looking around. "Look, there's some pieces over there," and Maria ran into the forest.

"Don't go far," Mrs. Bird called after her. "Stay where I can see you."

"It's all right, I've found some pieces of tree. Look!" Maria was picking up broken branches. "Oh, this one's nice. Nope, this is better." She ran back to Mrs. Bird waving a branch. "How about this?"

Mrs. Bird took it and shook her head. "No, it's too small, too thin. We need a fatter branch so we can poke holes in it."

"Okay, I'll get a better one," and Maria ran off into the forest again. She picked up a few pieces and brought them back hopefully.

"No, they're still too skinny."

Maria quickly went back to the forest with the rejected branches. She hunted around for a while and then came back carrying a much thicker branch. "How about this?"

"Oh dear, I think that one's too heavy." Mrs. Bird shook her head.

"This time I'll get a good one!" Maria ran merrily back into the forest, enjoying the hunt for the perfect branch. This time she chose a piece that had broken off an old tree, and then broken again when it landed on a rock.

"This is good," she said as she made her way back. "Isn't it good?" she held it out to Mrs. Bird.

"Yes, that's very good. Perfect I think. Just put it on the chair and we'll make a nice hanging feeder. But maybe we should eat lunch first?"

"Oh yes. And I need to use the bathroom. And wash my hands I suppose," Maria looked at her hands which were all dirty from carrying the broken branches.

"Right. Come on dear. I'll show you where the bathroom is."

Maria followed Mrs. Bird into her house. The front door opened directly into the main room, which was rather sparsely furnished and Maria thought didn't look particularly comfortable. Off to one side Maria could see a small kitchen and Mrs. Bird led her towards a door down a narrow hallway. There was another door, which Maria assumed led to her bedroom. The bathroom was small, but very clean. There was even a pretty towel beside the sink so Maria washed her hands thoroughly not wanting to make it all dirty when she dried her hands.

When she was done she found Callie sitting in the hallway waiting for her. "Hello, Callie. What a nice little house you have." Callie stood up and walked towards the front door with her tail standing up straight. She paused at the door and turned to see if Maria was following her. "I'm coming Callie," Maria called as she hurried to catch up to the cat. "I'll close the door behind us I suppose?" Callie sat on the front porch and watched.

"Everything alright?" Mrs. Bird asked as Maria returned to the table.

Maria nodded and opened her backpack to take out her lunch. There was a notebook on top of her lunch bag and she put it on the table. "Momma gave me a notebook to write stuff about the birds. That's to go in my scrapbook with the photos. But I want to have lunch first!" and she took out a large sandwich. "Mmm, tuna salad, that's nice." She felt something touch her leg and looked down to see Callie had arrived and was rubbing against her. "No, Callie this is my lunch!"

Mrs. Bird laughed. "She likes fish!"

"Well, this has mayo and stuff mixed in it, so it's not good for her, right?"

"You're right. Callie, let Maria eat her lunch in peace."

Callie moved away and sat down, still watching closely. Suddenly there was a disturbance at the bird table which attracted their attention, including

Callie's. The last piece of bread was being fought over by two birds, who were both squawking loudly. In the middle of the commotion, another bird swooped down and grabbed the piece of bread, flying away with it firmly grasped in its beak.

"Oh, he took it!" Maria was shocked. "Now those two noisy birds have no bread!"

"Well, that'll teach them not to fight!" Mrs. Bird was nodding her head. "Now they'll just have to wait till we put out more food."

"Oh, I feel bad for them!" Maria was looking in her backpack hoping to find some more bread. "I've got half a cookie still. Can I put that on the table for them?"

"If you've had enough to eat yourself."

"Yes, I'm full now." Maria jumped up and made her way to the bird table. "I'd better break it into pieces or they'll just fight again," she said to herself. As she put the pieces on the table she looked into the nearby bush and saw the two birds perched there, watching her. She smiled at them and backed away.

"I saw the birds in the bush. I hope they come and share the cookie now."

Mrs. Bird was smiling as they both watched attentively. And sure enough the two birds came one after the other to the bird table, each grabbing a piece of cookie and flying off.

"Well, that worked out nicely."

"Yes, it's good I had more food." Maria had picked up her notebook and pen. "What kind of birds were those? Oh, I forgot to take their photo!"

"Don't worry, they'll be back. They're starlings, noisy birds, always seem to be squabbling about something!"

"Right, starlings. And I met the chickadees this morning, he told me his name, and his wife looked the same as him. They both wear black caps on their heads. I got their photo but I want another one when we've made the bird feeder." Maria was concentrating hard as she wrote down notes about the birds they had seen. "This is going to be a great project! Thank you Mrs. Bird, I'm having so much fun!" she declared as she finished writing. "How are we going to make the branch into a bird feeder?"

"Well, we have to make some holes in it. I have to find something sharp to do that with." Mrs. Bird was looking at the branch closely. "Then we can put some wire, or some string, around here where the twigs broke off. That should hold it securely when we hang it up on the tree."

"Ooh, yes, there's a branch over there you can reach if you climb on a chair!" Maria was clapping her hands enthusiastically. Just then though the alarm on her phone sounded. It wasn't as loud as before but it still made them jump.

"Goodness, that is still quite loud!" Mrs. Bird said. "But at least we won't miss it. I think that means you have to go home now."

Maria packed up her things. "Yes, Momma will be mad if I'm late. Bye, Mrs. Bird. Bye, Callie. See you tomorrow!" and she set off along the path. Then she stopped and turned. "Peanut butter, right?" she called out.

Mrs. Bird smiled and nodded. And Maria turned and skipped along the path on her way home.

The next morning Maria arrived full of excitement. "Mrs. Bird, I've got peanut butter! Can we make the bird feeder?" She bounced into the yard and almost tripped over Callie, who gave her a most disapproving look. "Oops, sorry Callie!" Maria stopped and bent down to stroke the cat. She looked up when she heard a laugh.

Mrs. Bird was coming over to the table. "Callie was waiting for you. Silly cat, did Maria step on you?" She gave Callie a stroke too, and the cat gracefully walked around both of them to take up a position where she could see the birds coming to eat whatever food Maria had brought.

"Did you make holes in the branch? I've got peanut butter to put in, see," Maria put her backpack on the table and started pulling things out of it. "Momma gave me a whole jar, so we can refill it if the birds eat everything. It's the healthy kind, all natural. Is that good?"

Mrs. Bird looked at the jar. "This looks excellent," and she unscrewed the lid and sniffed it. "Mmm, smells delicious. I'd like to eat some myself!"

Maria laughed. "Momma said we'd want to eat it too, so she gave me a big jar!"

"Well, I do like your Momma!" Mrs. Bird said and they both laughed.

"I guess we should make the bird feeder first though," Maria was serious. "Then we can have some of the peanut butter all together!"

"That's a good plan," Mrs. Bird approved. "Now, let me see. I've got the branch here and some wire to hang it. We just have to make some holes," and she brought out a screwdriver from her pocket. "Here, see if you can make a hole with this."

Maria tried poking at the branch, but it was rather hard. "Hmm, maybe I have to try a different place," she muttered. She found a softer spot and was able to dig out a reasonable sized hole. "Better make more, right?" she asked, as she poked again at the branch. "Got the hang of it now," she said as the screwdriver sank into another place.

"Excellent," Mrs. Bird was watching closely. "One more hole and that should be enough."

Maria kept working and suddenly she heard the sound of the blue jay squawking loudly. "Oh no, Mister Blue Jay is waiting for his food!" She grabbed a piece of bread from her backpack and went over to the table. "Here, Mister Blue Jay. I've got bread for you!" and she broke up the bread into smaller pieces and scattered them around on the table.

"I'm going to get some peanuts for him soon," she said as she made her way back to their table to finish her job on the branch. "Momma said she can buy some whole peanuts in their shells. He'll like that, won't he?"

"Yes, I'm sure he will. And you should get a nice photo of him eating them."

"I could take his photo eating the bread too," Maria decided, picking up her phone and aiming it at the bird table. "Come on Mister Blue Jay! Your bread is waiting!"

Almost immediately she heard the sounds of a bird descending, and there he was on the table looking at the bread. He fixed one of his beady eyes on Maria, and she quickly hit the button to take his photo. Although the click startled him, it wasn't enough to make him fly away. Giving a squawk, he reached forward and grabbed a piece of bread in his beak. Maria took another photo. This time the bird decided enough was enough and flew up to the safety of a branch in the tree.

"I have to stop it making that noise when I take a photo," Maria said, fiddling with her phone. "Ah, there it is. 'Shutter sound off.' Got it. Now the birds won't know I took their photo!"

"How clever you are to know how to work that camera phone so quickly," Mrs. Bird looked at Maria in admiration.

"Oh it's nothing," Maria smiled. "All my friends have phones, well most of them anyway, so I know how it works already." She turned her attention back to making the third hole in the branch. "Alright," Maria held the branch up for Mrs. Bird to see a few minutes later. "That's three holes now. Can we put the peanut butter in?"

Mrs. Bird produced a spoon and gave it to Maria. "Go ahead, put some in each of the holes."

Maria took the spoon and carefully put peanut butter in each hole. She tried to stuff as much as possible in each hole and of course it made a bit of a mess around the edges, and some went on her fingers. "Mmm, this does taste good," she said, licking it off her fingers. "The birds will love this. But not you, Callie," she saw the cat was watching her with great interest.

Mrs. Bird took the branch and started to wrap the wire around it, being careful to make it secure by going under the knobs that were all that remained of the smaller twigs that had broken off. It was a bit difficult, and Maria noticed that Mrs. Bird's fingers were rather stiff. Still, she was able to attach the wire firmly. Then came the task of hanging the feeder on the tree.

They both stood up and looked at the tree. "That branch is quite low," Mrs. Bird said. "And it's growing over the same area where the birds are already coming to eat. We should try to hang the feeder from there."

"Okay," Maria ran over to the tree. "But how can we reach it? It's too high for me."

Mrs. Bird nodded. "Maybe if we bring our table over, you can stand on top of that and reach it?" she suggested.

Maria came back and the two of them struggled to maneuver the wrought iron table over to a position under the branch. "It's a bit wobbly," Maria said doubtfully.

"But it's a strong table, it'll hold your weight. Here, I'll hold the table steady. You climb up."

With Callie watching attentively, Maria clambered up onto the table and gingerly stood up, holding onto Mrs. Bird's shoulder for support. Mrs. Bird handed the feeder to Maria with one hand, keeping the table steady by keeping her other hand on it and leaning her body against it at the same time.

Once Maria had a firm grasp of the feeder, Mrs. Bird held onto the table tightly and encouraged the girl to loop the wire over the branch. "That's it. Now grab the end and wind it around the long part that's hanging. Good, good."

162

Maria almost slipped when she let go of the feeder and took a step back to see if it held. "Oops, almost fell!" she said with a laugh. "Can I come down now?"

Mrs. Bird helped her down and the two of them breathed sighs of relief when they were both safely on the ground and their bird feeder was hanging nicely from the branch. "Now we just have to take the table back and wait for the birds to find it!"

"And we can have some peanut butter too!" Maria said eagerly as they dragged, rather than carried, the table back to its original location.

"Do you think we scared the birds away doing that?" Maria asked as they settled down again.

"Probably. But they'll be back soon," Mrs. Bird was looking at their feeder. "It looks very good, Maria. I think they'll like it a lot."

"Well, I want to enjoy this peanut butter!" Maria was putting the food back on the table and searching in her backpack. "I brought some bread and jam, I hope. Yes, here it is!" She took a slice and started spreading peanut butter on it. "Can I use the same spoon for the jam, or do you have another one?" she asked cautiously. "Momma doesn't like me to mix them."

"Well, I don't mind," Mrs. Bird said with a smile. "You're going to eat it all together anyway, aren't you?"

"Yes," Maria nodded, spooning jam on a second piece of bread, and then putting them together. "Mmm, this is so good. Have some Mrs. Bird!"

Mrs. Bird was looking at the jam with interest. "Blueberry preserves?" she said looking at Maria. "That sounds delicious. I do like blueberries. I would appreciate some," and she made herself a smaller sandwich, using only one slice of bread.

"Oh, sorry Callie," Maria said turning to the cat who had approached silently in the meantime. "This isn't cat food. And anyway, it's only a snack. You should wait till lunchtime. But it is really good, isn't it Mrs. Bird?"

"Yes, indeed!" Mrs. Bird was clearly enjoying her sandwich. "I do love berries and this peanut butter is excellent too."

"Oh, there's some of the jam in the peanut butter jar now," Maria had taken the lid to close it up. "Will that be alright for the birds?"

"Oh yes, birds like berries. Blueberries are good for them."

"Well, we could mix some in next time we fill up the holes," Maria smiled as she closed up both the jars. "When will they come and eat it?"

They both looked at the hanging feeder, which had not yet attracted any birds. Some birds had landed on the table and were eating the bread, but Maria wanted someone to come and eat the peanut butter. Mrs. Bird was looking in the tree and she motioned to Maria to look at the trunk just above the branch where the feeder was hanging. At first Maria didn't see anything, but then there was a movement and she saw a bird moving down the trunk head first.

"It's upside down!" Maria said quietly, with a chuckle.

"Yes, it's a nuthatch," Mrs. Bird responded. "They go head first down the tree trunk."

Just then the bird flew over to the hanging feeder and grabbed on to it, quickly finding one of the holes with the peanut butter inside. Maria almost scared it away when she knocked her phone off the table in her excitement. "Oops," she whispered. "I want his photo," and she stood up carefully. The nuthatch shifted position, making its way down to the next hole, still head first. Maria was able to get a couple of photos before he flew away.

Nuthatch

"Oh, he was good," Maria said sitting back down. "I like his colors too. He's got a white face and black head, but his back is blue isn't it?"

"Yes, it is. He does look very smart with those markings," Mrs. Bird agreed.

"And he liked the peanut butter!" Maria was smiling. "Will he tell his friends to come and eat too?"

"Well, he might. Oh look, that might be his wife," Mrs. Bird pointed to the feeder where another nuthatch had just arrived.

"She looks the same!" Maria exclaimed. "Like the chickadees, they both look the same."

"That's right," Mrs. Bird was nodding.

"But not all birds look the same, I mean the girl and boy ones."

"No, indeed. There are plenty that are different," Mrs. Bird agreed. "Look, there are a bunch of house sparrows there eating the bread. Can you see?"

Male House Sparrow

"Oh yes, I see. Those are the sparrows, right? Brown birds with white on their faces and a black patch down the neck and chest and white tummies. And I can see white stripes on the wings too. But those other ones are just brown with stripes on the back. You mean those are sparrows too?"

"Yes, indeed! The brown ones with stripes are the female sparrows."

"Oh, I didn't know that! I have to take their photos." Maria bounded up and started taking photos as the birds continued eating. She sat down again and looked at the collection of photos on her phone. Then she took out her notebook. "I have to write down all this stuff!" she said, and taking up her pen she started writing notes diligently. "I think it's a pity the girl sparrows have such dull colors," she commented. "They should be prettier than the boys!"

Mrs. Bird laughed. "Well, that's interesting. In the bird world it's the males that strut around looking handsome to attract a female. Don't you think that's a good system?"

Female House Sparrow

"Hmm, yes in a way," Maria was thinking about it. "But lots of girls like to look pretty. My Momma always looks nice when she goes out to work or something. She likes to get dressed up and look pretty. If the girls can't be prettier maybe they're better off looking the same as the boys!"

Just then they heard the unmistakable sound of a chickadee calling, "Chickadee-dee-dee!"

"Oh, it's the chickadee! Where is he?" Maria looked eagerly at the bird table.

"There, he's in the tree," Mrs. Bird pointed. "I think he's seen the peanut butter feeder."

But before he could reach the feeder another bird swooped down and landed on it.

"Oh! Who's that! He's taking the peanut butter before the chickadee!" Maria was almost indignant. "But he's really cute. Look at his little face and he's got a tuft standing up on top of his head!" Maria jumped up to take a photo. As she was taking his photo the chickadee landed on the branch and started pecking at a different hole. "Oh my, the chickadee's eating too! Got to take more photos."

As Maria stood taking photos, several chickadees came and went, and another of the birds with the tuft on its head flew in to take the place of the first one. "Mrs. Bird, what's the one with the tuft called?"

"That's a tufted titmouse."

"Titmouse!" Maria laughed. "Well, he does have a tuft on his head so that's a good name. But why titmouse, he's not a mouse!"

"Indeed he's not!" Mrs. Bird laughed too. "I think it's because he's small and cute."

"Well, he's cute alright," Maria agreed. "Oh, that was a lot of birds already. It's great they like the peanut butter feeder. And the sparrows ate all the bread! Is it lunchtime now? I'm hungry."

Mrs. Bird smiled. "Yes, let's have lunch. Would you like some lemonade or do you have your own drink?"

Tufted Titmouse

Maria hunted through her backpack and brought out a lunchbox. "Let's see." She opened it up and there was a juice box, a sandwich and a plastic container with strawberries inside. And underneath she found a bag with two cookies. "I've got a juice box today," Maria said.

Mrs. Bird nodded and got up to go inside to get something for herself. Maria stuck the straw in the juice box and took a sip. Then she started eating the sandwich. Immediately she noticed Callie was rubbing against her leg. "Callie, this is my lunch, not yours!"

Just then Mrs. Bird came back and laughed. "Well, when you were eating your snack you told her to wait till lunchtime!"

"Oh, yes. Well let's see. Can she have a bit of ham?" Maria opened up her sandwich and was checking to see if she could extract a small piece.

Mrs. Bird looked at her. "Yes, ham would be alright. Just a small piece, mind. But no chicken, or turkey." She shuddered. "Can't have her eating any kind of bird."

"Oh, no of course not." Maria nodded her agreement. "This is ham, so that's okay isn't it, it's from a pig," and she held a small piece out to Callie who sniffed at it delicately before accepting the offering. Maria gave her another piece and then closed up the sandwich so she could eat the rest herself. They all sat together enjoying their lunch. "Do you want a strawberry, Mrs. Bird?" Maria offered.

"Oh yes, please! I do love berries," Mrs. Bird reached out immediately. "Delicious!"

"You do like all the things birds like, don't you?"

"Indeed I do! Birds eat rather a healthy diet you know!" Mrs. Bird nodded vigorously. "May I have one more strawberry?"

Maria nodded and between them they had soon finished all the berries. Maria gave a big sigh and settled back in her chair. "That was a good lunch!"

"Yes, and please thank your mother for the delicious strawberries." Mrs. Bird had also made herself comfortable in her chair. "Did you get notes on all the birds we saw today?"

"Yes, I think so." Maria picked up her notebook and looked through the pages, comparing them to her photos. "Oh, I forgot the titmouse! I'd better write about him now."

As she was busy writing more birds started landing in the tree, looking with interest at the feeder. Mrs. Bird was listening to their chirps and started to shake her head. Then she looked up at the sky. "Maria, I think the birds have come to eat because it's going to rain soon. Look at that dark cloud over there in the distance."

"Oh no," Maria looked at where Mrs. Bird was pointing. Then she turned towards the tree where the birds had gathered. There was quite a crowd in the branches and as she watched two chickadees swooped down and started eating from the feeder. A moment later a titmouse joined them. Then she heard the blue jay squawking loudly and the three birds flew away, leaving the feeder open for the blue jay to eat! "Oh, he's chased them away!"

"Yes, he's a bit of a bully sometimes," Mrs. Bird was laughing. "There's no food left on the table, so he wants the peanut butter."

"Oh, I'll have to bring some bird seed so we can add more to the table. Alright, I'll ask Momma to get it. And he would eat whole peanuts too, right?"

"Yes he would love those!" Mrs. Bird was nodding vigorously. "And we could eat some of them too!"

Maria laughed. "That sounds like a good plan to me!"

They sat and watched the birds for a while longer. No new birds came, but Maria took several photos. She was so focused on the birds that she forgot about the rain cloud that was now approaching rather quickly.

Suddenly Mrs. Bird shivered as a raindrop landed on her hand. "Oh, the rain's starting!"

Maria turned and saw Mrs. Bird was getting up from her chair. As a couple more drops landed on her Maria saw her shake herself, almost like a bird would flutter its wings, to get the water off. "I'd better run home quickly," Maria said. "I won't get very wet in the forest with all the trees to protect me."

"Alright, dear. If you're sure you'll keep dry. It looks like a lot of rain is coming." Mrs. Bird was making her way to her front porch, where Callie was already waiting. "If it's still raining tomorrow I'm afraid the birds won't come to eat, and you would get very wet too. So I'll see you when the rain is finished?"

"Yes, Mrs. Bird. I'll be back when the sun is shining again!" Maria started to run along the path back home. "Bye Callie. Keep dry!"

Maria reached home without getting too wet but once the rain started in earnest it seemed like it would never stop. The next morning it was coming down steadily and Maria sat looking out the window disconsolately as she ate her breakfast. Then she brightened up. "Momma," she said eagerly, "Can we go to the store and buy bird seed today since it's raining? And some peanuts in their shells too? Then when the rain stops I'll have lots of food for the birds."

Looking at Maria's shining face, her mother was unable to resist a smile. "Alright, but I have to work all day today and I arranged for you to go to your friend Jane's house, remember?"

"Oh yes, but after?"

"We'll see. I saw the weather forecast said it would rain tomorrow too. If that's the case, I'd rather go tomorrow when I don't have to work so long."

It turned out that the weather forecast was correct. The rain kept up all day and night, and in the morning Maria looked out of windows streaked with rain to see puddles and raindrops splashing everywhere. "Oh dear, the birds will be so hungry! Momma, we must buy food for them today!"

Her mother laughed and told Maria not to worry. But she agreed to go shopping as soon as she was free from work. They were able to buy a bag of bird seed and a large bag of peanuts in their shells. Maria started to eat the peanuts, just to make sure they were good of course! "Mrs. Bird will love these!" she declared as she munched on the nuts.

The next morning the sun was shining and Maria was thrilled. Her mother told her to wear her boots since the forest would be rather muddy after all the rain, but that didn't dampen her enthusiasm. "I'll bring my sneakers in my backpack," Maria said eagerly. "Where's my lunch? Oh, I've got so much stuff to bring with all the food for the birds too!"

She set off for Mrs. Bird's cabin full of anticipation, even though her backpack weighed as much as it did on the first day of the school year when she had to bring all her new books. But this was so much more fun! "Mrs. Bird!" she called out as she approached. "Mrs. Bird, it's me Maria. And I've got food for the birds!" She stopped and looked around. There was no sign of Mrs. Bird or Callie. But then she heard the squawking of the blue jay and started to laugh. "Well, Mister Blue Jay, you're waiting for me, I see!"

Putting her backpack on the table she opened it up and pulled out the bag of bird seed and the bag of peanuts. "Which should I give you first?" Maria muttered. Just then, the front door opened and Mrs. Bird appeared with Callie at her feet.

"Oh, Maria, you've come! We weren't sure if you would make it today. It's still rather wet outside isn't it?"

"Yes, but I've got my boots on so I'm fine. Come on out. I have food and Mister Blue Jay is waiting!"

Mrs. Bird cautiously took a few steps outside onto the ground. Callie, however, sat on the front step and looked at the mud with disdain. Maria laughed seeing the cat not wanting to get her feet wet. "I'll get a towel to dry the table and chairs," Mrs. Bird said, turning to go back inside.

Maria waited impatiently, although she had to agree sitting on a wet chair would be no fun. Eventually Mrs. Bird reappeared and came over to join her at the table. "We'll just wipe these chairs off and the table too, and then we can get settled. Callie will come when she sees we're all comfortable."

"Oh, that's much better," Maria said appreciatively, sitting on a dry chair. "Now, which food should I give first? We have a bag of bird seed and some peanuts in their shells. Would Mister Blue Jay like the peanuts?"

"Yes, I'm sure he would." Mrs. Bird was looking at Maria's collection. "Why don't you give him some and then we'll see how best to deal with the bag of seeds."

"Alright," Maria jumped up and took the peanut bag over to the tree. She spread several nuts on the table and looked up at the feeder. "Oh good, still some peanut butter in there," and she walked back over to the table. The blue jay landed on the table before she even sat down, and stood, cocking his head to look at the nuts.

Maria sat down and watched. Soon he pecked at one with his beak, but it bounced away. Then he tried again and this time he got the whole peanut shell in his beak. Triumphant, he flew away. "Oh, he took it!" Maria exclaimed in disappointment. She had hoped to see him eat the peanuts. She didn't stay disappointed for long though. Almost immediately another blue jay landed on the table. "Is that second blue jay the wife?" Maria wondered. "It looks exactly the same as Mister Blue Jay."

Blue Jay with Peanut

"Yes, the females look the same, and that is certainly a female. It could be his wife." Mrs. Bird cocked her head to one side and seemed to be listening. "Well, I do think she's his wife," Mrs. Bird nodded. "They seem to be talking to each other. I'm sure he told her there was good food here to eat!"

"Oh how cute!" Maria was smiling. "Mrs. Bird you look just like a nice old bird yourself, listening to them talk!" Seeing Mrs. Bird's expression, Maria quickly added, "A very cool bird, you know, kind of special."

"Well, thank you, Maria. I'll take that as a compliment." Mrs. Bird sat back in her chair.

While they watched, the second blue jay pecked at the peanut until it opened and she was able to grab the nuts in her beak. As soon as she flew off another bird arrived.

"Oh look, the titmouse has come!" Maria whispered to Mrs. Bird. "Will he eat the peanuts?"

"Oh, yes, I'm sure he will," Mrs. Bird nodded. "Watch him, he's already thinking about it!"

They sat still, Maria holding her breath, as the bird hopped over to a peanut. She could see his black beady eye checking out the peanut shells. Suddenly he hopped right up to one and started to peck at it. His first attempts weren't completely successful – the peanut rolled away and fell off the table onto the ground. He didn't give up though, and by the time Maria had realized she should get her phone out of her backpack to take his photo he had already succeeded in breaking open a shell and had the nut in his beak. Maria managed to get a couple of photos before he flew off.

"Oh, that was great!" Maria was elated. "Look, Mrs. Bird. I've got his photo eating the peanuts!"

"That's wonderful, dear," Mrs. Bird was all smiles, enjoying her young friend's delight.

"Do you think someone will find the peanut that fell on the ground?" Maria was concerned.

"Oh yes, there are plenty of birds that like to eat on the ground. Those starlings may come back, and they will find all the food!"

"Alright, then. But should I put some seeds on the table too? Some of the birds might like them better don't you think?"

Mrs. Bird looked at the package of bird seed. "Yes," she said thoughtfully. "But once we open this bag can we close it up securely? Otherwise the seeds will all spill out."

Maria looked at the package. "Look, it has a thing to close it. I thought so; we tried to choose a good bag. We just have to cut it open carefully and then we can close it up again. Do you have scissors?"

"Yes, I'm sure I do somewhere. I'll go and look. And I'll encourage Callie to come and join us too. With all this food the squirrels will be sure to come if Callie isn't on guard to chase them away!" Mrs. Bird was on her way indoors.

Maria sat and watched as several more birds flew down to check out the peanuts on the table. The chickadee seemed to prefer the peanut butter in the hanging feeder and she was soon laughing at his antics.

Mrs. Bird reappeared holding two glasses of lemonade. She walked over to join Maria, but Callie sat on the very edge of the step determined not to get her feet wet. Mrs. Bird turned back to remind her that she must keep the squirrels away, and Callie just turned to look at the birds.

"Ooh, lemonade! Yay!" Maria picked up her glass and took a drink. "I mean, thank you," she said quickly, remembering she should be polite. "Does Callie really chase the squirrels away?" she asked, not so much to change the subject but more because she really was interested.

"Oh yes, there would be no food left for the birds if we didn't chase those thieves away!" Mrs. Bird seemed quite indignant at how much the squirrels would eat if allowed.

"But can't you put the food out of their reach?"

"Unfortunately not!" Mrs. Bird shook her head. "Those squirrels can climb any tree, run along any branch even the thinnest one, and jump to land on another tree or of course a bird feeder. And they're the best acrobats, hanging by their back feet and using their front legs like arms to grab all the food. Their tails help them keep their balance you see. And they're so greedy!"

"More than the noisy starlings who eat all the food?"

Mrs. Bird laughed. "Well, that's true enough. A whole flock of starlings can certainly eat all the food we put out. But then they move on and the other birds have a chance. Squirrels just keep coming all day." She shook her head. "Callie caught a few and taught them a lesson, so now they don't come here very often. But with all this new food, I'm afraid they will be back."

"Callie doesn't kill the squirrels she catches, does she?" Maria's eyes were wide with horror at the thought.

"Oh no! I wouldn't want her to kill them. She just shakes them up a bit and plays with them, you know how cats do. Leave them to try to escape and then pounce and catch them again. It's a fun game for a cat, not so much for their prey."

"Oh, poor squirrels!" Maria felt bad for them. "I hope she doesn't have to teach any more of them a lesson."

"Well, if she stays on the step there too long they might just get brave enough to venture close."

"Maybe if we make noise and move around they won't come?" Maria suggested.

Mrs. Bird nodded. "Yes, of course they would be wary of you. Now, let's see about this bird seed shall we?"

"Oh, yes. Cut the bag and we can put some on their table!" Maria instantly turned her attention back to the bird seed.

Mrs. Bird carefully cut the top of the bag with her scissors while Maria watched impatiently. As soon as the bag was open she jumped up. "Alright, bring it over to the table!"

"Maybe I should have cut it open on the bird table!" Mrs. Bird wondered as she carried the full bag of seeds carefully over the muddy ground to the table under the tree. "Good, I didn't spill them!"

Mrs. Bird put the bag on the table, and Maria put her little hand in and scooped out some seeds. "I'll put them on this side away from the peanuts," she said, letting the seeds drop from her hand. "A bit more don't you think?"

"Yes, we can put a couple of piles of seeds on the table for now."

Maria finished and looked at the bag. "I think this is how to close it. Yes, that worked! Alright, now we just have to wait for the birds to eat the seeds!" she made her way back to their table carrying the bag.

"I'm sure the birds will be excited to see what kind of new food you brought them," Mrs. Bird commented as she sat down on her chair.

Before the birds came for the food though, Maria noticed some birds flapping their wings on the ground. "What's going on over there?" she asked.

Mrs. Bird turned to look. There were several birds lined up around a puddle full of rainwater. One bird was in the puddle ducking down into the water and then shaking itself and fluttering its wings. "He's taking a bath!" she exclaimed. "That robin is taking a bath in the puddle."

"A bath! In a puddle. How funny!" Maria was laughing. "That won't get him very clean, it's all muddy!"

Mrs. Bird laughed too. "But it's cleaner than his feathers, probably. And the bath helps get rid of nasty bugs."

"Oh, bugs are bad! I wouldn't want bugs if I had feathers!"

"No indeed," Mrs. Bird nodded wisely. "Birds spend a lot of time cleaning their feathers. Without good healthy feathers they can't fly well. See how each bird is cleaning his feathers with his beak after his bath?"

"And they're lining up to take turns at the bath!" Maria was fascinated. "Oh, two of them are in the puddle now, splashing each other! Oh but one of them flew away. I guess they weren't really friendly."

"No, that one was too impatient. Usually they wait their turn. And that puddle is too small for more than one bird at a time."

Maria was looking around thoughtfully. "You know, it would be nice for the birds to have a bath all the time, not just in a puddle from the rain, wouldn't it?"

"Yes they would love that," Mrs. Bird was smiling. "But we don't have anything to make a bird bath out of, I'm afraid."

"Well," Maria's eyes started to sparkle as they did when she had an exciting idea. "When I went with Momma to the store to buy the peanuts and the bird seed, I saw a bunch of other things there. I bet they have something we could use as a bird bath!"

"Oh, Maria, don't ask your mother to spend so much money! That's too much."

"But I can ask." Maria looked disappointed. "If it's not too expensive, you would like to have a bird bath out here right?"

"Yes, I would," Mrs. Bird affirmed Maria's idea. "Just tell your mother not to buy anything expensive. I wish we could just make one, like we made the bird feeder, but I don't think I can do it."

"Oh, look, Mrs. Bird, they're coming to eat the seeds!" Maria's attention was drawn back to the bird table by some excited squawks. "It's Mister Blue Jay! He's found the seeds and he's telling the others!"

They both turned to watch the table. The blue jay was busy pushing at the pile of seeds and grabbing the ones he liked. Soon seeds started flying off the table and onto the ground as he swept them aside with his beak. "That Mister Blue Jay is making a mess!" Maria said in surprise.

"Yes, he's choosing the seeds he likes and sweeping the rest out of the way." Mrs. Bird was watching intently. "Maybe we should put the seeds in the center of the table next time, so more of them stay on the table."

"What about the ones that fell on the ground?" Maria was worried about the wasted seeds.

"Oh, some other birds will come along and eat them, don't worry," Mrs. Bird said with a smile. "Probably some mourning doves will come. They like to eat on the ground."

"Oh, I hope so!" Maria was looking around. "I want to see so many kinds of birds, and put them in my notebook. I have a lot to write about Mister Blue Jay already. But, oh I didn't get a photo of the birds in the puddle! Hmm, now they're gone. I hope Momma can buy a bird bath so I can see more birds taking a bath." Maria had pulled her notebook out of her backpack and started writing in it. "It was a robin we saw taking a bath, right? He has red on his front. If he comes back, I'll get his photo."

Maria finished writing and sat back to watch for birds coming to eat at the bird table. She had her phone ready now to take their photo, but there were no birds. Suddenly she had an idea, and picking up her phone she aimed it at Mrs. Bird who was also watching the tree and had her back to Maria. Knowing that Mrs. Bird didn't enjoy having her photo taken Maria was trying to do it without telling her. She had just got the camera zoomed in to make a nice shot and was about to take the photo when Callie suddenly jumped up on their table. As Maria's finger pushed the screen Mrs. Bird whirled around to stop Callie from knocking over her glass of lemonade, her arm in the air completely ruining the photo.

"Oh, Maria, I told you not to take my photo!" Mrs. Bird scolded her. "And Callie, what are you doing jumping on the table!"

Both Maria and Callie hung their heads down, chastised. "Oh, it's not that bad!" Mrs. Bird said with a smile. "Just please don't take my photo, Maria. And Callie, it's alright. The lemonade didn't spill."

"I'm sorry, Mrs. Bird," Maria apologized. "It's just there weren't any birds coming to eat and I thought I could get a photo of you looking at the bird feeder. I won't do it again." Maria felt bad. She smiled at Callie, though. "At least Callie has come to join us. That will help keep the squirrels away, won't it!"

"Yes, but she really shouldn't sit on our table," Mrs. Bird was still looking rather stern.

"Maybe she needs her own chair, 'cos it's still wet on the ground," Maria suggested. "If I dry this chair can she sit on it?" Maria took the towel to dry the third chair, and Callie immediately jumped onto it, turning to look at Mrs. Bird as if to say this was the solution. Mrs. Bird gave her a nod and Callie settled down to clean herself, especially her feet that had gotten a bit muddy.

Now that everyone was settled Maria noticed that the birds were beginning to gather in the tree again. Soon the blue jay ventured onto the table and hopped over to the peanuts. He gave a loud squawk and took one in his beak and flew away. Immediately a second blue jay landed on the table, probably his wife Maria thought. She watched as the bird investigated the nuts. The blue jay started pecking at the shell of one large peanut and Maria lifted her phone to take a photo. As soon as she had a couple of good shots, she let out a big breath. "Ooh, this is so much fun, watching the birds eat the peanuts. I was holding my breath till that blue jay got one open!"

Mrs. Bird smiled contentedly. "Yes, it's a nice way to spend the summer." She could see Maria was learning a lot about the birds, and of course the birds were enjoying all the food. Even Callie had settled down in her chair and seemed quite relaxed.

"Is it lunchtime yet?" Maria realized that watching all these birds eating their food she was getting a bit hungry herself. As soon as she said it, Callie opened her eyes and looked at her backpack. "Yes, Callie, my lunch is in there!" Maria said with a laugh. "I don't know if I have anything for you though."

As Maria pulled out her lunch boxes from her backpack both Callie and Mrs. Bird watched. "Do you have any more berries today?" Mrs. Bird asked hopefully.

"Let's see," Maria was looking in the bag. "Let's see, this has chips. Hmm, I bet some birds would like those if I don't finish them. Oh, look, here's the fruit! Yes, there's strawberries again, yum." Maria triumphantly offered the container of strawberries to Mrs. Bird, glad that she had mentioned to her mother how much she had enjoyed them. "Oh, Callie, alright, here's some ham for you," she opened her sandwich and tore off a small piece of ham for the cat, who had been inching closer all the time. "Now we can all eat!"

The three of them sat around the table eating Maria's lunch. Of course Mrs. Bird had supplied the lemonade and Callie's presence was enough to justify her share. Maria wished she could get a photo of the charming scene, but she had learned that Mrs. Bird was serious about no photos so she just stored it up in her memory.

Before they finished eating, a new bird arrived at the feeder. Maria noticed and stared closely at the newcomer. "Who's that Mrs. Bird?" she asked quietly.

"Oh that's a woodpecker," she replied immediately. "She will love the peanut butter!"

"That's the wife?" Maria asked, getting her phone ready to take a photo. "How can you tell? Does the husband look different?"

"Well, the male has a red spot on the back of his head, that's how you tell. Otherwise they look the same."

"Oh, I see. Right, no red spot." Maria took a couple of photos and put her phone down to watch. After a while another woodpecker arrived and landed on the other side of the branch, and started eating. The first woodpecker moved downwards to a new hole to eat the peanut butter and Maria couldn't restrain her laughter. "Oh, she's going down backwards! Not headfirst like that other bird, the nuthatch. I like these woodpeckers, they're cute!"

"Can you see a red spot on the new one?" Mrs. Bird was reminding her of the difference.

"Oh, yes, that must be her husband! He does have red on his head. Cool! I've got his photo too now, and one with both of them." Maria went back to eating her lunch, still watching the two woodpeckers. "Mm, this lemonade is good! I'm getting thirsty with these chips."

"Have some more of your strawberries, dear," Mrs. Bird pushed the container back to Maria. "I don't mean to eat all of them! Shall I get some more lemonade?"

"Oh yes, please!" Maria smiled appreciatively. "I think I'm going to eat all my chips, those birds have enough of their own food today, don't they?"

"Well, we might need to refill the peanut butter later. Those woodpeckers are doing a good job at eating it."

Downy Woodpecker

"Okay. Can you bring the jar and a spoon with the lemonade?" Maria looked at her chips. "I bet these chips would taste even better with some peanut butter on them."

Mrs. Bird laughed and made her way back to her house. Callie turned to watch, but decided to stay on the chair. To Maria's surprise, the little woodpeckers didn't fly away as Mrs. Bird walked past. "I have to write that in my notebook," she muttered, picking up her pen. "Brave woodpeckers, they're not afraid of us," she wrote. "Is that right Callie?" she turned to the cat who was still sitting on the chair watching all that was going on around her. At the sound of her name, she turned to look at Maria and gave a small chirp sound. Maria laughed, "Are you agreeing with me?" she said reaching out to stroke the cat. Whatever Callie had been communicating, she clearly liked being stroked, rubbing her head against Maria's hand and purring loudly.

Mrs. Bird reappeared carrying a tray and Maria jumped up to give her a hand. "Let me help carry that," she said taking the pitcher of lemonade in both hands. "Ooh, you brought cookies too. What a feast!"

"I hope your mother doesn't mind," Mrs. Bird commented as they set everything on the table. "But if we're going to watch all the birds eat all that delicious food it seems only fair that we have plenty too."

"Those woodpeckers are brave aren't they?" Maria asked. "They are still eating even though we've been walking around quite close to them."

"Oh yes, they're tough birds. Chickadees too. They won't leave unless you threaten them by getting too close and moving suddenly."

"Funny! They're the little birds but they're not scared. The big blue jay watches me but doesn't want me to get close."

As they sat and watched more and more birds took their turns eating at the table. Maria saw a couple of nuthatches as well as a number of sparrows. The piles of seeds soon disappeared, many of them eaten or taken away in some bird's beak, while those that remained were scattered across the table and on the ground. As Mrs. Bird had said, several birds came to eat the seeds on the ground. Maria took photos of the starlings who returned in a group, some landing on the table, others on the ground, and one hanging on the feeder, all eating quickly and squawking at the same time. They made so much noise Callie glared at them!

Once the starlings had left Maria was going to get up to see if there was any food left but she realized there were still sparrows hopping around on the ground, eating whatever the starlings had left behind. A couple flew up onto the table and pecked around finding the last of the seeds. When they left the table was empty and Maria got up to check on the feeder.

"Oh, there's almost no peanut butter left! Can I put more in the holes?"

"Of course, dear," Mrs. Bird responded. "Can you reach, or do you need to climb on a chair?"

"I think I need a chair," Maria decided. "At least I don't need to climb on the big table again!" She started carrying her chair over to the tree. "Oh, I'd better not wear my boots. It'll get all muddy." Leaving the chair under the feeder she ran back to their table and rummaged in her backpack. "See,

I brought my sneakers for when it dries up. I can wear them now and not get the chair all muddy from my boots!"

Mrs. Bird smiled approvingly. "You are a clever girl, Maria, thinking all of that. I'll bring the peanut butter and the spoon, and hold the chair to keep it steady."

Starling

Maria quickly exchanged her boots for clean sneakers and climbed on the chair, grabbing the feeder with one hand. Mrs. Bird scooped out some peanut butter and held the spoon out to her. "Careful now," she held onto the chair and watched as the girl carefully pushed the food into the hole. They repeated the operation several times before the feeder was overflowing with peanut butter again, and Maria's fingers had their fair share covering them too.

"Alright," Maria announced climbing down from the chair. "Mmm, this peanut butter does taste good," she licked it off her fingers as Mrs. Bird picked up the chair and carried it back to their table. "These birds are lucky I came to do my project here this summer, aren't they!"

The rest of the afternoon passed all too quickly. Maria's phone alarm went off and Callie looked around in annoyance. "Oh sorry, Callie, it means I have to go!" Maria reached over to give the cat a final stroke. "And I won't be back till Monday. But I hope Momma will buy a bird bath. That will be so much fun!" She started packing everything in her backpack and then frowned as she saw her boots under the table.

"Maybe you shouldn't put those muddy boots in your backpack," Mrs. Bird said. "Can you carry them, or do you need a bag to put them in?"

"Um, yes, maybe a bag would be good." Maria knew her mother wouldn't be thrilled if she got everything muddy.

"I'll just get a bag then," Mrs. Bird was on her feet heading for her cabin. By the time Maria had everything organized she was back carrying a paper grocery bag. "This will work, won't it?"

Maria thanked her and stuffed her boots in the bag. Hoisting her backpack on her back she headed out. "Bye! See you on Monday, with a bird bath I hope!" With a cheery wave she ran down the path towards her home.

Mrs. Bird waved back and then turned to Callie. "A bird bath. Now that will be interesting, won't it?"

As soon as she got home Maria started to tell her mother about the bird bath. She explained in excited tones that the birds were trying to take a bath in a muddy puddle. "They were so funny, Momma, they lined up to take their turn. Except for one that went ahead and the other birds got angry with it. They chased it away!"

Her mother was busy unpacking Maria's backpack, taking out the various containers that had held her lunch. "Where are your boots, Maria?" she asked, seeing that her daughter was wearing her sneakers.

"In that bag. Mrs. Bird gave it to me 'cos they were all muddy." Maria picked up the bag and showed her mother. "Can we get a real bird bath for the birds, please?"

Her mother looked at her in surprise. "Well, I don't know about that dear. What did Mrs. Bird say?"

Maria smiled. "She said she would like a bird bath. But not to spend too much money," she added quickly. "I saw some in the store where we got the bird food. Can we go and check, please?"

Her mother sighed and finished sorting out Maria's things. "We can look tomorrow. But I'm not promising anything, mind. We'll just look."

But Maria knew looking meant they could probably get one so she was already giving her mother a big hug. "Momma, I'll take photos of the birds taking a bath for my notebook. You'll see, it will be great! You can see the photos I have already on my phone," and she got her phone out and opened her photo gallery. "See, these are chickadees, and here's Mister Blue Jay. And this is a nuthatch, and some sparrows, more chickadees. Oh this one's called a titmouse, isn't that a funny name! And here they're eating the peanuts. They can open the shells with their beaks. And look, these woodpeckers are so brave they let us get close while they're eating. And here are the noisy starlings, they come in a big group and eat a lot!"

Her mother looked at all the photos in amazement. "That's wonderful, Maria. Those photos are lovely, and so many different birds. You've learned a lot! And that's the feeder where you put the peanut butter?"

"Yes, that's it. Some of the birds hang upside down on it! I wrote about them in my notebook, but I'm not finished. There's lots more to learn still. Momma, this is the best summer camp ever!"

Maria's mother smiled and nodded. The summer "camp" was certainly a success so far. "I'm glad it's working out so well. We can go and look for a bird bath tomorrow. I have some shopping to do anyway. But now can you help me with the laundry?"

Maria was so elated she readily gathered her dirty clothes and helped her mother get the laundry started. Then she went and tidied up her room while her mother started to prepare dinner. As she sat on her bed texting her friend Jane, she smiled contentedly knowing that she was going to spend a wonderful summer with Mrs. Bird. Her mother hadn't mentioned the trial period of a week again, and Maria certainly wasn't going to remind her.

Jane was still suspicious of the "witch in the forest" as she continued to call Mrs. Bird. But Maria didn't care. She sent Jane the photos of the birds she had seen and Jane was impressed, but then she asked if she had a better photo of the cat yet. "I'll get Callie's photo next week," Maria promised. Both girls had asked their mothers if they could have a cat, but so far to no avail. "It's almost like having my own cat," Maria told Jane, referring to Callie. "It's just for the summer, though," Jane replied. Maria didn't want to think about that. Fortunately, her mother called her for dinner just then so she was able to put that unpleasant thought out of her mind.

As promised, Maria's mother took her shopping on Saturday and they spent a long time in the store looking at bird baths. With the help of an assistant they chose one that was a reasonable size and price. It wasn't too heavy so Maria thought she could carry it to Mrs. Bird's cabin.

When Monday came around though, Maria found it hard to walk any distance carrying the awkward shaped box and of course her backpack on her back. "Momma, can you help me?" she asked. So they both made their way through the forest, Maria bouncing merrily along the path with her mother following behind rather more slowly.

When they reached the cabin Maria called out to Mrs. Bird and Callie, "We're here! And we've got a bird bath!"

Callie was outside waiting and immediately came over to investigate. Mrs. Bird took a bit longer to appear, but came out in time to see the bird bath emerge from its box. "My goodness," she said. "What do we have here? Enid, how kind of you. I hope it wasn't too much trouble?"

Maria laughed. "We got a bird bath, Mrs. Bird! Look, isn't it great? We can put it, over there, or over there … where shall we put it?" Maria's excitement was infectious and her mother and Mrs. Bird laughed together enjoying her enthusiasm.

"I'm afraid I have to go to work now," Enid said. "But I'm pleased to see you again Mrs. Bird. And thank you for making Maria's summer so wonderful."

"Bye Momma! Thank you for bringing the bird bath. See you later," Maria was impatient to set up the bird bath. "Mrs. Bird, where can we put it?"

"Well, let's see. How does it work? Oh, I see, it's quite flat on the bottom so it can go anywhere on the ground."

"Yes, they had some that went on these table things, 'peddy stools' or something," Maria frowned, trying to remember the word. "But the lady in the store said this kind that goes on the ground is better for us. Is that OK?"

"Oh yes, this is wonderful," Mrs. Bird nodded. "Let's see. We can try it over there, close to where all the food is but not too close. It's probably better not under the tree or too many leaves and things will fall in it."

"Over here?" Maria was carrying it over to the place Mrs. Bird had pointed out. She placed it on the ground, and then shifted it around a bit till it seemed secure. "Can we put water in it now?"

Mrs. Bird was already moving to the cabin, "I've got a bucket inside. I'll fill it with water."

Meanwhile Callie came over to investigate. She sniffed at the bath and carefully touched it with her paw. Satisfied that it was safe she delicately climbed in and sat down in the middle. Maria laughed, but the cat merely looked at her as if this new contraption had been brought just for her. "Alright, Callie, you enjoy it until the water comes," Maria said. "I'm getting my phone and will take a photo of you sitting there. Jane will enjoy it!" This time Callie cooperated. She sat quite regally in the bath, surveying her "kingdom" while Maria was able to take several photos before Mrs. Bird returned with a full bucket of water.

"Well, I see you approve of the bird bath!" she said to Callie. "You'd better move now though; I'm going to fill it with water."

As Mrs. Bird lifted the bucket Callie instantly moved out of the way, nimbly avoiding getting wet. "It's a very nice bath, Maria. It's wide enough for several birds to enjoy and not too deep for the little ones. And they should be able to perch on the rim here quite nicely. Well done!"

"Oh, I do hope the birds like it!" Maria responded. "At least Callie approved, so maybe that's a good sign."

"Well, let's get settled at our table and see what happens. Oh, I suppose we should put some more food out on their table. I can take this bucket back and get the seeds and nuts, and maybe the peanut butter too." Mrs. Bird looked up at the feeder.

"Oh yes, it looks like they ate a lot over the weekend when I wasn't here!" Maria exclaimed. "I'll get the chair and I can climb up and put more in."

Callie had taken up residence on one of the chairs, and she sat there watching while Maria and Mrs. Bird replenished the food for the birds. When everything was organized the three of them sat around the table in anticipation. Maria noticed that Callie was eying her backpack. "Mrs. Bird, maybe we can have a snack too, while we watch the birds? And I think Callie wants something too."

"Well, I think Callie has to wait until lunchtime!" Mrs. Bird was firm. She got up again and went inside.

Maria looked at Callie, who was watching with a pretended indifference. Suddenly though, her ears pricked up and she turned to face the tree where the birds ate. Maria turned too, just in time to see the blue jay land on the table and start pecking at the peanut shells and seeds, spilling a bunch on the ground. Maria could hear some rustlings in the tree and knew more birds were gathering. Sure enough, within a minute there were several small birds on the table, busy eating the seeds.

Maria watched hopefully and shook her head. "Sparrow, chickadee, titmouse, got them all already. I need someone new to come!" Just then a bird flew towards the feeder, landing on the branch and then making its way down to one of the holes with the peanut butter. "Oh, another woodpecker," Maria recognized the black and white pattern on its wings and its white back. "Got a red patch on its head, must be the husband," she nodded, proud of remembering that detail.

Suddenly she frowned, and stood up to looked more closely. "It's bigger!" she exclaimed, and picking up her phone she got the bird in focus and started taking pictures.

The door opened and Mrs. Bird came out carrying a tray. Maria immediately put down her phone and went to help. As she ran over to the cabin the bird flew away. "Mrs. Bird," she said excitedly, "another woodpecker came! It was bigger than the ones we saw before, but it looked exactly the same! Was it the Dad, and they were children?"

Mrs. Bird put the tray down on the table with a smile. "You saw another woodpecker with the same markings but bigger?"

"Yes, yes, bigger, much bigger. Almost like the blue jay. Well, maybe one of those noisy starlings. See, I got photos of it." Maria handed her phone to Mrs. Bird who looked at the images carefully.

Hairy Woodpecker

"Well, Maria, that was a hairy woodpecker. The ones we saw before were downy woodpeckers. They look almost exactly the same, only the downies are smaller."

"Really? How funny!" Maria laughed. "I hope they both come back. I'd like a photo of them together to show that."

"I'm sure they'll be back," Mrs. Bird smiled and poured out a glass of lemonade. "Here you are, Maria, and have a cookie too if you like. None for you though Callie!" she said, even though the cat wasn't actually watching the food. "Ooh, thanks. Delicious. Now we just need some birds to take a bath!"

For the rest of the morning, though, all the birds seemed to avoid the bath. When a group of starlings arrived to eat the food, some hopped very close to it. But they seemed more interested in eating and none ventured into the water. Watching the starlings busy pecking on the ground and on the bird table Maria realized that a couple of the birds in the group were bigger, and even shinier than the starlings.

"Who are those bigger birds?" she asked. "Look, they're so shiny."

"Ah, those are grackles," Mrs. Bird responded. "Yes, they are rather similar to the starlings."

"They seem kind of proud, marching around like they own the place!"

Grackle

Mrs. Bird laughed. "I suppose so. It's good the blue jay spilled seeds on the ground so the little birds can eat on the table and the grackles stay on the ground and don't bother them."

"Oh yes, I see. He's helping them." Maria was busy taking photos of the grackles.

"You know, another bird that's related to the grackle is the red winged blackbird. I think they might come soon, I thought I heard one singing."

"Ooh, really, red wings?" Maria was very interested.

"Well, just the top part of the wing is red, and there's a yellow stripe below the red patch."

"Are they black? That's why they're called blackbirds?"

"Yes, very black and shiny. Except the females are brown and striped, kind of like big female sparrows."

"Oh, another boring female!" Maria sighed. "I still think that's not fair!"

Red Winged Blackbird

"Look, here they are!" Mrs. Bird pointed to the table where a black bird had landed. "The female just landed in the tree, waiting to see if it's safe."

"I don't see any red wings!" Maria complained trying to take photos. "He's all black!"

"Wait a minute. He will show his colors soon."

Just as she said that the bird seemed to shrug his shoulders and suddenly Maria saw the brightest scarlet and yellow appear at the top of his wings. "Yes, yes that's beautiful!" The blackbird turned to look in her direction, cocking his head on one side, as if he was listening to her praise. Then a brown striped bird landed on the table close to him. "Oh, is that his wife?" Maria was so interested she missed her chance to get a photo of both of them together before they flew away. "Oh, I missed her. But I got him with his red and yellow wing, look," she showed Mrs. Bird.

"Very nice, Maria. He is handsome isn't he?"

"Well, I hope his wife thinks so!" Maria replied, and they both laughed.

While plenty of birds came to eat the food on the table, and some chickadees and downy woodpeckers came back to eat the peanut butter out of the hanging feeder, Maria waited in vain for a bird to take a bath. After watching for what seemed like a very long time, she declared, "I'm hungry. Can we have lunch now?"

"Of course, dear. I have some bread inside, let me get it."

Maria started pulling things out of her backpack. Callie of course moved closer as she put her food on the table. "Tuna sandwich and it doesn't have mayo this time so I suppose you want a piece?" Maria looked at the cat. They were both happily eating when Mrs. Bird returned with her bread and a spoon.

"I'll just have some peanut butter if you don't mind," she said, scooping it out of the jar and spreading it on a piece of bread.

"I have some blueberries if you want some," Maria offered. "And this is trail mix I think, nuts and dried fruit. Looks yummy."

Mrs. Bird nodded, her eyes sparkling in anticipation.

"You really like nuts and fruit, don't you Mrs. Bird?" Maria said with a big smile. "Momma is pleased you like these healthy things, she doesn't like me to eat junk food."

"Junk food, no, no, you should eat healthy food," Mrs. Bird agreed. "Right, Callie? I see you have been enjoying Maria's lunch too!" The cat was licking her lips with a satisfied expression.

"Yes, I have a tuna sandwich so I gave her a bite. There's no mayo."

Just then Maria heard a splash. They turned to look and sure enough there was a bird in the bath. "Oh," Maria breathed. "He's taking a bath!" She put down her sandwich and picked up her phone, standing up to get a better angle. After she got a few shots, she sat down again, still watching the bird. "It's a robin, isn't it? I can see his red front."

"Yes, he is. And look, there's another one coming to take his turn."

Maria forgot about her lunch for a while, watching the robins bathing and taking their photos. As soon as the robins left a blue jay arrived. He perched on the edge of the bath for a minute and then went in the water.

"Oh look, Mister Blue Jay is having fun. He's got so wet!" Maria jumped up to take his picture too. "I hope they don't get cold, getting all wet like that."

Robin taking a Bath

"No, no, it's warm today and anyway their feathers are water proof. They don't get wet all the way through," Mrs. Bird reassured her.

"Oh look, they're fluffing up to dry off!" Maria saw the two robins had settled on branches in the tree and were cleaning their feathers and drying themselves. "I'm glad they like the bath. Momma will be happy too when I tell her, and show her my photos. Hmm, did you take some blueberries? These are so good!"

Callie had been keeping watch on the proceedings over at the tree. After a while she got up and slowly went over to the bird bath. Aware that it was full of water she didn't jump in but rather sniffed the edge and then sat down beside it, watching the water intently.

"Oh, is Callie waiting for more birds to come and take a bath?" Maria noticed what the cat was doing.

Mrs. Bird looked at her and laughed. "Callie, they won't come if you're that close. Take a drink if you want, but then come back here so the birds can enjoy the water."

Callie's ears had pricked up when she heard them talking, and now she put her head on one side, considering the situation. She decided to put one paw in the water and then brought it to her mouth and licked it. She repeated the process and then stretched her head forward and started lapping the water directly from the bath. After a while she stopped and stood up, turning to walk back towards her chair.

"Do you like the bird bath then, Callie?" Maria asked the cat. "Did the water taste good after the birds took a bath in it?" Callie rubbed herself against Maria and purred. Then she settled down on her chair for a nap.

"Is it OK for Callie to drink that water?" Maria asked.

"Yes, it will be fine. I'll put fresh water in every morning. I'm sure she won't drink it if it's nasty."

"Okay. Let's see. Which birds came today? I have to write it all in my notebook." Maria pushed aside the lunch boxes and opened her notebook. "The hairy woodpecker came; he was on the feeder. The downy woodpeckers came back, and chickadees, and sparrows and starlings, and titmouse and nuthatch, and of course Mister Blue Jay! And then the grackles were eating on the ground. The red wing blackbirds came on the table. And then the robins and blue jay took a bath! That's a lot of birds. It's …" Maria started counting. "Ooh, that's eleven different kinds of birds already! Mrs.

Bird, what other birds will come? I hope twenty kinds of birds come this summer. Do you think they will?"

"Well," Mrs. Bird was smiling. "Let's see. I'm sure a few more will visit. We didn't see any cardinals yet did we?"

"No, cardinals are red aren't they? I've seen them on Christmas cards. They're red all over not like the robins that are only red on the front."

Mrs. Bird frowned. "Well, yes, the male cardinals are very red. A dazzling red really. The females are different. But you'll like them Maria, they're very beautiful too," She added quickly seeing the girl's face. "And then there are more kinds of woodpeckers, and probably a little wren will come sometime, and maybe some finches. Then there are the cowbirds …"

"Cowbirds! That's a funny name! Do they look like cows?" Maria was laughing.

"Not exactly!" Mrs. Bird had to laugh too. "Mostly they look a bit like blackbirds but with a brown head, and no red and yellow on the wings of course."

"Hmm, OK. Any others with funny names?"

"Well, there's the catbird. He makes a sound like a cat."

Maria laughed. "Will Callie be confused?"

"No, no, Callie knows it's not a cat. But she does find them interesting. Oh, of course, I forgot. Surely some crows will come. They always show up when there's something going on."

Maria was smiling. "I can't wait for so many different birds to come. But I'd better write all about today's birds now before I forget. Let's see, if I look at the photos I can remember." She wrote industriously in her notebook, checking off each of the photos with the information about each bird. By the time she had finished a group of sparrows had discovered the bird bath. Some were perched on the edge taking a drink while others were splashing vigorously around in it.

"You can tell your mother the birds enjoyed the bird bath," Mrs. Bird said with a smile.

"Callie too!" Maria joined in, having just taken some photos of the sparrows.

Back home later that afternoon Maria decided to text Jane more of her photos, even if she did think Mrs. Bird was a witch. Her mother had admired the photos and was interested to hear all about the bird bath. She laughed at how Callie had sat in it before it was filled with water and then drank from it after the birds had found it. Jane was interested too, even a bit jealous of the fun time Maria was having. She was going to the local park for summer activities every day, but the organizers kept changing the teams around for sports and Jane had ended up with a group of girls she didn't like much. Still, they were going swimming next week and she was looking forward to that.

When Maria mentioned it to her mother over dinner, she got a surprise. "Well, you'll be able to do plenty of swimming the next two weeks at Uncle Harry and Aunt Sarah's cabin. It's on a lake and you can swim every day."

"We're going to their cabin next week?" Maria was shocked. "I didn't know, well I forgot."

"Yes, dear. I told you that was our plan for my summer vacation from work. And you'll have your cousins to play with. It will be so much fun."

"Oh, but I'm having fun with Mrs. Bird. There are still so many more birds to see!" Maria was almost in tears.

"But, Maria. The birds will be there when we get back. There's still five more whole weeks of summer before school starts."

Maria smiled. "Yes, OK, five more weeks. That should be enough to see all the birds. I'll have to explain to Mrs. Bird and Callie though."

"Of course, you will. It's just two weeks out of the whole summer. Now, are you ready for dessert?"

Maria's high spirits returned with the realization that the trip would be fun. "Maybe there will be some birds there I can take photos of and ask Mrs. Bird about when we get back?"

"There you go, that's a great idea," her mother was thankful Maria was accepting the plan. "I'm sure there will be different birds on the lake than the ones you see around here."

Maria told Mrs. Bird about her trip to the lake and she nodded seriously. "Yes, Maria, your mother is quite right. I'm sure you will be able to see many birds there if there's a lake. You can take photos and show me when you get back. I'll certainly look at them and tell you what I know about the birds."

They spent the rest of the week happily watching birds come to eat at the feeder and on the bird table, and of course to take a bath. On Friday, as Maria was watching the bird bath she saw two new birds hopping around near it. One of the birds was quite red, and she whispered excitedly "Is that a cardinal?"

"Indeed he is," Mrs. Bird smiled. "Isn't he handsome?"

Maria had her phone out and was already taking his photo. "He has a tuft on his head like the titmouse!" she remarked. "And black on his face and under his beak. How special he looks. But what about his wife, is that her? The lighter colored one?"

"Yes, that's her. Look closely and you'll see she has very beautiful colors too, just not as red as him!"

"You're right Mrs. Bird," Maria agreed seeing the orange and almost golden colors on the bird's wings and body, and the crest on her head that had red on the tips. "Mrs. Cardinal is lovely. She's as beautiful as her husband is handsome!"

They both laughed and the birds flew up into the tree.

Male Northern Cardinal

"Oh no, did we scare them?" Maria was concerned. "Will they come back to eat something?"

"I think so. They're just sitting in the tree to make sure it's safe." Mrs. Bird was watching them. "See, he's checking out the bird table. There he goes, he's found the seeds."

"Oh good. Do they like peanuts, or the other seeds?"

"Usually cardinals like sunflower seeds, those big ones. See, he's eating a sunflower seed now."

"Is his wife coming to eat too?" Maria wanted to get a photo of the female cardinal.

Mrs. Bird smiled. "I'm sure she will. She's probably waiting for him to finish and then she'll have her turn while he watches in the tree."

"So they take care of each other?"

"Yes, and he watches out to make sure no other male cardinals come, except their children of course. Cardinals don't like to be in a big group."

Female Northern Cardinal

"Oh, not like the noisy starlings then?" Maria was smiling.

"No, indeed. But cardinals have loud voices so they're quite noisy too."

They both laughed again. "Oh, Mrs. Bird I'm going to miss you while I'm away, and Callie too," she added quickly as the cat rubbed against her leg.

"You'll be back soon and you can tell us all about it. It will be fun for you to be with other young people, and to go swimming in the lake." Mrs. Bird encouraged her.

"Yes, I know, but still," Maria had packed up her backpack and was ready to leave. She hesitated, and gave Callie another rub. Then she walked over to Mrs. Bird and gave her a hug. "Bye Mrs. Bird, I'll see you soon," and she ran off.

Mrs. Bird watched her leave and then turned to Callie. "Well, she'll be back soon. But we'll miss her won't we?" The cat rubbed against her leg in response.

For Maria the two weeks at the lake went by very quickly. They had good weather and everyone spent a lot of time in the lake swimming, jumping off the dock into the water, and paddling around in a small rowboat. All too soon it was time to say goodbye to her cousins and her uncle and aunt, and return home.

Unfortunately, it was raining when they got back and Maria was almost in tears on Monday morning when she realized she couldn't go to see Mrs. Bird. Her mother arranged for her to go to Jane's house instead, since her program was cancelled as well, due to the rain.

By the evening the rain had almost stopped and Maria was excited to go to see Mrs. Bird the next morning. She ran along the path so fast that she was quite breathless when she arrived at the cabin. "Mrs. Bird, Callie," she called out, gasping for breath. "I'm here!"

The cabin door opened and Callie came running out, with Mrs. Bird following behind. "Oh Callie, I've missed you! Mrs. Bird I saw lots of new birds, it was great!"

Mrs. Bird laughed, "Didn't I tell you it would be fun? Sit down and I'll bring our snack. I've got it all prepared." She darted back inside as Maria and Callie made their way to the table. Maria opened her backpack and took out her notebook and her phone. "I had such a good time. Callie, were you good while I was gone?" The cat had jumped up on "her" chair and was watching keenly as Maria took things out of her pack. "Nothing for you yet, wait till lunchtime," Maria said firmly. "Oh look, it's lemonade time! Thank you Mrs. Bird!"

Mrs. Bird set the tray on the table and they each took a glass. "Cookies, too, yum." Maria started munching immediately. "Oh, it's nice to be back!"

"So tell us all about your trip? Do you have photos of the birds?"

"Yes, yes. I'll show you." Maria picked up her phone and found the right photos. She moved her chair to be closer to Mrs. Bird so they could see them together. "This is the cabin and the lake, and here's my Uncle Harry and Momma, and here's Aunt Sarah, and these are my cousins.

Nancy is nice and Derek, but Owen is a pain!" Maria was flicking through the photos to get to the birds. "Alright, here we are. I know what this bird is, do you?" She gave Mrs. Bird the phone.

"Oh my, yes, that's a loon! What a lovely photo." Mrs. Bird was staring at the phone. "Did you hear him too?"

Loon on Lake

Ducks on Lake

Geese on Lake

"Yes, yes, he had a strange song!" Maria was smiling. "Uncle Harry told me it was a loon that made that sound. I was a bit scared the first time I heard it. But then I thought it was kind of sad sounding, and lonely. He said they always sound like that. Are they sad?"

"No, not sad at all. That sound just carries really well across the water so they can call out to other loons all the way across the lake. It's a rather beautiful sound, don't you think?"

"Yes, after I got used to it," Maria nodded.

"What else did you see?"

"Well, there were these, see?" Maria flicked through her images which included a number of shots of ducks and geese on the lake.

"Ah, of course. Beautiful pair of ducks, very nice," Mrs. Bird was nodding approvingly. "And geese too. How lovely this lake is!" She had a wistful expression on her face which made Maria wonder if Mrs. Bird wished she lived by a lake.

Scarlet Tanager

"There were other birds in the forest too," Maria said looking through the photos. "Here, look at this bird. It's very red but I don't think it's a cardinal. It's wings and tail are really black. What do you think?"

"No, no, that's not a cardinal. That's a scarlet tanager! He's beautiful isn't he?"

"Yes, he's really scarlet," Maria was smiling. "And he could fly fast! But I got his photo when he stopped on that branch."

"You know the female scarlet tanager isn't scarlet at all. She's a greenish yellow color and her wings aren't so black."

"Oh, I didn't know," Maria shook her head. "But I don't remember seeing another bird. Just him, the scarlet colored one."

"Any others?" Mrs. Bird asked.

"Well, of course I saw lots of birds like the ones here. Wait, there was one more different bird. Here, he was singing away and I think the next one is his wife, but she doesn't have all the colors."

Rose-breasted Grosbeak

Mrs. Bird took the phone and looked at the photo. "Oh, my, yes, that's a rose-breasted grosbeak. You see he has a dark pink breast, like a rose, and a big fat beak!"

Maria laughed. "So that's a good name for him!"

"And you're right, this next one is his wife. She has the same shape of beak but she doesn't have the same colors at all, just browns and white."

"But she's quite nice looking," Maria commented. "I think I'm getting used to the husbands having the bright colors."

"Yes, sometimes you have to look closely and then you can appreciate the subtler coloring of the females. They're not just all show!"

Just then they heard a loud squawking from the tree. Maria looked up and there was the blue jay glaring at her. At least she felt like he was staring at her in annoyance. "Oh, it's Mister Blue Jay! Did he miss me?"

Mrs. Bird laughed. "Of course he did! He knows you are the one who brings all the good food, and he thinks you should have put it out for him already instead of sitting there looking at pictures of other birds!"

"Oh, that's so funny!" Maria laughed and reached into her backpack. "Well, let's see. Should I share my cookie with him, or do you still have the bag of peanuts?"

There was a rustling sound and then more squawking. The blue jay had landed on the bird table and was hopping around looking for food.

"Oh, I think you should share your cookie with him while I go and get the rest of the food," Mrs. Bird stood up with a smile.

Maria followed suit, having broken her cookie into several pieces. As she approached the table the bird flew up into the tree, but he perched on a branch watching her attentively. "Here, I've put some pieces for you, but I want the rest for myself!" Maria told him and walked back to her chair. She hadn't even sat down before she heard him flying down to the table where he immediately pecked at a piece of cookie. "Goodness, anyone would think you'd been starving without me," Maria said eating her own piece. "I'm sure Mrs. Bird fed you while I was gone."

The blue jay stared at her and then continued eating. He took the last piece of cookie in his beak and flew off. At the same time Maria saw a couple of new birds land on the ground under the tree. They walked around obviously looking for food. Unfortunately for them, the door opened and Mrs. Bird came out and they flew away before they found any.

"Oh, Mrs. Bird," Maria called out. "There were two new birds on the ground. But they flew away when you opened the door so they didn't get any food. Do you know what they were?"

Mrs. Bird made her way over to the table with the bags of food and the jar of peanut butter. "Well," she said setting the bags down. "Were they quite large, with pointed tails and small heads, kind of light brown color with some spots on their wings?"

"Um," Maria thought for a moment. "Yes, I think so. They did have small heads and kind of bigger bodies, and they were walking on the ground, not hopping."

"Ah, yes, then they were doves. A pair has been coming to eat recently. They make lovely cooing sounds; you'll hear them when they come back."

"Oh, good, I do hope they come back. I felt bad they didn't get any food. Let's put some seeds out now, and peanuts!" Maria picked up the peanut bag and took it over to the bird table. "Mister Blue Jay already ate all the cookie so we have to put more food quickly!"

Mourning Dove

They quickly put out the bird food, and as soon as they had returned to their chairs the birds started to arrive. Maria saw chickadees, nuthatch, titmouse, and a group of sparrows all alight on the table one after the other to eat the seeds and nuts. A downy woodpecker joined in and quickly flew up to the hanging feeder to feast on the peanut butter.

She was just beginning to wonder if the doves would really come back when they arrived. They landed under the tree as before and began walking around.

"Oh, they nod their heads when they walk. How cute!" Maria got her phone ready to take their photo. The cardinal pair arrived as well and soon there was quite a crowd under the table as well as on top. Even a robin came to take a bath! As soon as Maria had a few photos she put her phone down and smiled gleefully.

"Oh Mrs. Bird, it's so lovely to be back! I feel like these birds are my friends."

"Well, they are dear. They are happy you feed them, you know."

Maria smiled. "Oh, good. I was wondering, though, why do some of them walk on the ground like those doves, but others hop around like the sparrows and Mister Blue Jay?"

"Well," Mrs. Bird said thoughtfully. "Mostly it's the birds that eat on the ground that walk and those that like to stay up in the trees hop. And little birds that have short legs like to hop. But some birds can do both, like robins."

"I see," Maria nodded. "Long legs are better for walking! I remember when I was very young I used to hold my Momma and my Papa's hands and have them swing me while they walked. My little legs couldn't walk fast enough to keep up otherwise!"

Mrs. Bird laughed. "What a nice memory." She hesitated, "Maria, would you like to tell me about your father? What was he like?"

"Oh he was the best dad!" Maria nodded. "He used to play fun games with me, picking me up and carrying me on his back, and all kinds of stuff."

"You miss him a lot?"

"Yes, me and Momma, we get sad sometimes, and then we look at photos and videos we have of him and us." Maria's lip quivered and her voice got a bit shaky as she said that. Then she straightened up and smiled. "Me and Momma, we take care of each other now and it's OK. Even if

Papa isn't here now I'm still glad he's my father. I know he loves me and wants me to be happy."

Just then they heard what sounded like a cat, but when Maria turned to look Callie was asleep on the chair beside her. She heard the mewing sound again, and this time she realized it was coming from the tree. "Mrs. Bird, is that another cat?"

"No," Mrs. Bird laughed. "That's a catbird!"

"Oh," Maria's eyes opened wide and she grabbed her phone. "Where? I want to see it. It really sounds like a cat! What does it look like?"

"It's a grey bird with a black cap on its head, and a reddish-brown patch under his tail. He's probably in the tree, but maybe he'll come onto the table to eat if we're quiet."

They sat quietly watching and eventually were rewarded when the bird flew down onto the table. Maria quickly took photos as the bird first investigated and then pecked at the seeds. After he flew away she smiled triumphantly at Mrs. Bird. "Well, I got his photo. Now we just need the cowbird to come too!"

Catbird

"Ah yes, the cowbird. I haven't seen one yet, but there's plenty of time for them to show up. By the way, catbirds love fruit so if you have any small berries we could put them on the table for him."

"Let me see, oh I don't see any berries," Maria was hunting through her backpack. "There's a peach, but that might not be good, too messy. If I had trail mix that would have some fruit in it. Maybe tomorrow. But I'm hungry now, I'm going to eat my peach!"

"Yes, feeding the birds always makes us want to eat too, doesn't it!" Mrs. Bird said.

"And then I have to write in my notebook, about the doves and the catbird, and all about the birds from the lake too! Oh, that will keep me busy till lunchtime." As she said that Callie's ears pricked up and she opened her eyes. "Callie, not yet! I said I've got a lot to do before lunch." Maria was laughing.

She ate her peach and was diligently writing her notes about all the birds in her book when she heard the sound of more birds arriving. Looking up she saw the cardinal on the bird table. "Oh, look the red cardinal has arrived!" Maria put down her pen to watch. "It's funny, he's still really red but now he doesn't look so bright as that other red bird I saw at the lake, the tanager. But he still acts like he's the most beautiful colored bird!"

"Yes, he does think he's special," Mrs. Bird agreed.

"Oh, Mrs. Cardinal is here too! She's coming to eat as well. You're right, she is kind of special looking. I have to get a photo of them together."

Satisfied with her photos, Maria returned to work on her notebook. Mrs. Bird sat and watched, as content as Callie who kept her ears alert for any new happenings while serenely dozing on her chair. Finishing her notes Maria looked at them both and smiled. "I'm so happy to be back. And it must be lunch time!" At that both Mrs. Bird and Callie came to life and the three of them settled in to enjoy all the items in Maria's backpack, supplemented by Mrs. Bird's stash of goodies.

They didn't see any new birds the rest of that day, or the next few days, although plenty of their "friends" returned for food or a bath each day. On Friday, just when Maria was thinking that was it for the week, a new bird arrived. She wouldn't have noticed if Mrs. Bird hadn't called her attention to the little bird hopping around in the tree.

"Do you see that small brown bird, Maria?" she pointed to a branch right above the feeder.

"With the sticking up tail?"

"Yes, that's her. She's a wren. They're a bit shy, but she'll come down soon. She sees the bird bath and wants some water. Just keep watching."

Maria carefully lined up her phone hoping that she could get a good photo. "She is little," she said softly, hoping not to scare her away. "Oh, she came to the bath. How cute!" She quickly took a couple of photos and then kept watching, fascinated. "I love the way her tail sticks up!"

The bird finished drinking and flew away, but not far. Mrs. Bird was watching and she cocked her head to one side listening. "Maria, she's singing now, can you hear her?"

"No." Maria shook her head. "I can only hear a loud bird, that can't be her!"

"Oh yes, it is! Wrens have a loud voice for their small size." Mrs. Bird smiled. "I don't know why, but people often call her "Jenny Wren.""

Wren

"Oh, goodness. Now I love her even more!" Maria clapped enthusiastically as the song seemed to reach a finale. "Oh, sorry Mrs. Jenny Wren, I didn't mean to scare you away. But I have to go home now any way. Please come back tomorrow!" Maria had jumped up and was gathering her things. "Oh that was so fun to see the wren! I'll have to write about her with her tail and her loud song after I get home. Momma will be waiting. Bye Mrs. Bird, bye Callie," and she ran off along the forest path.

Over the next two weeks Maria visited Mrs. Bird every day. The birds and Callie seemed to have learned Maria's schedule. As soon as she arrived in the morning Mister Blue Jay started his "announcement" and birds started to gather in the trees.

They ate so much that Maria's mother had to buy a new bag of bird seed. Callie would slowly stretch and greet Maria by rubbing her legs and then take up residence on "her" chair. The sun shone every day and Maria was grateful for the shade offered by the trees. Even Callie moved out of the sun on occasion, although she made it clear that warmth was always preferable to the rain and cold of some of the earlier summer days.

Goldfinch

One morning, just as Maria had begun to wonder if she would ever have any new birds to enter in her notebook, she saw a yellow-colored bird arrive on the bird table. "Mrs. Bird," she exclaimed in excitement, "there's a new bird! What is it?"

"Aha, that's a goldfinch," Mrs. Bird nodded with a smile. "He's still got his summer golden colors, isn't he handsome?"

"Oh yes," Maria agreed aiming her camera at the little bird. "Is that his wife, the greenish colored one?"

"Yes, that's her. In the winter his colors will change to match hers."

"Oh that's funny!" Maria laughed. "So he can't think she's ugly if he looks like her for half the year!"

"No indeed! I think she's quite attractive too, don't you?"

Maria looked again at the two birds who were still eating busily. "Yes, she is pretty. It's just he has such a bright yellow color he looks special." She finished taking photos. "What are they eating? They seem to like something a lot."

"Hmm, goldfinches love thistle seeds," Mrs. Bird said. "Those are the little black ones. There must be more of them in this bird seed than the other kind. That's why they've come today."

"Oh yes. It is a different kind. Momma said that was all they had at the store. I'll tell her the goldfinches love it!"

Maria started writing in her notebook about the goldfinches. "I've got so much in my notebook now!" she commented. She was just finishing up when another bird landed on the ground beside the tree. It started rummaging among the leaves and scratching as it searched for something to eat. "Mrs. Bird," Maria said quietly. "Look, another new bird has come! It's on the ground. What is it? It kind of reminds me of that grosbeak, but it's got orange colors on its side instead of red on its front."

"Ah," Mrs. Bird looked over at the new bird. "Well, that's a towhee. They are a bit like the grosbeak, good job noticing that Maria."

"Towhee? That's another funny name!" Maria wrote it down in her notebook and then got her phone ready to take a photo. "He's kind of cute isn't he? Oh he flew away!" Maria looked in the tree to see if she could see him. "Where did he go?"

"Well, can you hear that bird singing? He sounds like he's saying "Drink your teeee!"

"Oh, yes. That's so funny!" Maria started laughing. "Is that really him?"

"Yes, indeed. I always enjoy his song. And I do enjoy a cup of tea."

"Oh, he's the right bird to visit you then," Maria had a big grin on her face. "I don't like tea, but my Momma does. I'll have to tell her there's a bird that likes people to drink tea! Talking about tea makes me think of cookies and so I'm hungry." Maria opened her backpack and started pulling out her lunch box. Callie of course perked up right away and soon the table was covered in goodies and the three of them were munching contentedly.

Mrs. Bird brought out the usual lemonade, despite Maria's protesting that the towhee would prefer her to drink tea.

"Alright, next time I'll make tea," Mrs. Bird promised. "But today I have lemonade ready so can we enjoy it?"

Maria laughed and accepted a glass. "Of course! We can both have lemonade every day. It's my joke now, though, that you should drink tea."

Towhee

"Well, in that case, you should drink tea too, young lady!" Mrs. Bird lifted her glass defiantly. And they both laughed.

Soon after they finished lunch, clouds began to appear and Mrs. Bird started to look nervous. "Maria, those clouds look like rain."

Mrs. Bird took the tray of drinks inside and Maria put all her belongings into her backpack. Callie watched with interest, still on her chair. "Callie, we think it's going to rain so you'd better go inside soon." The cat looked at her but didn't move.

Mrs. Bird came back outside and looked at the sky again. "Yes, that's a storm coming. Callie, we're going inside!" She picked up the bag of bird seed and headed indoors. "You make sure you don't get wet Maria."

"I'll be fine. I'll call Momma and tell her I'm coming home early," Maria had her phone out. "Callie you go inside with Mrs. Bird. I'll see you again tomorrow, or whenever it stops raining. Bye now Callie. Bye Mrs. Bird."

The rain started as she reached home, and continued all evening. Over dinner she told her mother about the new birds she had seen, especially the goldfinches who came to eat the new seeds. They laughed over the towhee and his declaration that they should drink tea.

The rain didn't last long and the next day Maria was able to head out into the forest again. Sitting at the table with Mrs. Bird and Callie she had her notebook out and her phone ready when a big black bird arrived. It strutted confidently across the ground and marched around under the tree as if checking out the scene.

"That's a crow, isn't it?" Maria asked, picking up her phone to take his photo.

"Yes, dear. A rather handsome one too."

Maria was able to get a nice shot of the crow as he stood looking around.

As she put her camera down, he found something on the ground and picked it up in his beak. Then, to Maria's surprise, he marched straight over to the bird bath and dipped it in the water. "Oh, what's he doing? He's putting the food in the water!"

"Yes, they do that sometimes," Mrs. Bird was nodding wisely. "Clever birds, crows."

"Is he washing it?"

"Maybe. Or maybe he's thirsty and he wants to get some water along with his food."

"Oh, there he goes." Maria watched the large bird fly away, carrying the now soggy piece of food in his beak. "I hope it tastes good now!"

They laughed and decided they should have a snack too. Of course Callie was interested, but Maria sternly told her to wait for lunch. "This cat never learns her food comes at lunchtime!" she protested.

"Oh she knows, but she just wants to see if there's something for her anyway," Mrs. Bird was shaking her head at Callie.

The rest of the day was uneventful, or at least filled with the events of birds Maria had already met. She was always happy to see Mister Blue Jay, and was thrilled when little "Jenny" Wren returned.

"I hope someone new comes soon," Maria said as she gathered her things before heading home.

Crow

"You have so many birds already, do you really need more?" Mrs. Bird looked at her with a smile.

"Well, you said there was a cowbird. I haven't seen him yet. And, I don't know, wasn't there another kind of woodpecker?" Maria said defensively. "I mean, I know I've seen so many birds, but I want more!"

The next day Mister Blue Jay greeted Maria loudly and she laughed. "I know you're here, Mr. Blue Jay. And I am glad to see you. But can you call some new birds to visit today?" The bird looked at her with his head on one side, as if considering the request. "Alright, here's your cookie. Now, go and tell the others the good food is here!"

Mrs. Bird appeared with Callie following and they all got settled at their table. Soon enough the other birds came to eat and Maria watched them while stroking the cat. "It's really nice here, Mrs. Bird. And I know I said I want more birds, but even if they don't come, it's still nice here with you and Callie."

"Yes, Maria. I'm pleased to hear that. We're happy to have you visit us too, aren't we Callie?"

The cat purred.

Just then Maria noticed something under the tree. On closer inspection she saw it was a largish bird and it was busy pecking away at the ground. "Who's that?" she asked. "It's quite fancy looking!"

"Ah, that's a flicker! They are related to woodpeckers, but they like to eat ants on the ground. I think that's what she's doing." Mrs. Bird was leaning over to get a closer look.

"That's Mrs. Flicker?" Maria asked. "She's beautiful. Look at those spots on her front and stripes on her wings, and that funny big mark on her front! And she has red on her neck. If she was a woodpecker I would think she was a he! What does her husband look like?"

"Well, they both have red on their necks. But the males have a 'moustache' from their beak to under their eye."

"Really, oh that's funny, a moustache!" Maria was laughing as she tried to line up the shot on her phone. "She's very busy eating."

"Yes, there must be ants living under the tree. They probably come out and take the crumbs the birds have left. It would have been helpful if she had come earlier in the summer before they built their whole nest there." Mrs. Bird was watching.

Flicker

"Kind of yucky to eat ants, isn't it?" Maria had taken her photos and was still watching the bird.

"Well, crunchy," Mrs. Bird said. "But nutritious."

Maria shook her head. "Not for me. I like peanuts and fruits, but no ants for me!"

Mrs. Bird laughed. "That's alright. Do you have any fruits to share today, by the way?"

Maria looked in her backpack and pulled out a container. "Ooh, yes, blueberries!"

"Excellent! Do you mind sharing them now for a snack?"

Of course Maria agreed and they enjoyed the berries while the bird continued pecking around on the ground. When she flew away Maria saw a flash of white on its back. "Bye, Mrs. Flicker!" she said. "That was a beautiful bird! I'm so glad she came to visit. I hope she ate all the ants, I don't want them to eat my food!"

The rest of the day passed agreeably. Several robins came to take their bath, splashing merrily in the water. Maria had tried to take photos of them as they bathed, but it was challenging so every time they came she would try again. "I might have to delete some photos soon," she said a bit worried. "I took so many my phone is getting full!"

"How will you get them out of your phone for your school project, your scrapbook?" Mrs. Bird was curious.

Maria smiled. "Mrs. Bird you're a genius! I have to get Momma to put them on the computer. Then she can print them for me. I don't have my own computer, yet," Maria hesitated just long enough to indicate that she had hopes, "so Momma will have to do it on hers. We get to use computers at school next year, though, so I'm going to learn how to do it myself soon."

"Goodness, computers and phones that take photos! You young people certainly know a lot more than us old folks!"

Maria laughed. "Yes, I guess I'm lucky that all this stuff is here now. Even Momma talks about 'the old days' when they didn't have any cell phones, just an old phone at home, and they didn't get to use computers until high school."

"Yes, yes, times are always changing," Mrs. Bird nodded. "You're a smart girl, learn to use everything well and put it to good use in your life." She hesitated and then smiled. "Now, let's not get too serious!"

Cowbird

Maria smiled. She was grateful Mrs. Bird was always supportive and even impressed by what she knew. Some older people complained that life was too easy for young people today, and she didn't like that.

"I guess it's almost time for me to go," she started to say. "Oh, there's a bird over there. I don't know it. Is it a new bird?"

Mrs. Bird looked and nodded. "Yes, yes, that's a cowbird. See his brown head?"

Maria had her phone ready. "Oh, funny. He's all black but with a very brown head!" She took a couple of photos and put her phone down. "There's a grey bird too! It looks like a catbird, kind of. Or is it his wife?"

"Yes, that's his wife. You're right, though, she is very grey like a catbird. But she doesn't have the black cap on her head."

"And I guess she doesn't sound like a cat!" Maria was taking photos of both birds. "They're not very big. Why are they called cowbirds?"

"Ah that's quite a story," Mrs. Bird said. "And it explains their behavior – do you know they don't build their own nests?"

"Oh, no, what do they do?" Maria sat back ready to listen.

"Well, cowbirds sneak their eggs into other birds' nests and let those birds take care of them. Sometimes they even remove one of the other bird's eggs to make room for theirs."

"That's not very nice!" Maria looked indignantly at the two cowbirds who were eagerly eating on the ground under the tree.

"No, it's not," Mrs. Bird agreed. "But it's their way so we just have to accept it. Some birds do notice the strange eggs and kick them out, but others sit on them to keep them warm till they hatch and then feed the chicks as if they were their own."

"But what happens to their eggs and chicks?"

"Well, sometimes they lose all their eggs, or if they have some that hatch the cowbird chicks eat all the food and the other little birds die. It's not very nice when that happens," Mrs. Bird was shaking her head.

"I don't like such mean birds!" Maria exclaimed. "We should send them away!"

Mrs. Bird laughed. "Yes, I understand how you feel. But I told you their name comes from how they learned to do this. They used to follow the big herds of buffalo, feeding on the insects that flew up when the buffalo herd moved through the grasses. That was a good way to get food, but it didn't allow them time to make nests. So they learned to lay eggs in other birds' nests, and even if they didn't get to see their eggs hatch, because they had to keep traveling with the buffalo herd, they hoped the other birds would take care of them."

"Oh," Maria was quiet. "That's kind of sad isn't it? I mean they never got to be with their children?"

"That's right."

"Well, then I can't hate them so much," Maria decided. "But there aren't any buffalo here, they should learn to make their own nests!"

Mrs. Bird laughed. "A lot of people would agree with you, and birds too. Maybe one day they will."

"Or some other bird could teach them," Maria suggested. "But then why aren't they called buffalo birds?" she asked, remembering her original question.

"Actually they were called buffalo birds originally, but when the buffalo were all gone they followed herds of cows instead, so they were called cowbirds."

"I see," Maria had her notebook out and was writing all this down. "That's a good story for my scrapbook. If the people hadn't killed all the buffalo herds, they would still have been called buffalo birds. That's even funnier than cowbirds!"

Just then her alarm went off and she hurried to finish her notes. "Got to go now. See you tomorrow, Callie. Bye Mrs. Bird. Thank you for telling me about the cowbirds."

As she ran off down the path through the forest Mrs. Bird watched her and smiled. "Not everyone's story is simple, is it Callie," she commented. "But Maria's a good girl, she understands things well. It will be alright."

The next day Maria noticed a group of birds at the birdbath and quickly took her phone out to try to get some more photos. "It's hard to get good photos of them in the bath," she explained. "They keep moving and the water splashes, but the photos don't show it right!"

Mrs. Bird laughed. "That's alright, Maria, I'm sure you'll have some good shots in your collection. You certainly work hard at taking photos."

"Well, that'll have to do," Maria said as the birds flew away. "Let's see, I might have cookies in my backpack. Yes, oatmeal raisin, should I give the birds some of this?"

"Well, you are generous Maria!" Mrs. Bird was walking over to her front door. "If you have several, maybe the birds can have one and we can have the others?"

"Yes!" Maria bounded over to the bird table cookie in hand. "Here, Mister Blue Jay if you're around, here's some cookie for you."

As she sat down again Mrs. Bird reappeared. Maria was watching the tree hoping the birds would arrive soon. "I don't see Mister Blue Jay," she commented taking her glass of lemonade. "Here, have a cookie. Mmm, they're good!"

"Thank you. Does your mother make them?"

"Um, well she puts them in the oven to cook but she buys the cookie dough from the store," Maria said. "She tried making them herself but they didn't turn out as good as these, so now she buys the dough. They still smell great when they're cooking!"

"And they taste delicious!" Mrs. Bird was obviously enjoying her cookie. "Tell your mother I approve of her 'home baked' cookies!"

"Oh look, the little woodpecker has come! He's going on the table for a peanut now. I should try and get another photo of him!" Maria stuffed the rest of her cookie in her mouth and picked up her phone.

"Look, Maria, that's a new woodpecker on the feeder!" Mrs. Bird said quietly.

"Oh, oh I see," Maria switched her aim to the feeder and took several photos. "What is it? It's got red on its head, is that the husband?"

"Yes, it is. The female has red on the back of her neck, but not the head. They're called red-bellied woodpeckers."

"Oh, shouldn't they be called red-headed?" Maria looked puzzled. "I can't see any red belly. Just a lot of black and white stripes all over his back and wings and his front looks kind of dirty white colored."

"That's true. The black and white on his back and wings is very noticeable," Mrs. Bird nodded in agreement. "The red on his belly isn't so easy to see, it's just a patch."

"But then why is he called red-bellied? His head is really red!"

"Ah, because there is a red-headed woodpecker too! That one has red all over its head, not just on the top."

"OK, I guess so." Maria wasn't satisfied, but she wrote all this information in her notebook. "I like this guy! He's so cool with his striped back, kind of like a zebra. I hope I got a nice photo of him." She started looking through her phone to check, but was interrupted by a loud squawking. "Goodness! What's going on?"

Red-bellied Woodpecker

Mrs. Bird was staring intently at the tree and the feeder hanging from it. "There's a bunch of greedy starlings trying to get that woodpecker to leave the feeder so they can eat the peanut butter. The woodpecker is standing his ground, and the blue jay is complaining about the fuss!"

"Oh, wow, they're like a bunch of crazy kids. We get into trouble if we behave like that at recess!"

Mrs. Bird laughed. "Well, it looks like your blue jay friend is telling them off for their bad behavior! That's amusing because usually blue jays are the bullies, taking all the food from the other birds."

Maria laughed. "Oh, Mister Blue Jay! Better to be the monitor than the bully. He does seem to have sorted them out. The starlings are leaving."

Things settled down for a while after that and Maria wrote some more in her notebook while Callie dozed on her chair. The red-bellied woodpecker came back again and Maria was able to take several good photos of him eating the peanut butter. Even the starlings returned and behaved themselves, eating food that had fallen on the ground and splashing around in the bird bath.

Maria was surprised the next morning to see Mrs. Bird standing up waiting for her, her finger on her lips. Maria opened her eyes wide and stood still. Mrs. Bird motioned her to come forward, which she did cautiously.

"Look, do you see?" Mrs. Birds said quietly, pointing to the spot under the tree where the birds ate.

Maria hesitated and then nodded eagerly. "What is it?" she whispered.

"That my dear is a female pheasant," Mrs. Bird replied.

"Oh she's beautiful!"

"Yes, I agree. That pattern on her wings and body is very fine."

Maria put down her backpack. She quickly took out her phone and started taking photos. The large bird kept pecking at the ground, obviously finding some food to her liking and Maria was able to get several nice shots.

Periodically the bird would look up, move her head from side to side as if checking that all was well, and then resume eating. Eventually, though, something startled her and she took off, running at great speed across the ground before stopping in the undergrowth of the forest.

"She runs fast!" Maria exclaimed. "She has really strong legs. I thought she might be slow with that big body."

Female Pheasant

"Oh no, she can run alright," Mrs. Bird laughed. "She does have a big body but I think it looks bigger because her head is so small."

"Yes," Maria laughed too. "Such a little head for that big body! And she has a long tail too, kind of pointed at the end, right?"

"That's right."

"She's a pheasant?" Maria had put her backpack on the table and was taking out her notebook to write down the information about the bird."

"Yes, she's a ring-necked pheasant. But you can only see the white ring around the neck on the males."

"Oh." Maria wrote it down. "Do you think her husband will come? I want to see him too."

"Hmm, that's a good question." Mrs. Bird looked over to where the bird had disappeared. "She might have just been looking for food on her own. They can cover quite a bit of ground running like that; she may have traveled far from home."

"Oh, I hope she's alright then," Maria looked concerned. "I mean, she might get lonely."

Mrs. Bird smiled. "Indeed. But let's wait and see what happens. She may stick around here for a while if she likes our food, or she may go back home."

Mrs. Bird had already brought the bags of bird food outside and so they were able to replenish the supply quickly, including extra food on the ground for the pheasant. Callie had moved from a spot where she could watch the pheasant without disturbing her to take up her usual position on the chair. She observed their activity at the tree before settling down for a nap.

"So, does the pheasant like seeds?" Maria asked once everyone was seated at the table.

"Yes, she eats seeds and fruits, as well as leaves and grasses, all kinds of insects too I think." Mrs. Bird replied.

"Oh, she would have had more ants if that flicker hadn't eaten them already!"

"Well, I'm sure there are still plenty of ants left for her," Mrs. Bird said with a laugh.

Maria joined in. "I have to write more about her," she picked up her notebook and pen.

"Look, she's coming back," Mrs. Bird said suddenly.

Maria put down her pen to watch. The pheasant made her way back towards the tree, more slowly but with determined strides, obviously intending to return to the food supply. "Oh good, she must like it here!"

The pheasant certainly seemed to like it, staying close for several hours. When there was a sudden noise or too many other birds came she took off into the forest, but always returned. Maria was thrilled. "I didn't expect to see such a big beautiful bird," she commented. "I mean, the crow was kind of big, but not as big or as beautiful as Mrs. Pheasant."

At that moment she heard a loud squawk and a fluttering as another bird landed on the table. It was the blue jay. He turned and looked at Maria with his beady eye and then marched around the table checking out the offerings. He squawked again and started pecking at a peanut. "Oh, Mister Blue Jay, don't worry I haven't forgotten you!" Maria was laughing. "Do you think he's jealous 'cos I said the pheasant was so beautiful?"

"I wouldn't be surprised," Mrs. Bird nodded. "He does seem to think he's your special favorite."

Maria smiled. "Well, he is kind of special," she agreed. Of course at that moment Callie gave a big yawn and stretched, her tail rubbing Maria's arm. "Oh Callie, and you're so special too, of course!"

Mrs. Bird sat back with a big smile on her face. "I'm delighted you and Callie are such good friends," she said. She looked like she was about to say more, but hesitated, and then said it was time for lunch.

The rest of the day passed enjoyably, with the pheasant taking her leave just before it was time for Maria to go home. "Bye Mrs. Bird, bye Callie," Maria said as she started down the path. "I hope the pheasant comes back tomorrow!"

Maria was not disappointed. The next morning as soon as she arrived she looked for the pheasant, but only heard the blue jay's squawk. As soon as they had all the food organized, and the three of them comfortable on their chairs, the pheasant appeared. She ran over to the tree and started hunting around on the ground for food.

Maria was so excited she clapped her hands, which startled the bird for a moment. However, she looked around and apparently decided it was safe and so carried on foraging. Maria breathed a sigh of relief. "I thought I scared her away, but she stayed. That means she likes it here, right?"

"I would say so."

"Well, she's found a good place," Maria said sincerely. "We take care of all the birds don't we?"

Mrs. Bird smiled at her young friend. "Yes, we do. You've learned so much about them. All these birds are lucky to have you as their friend."

Maria smiled happily, not at all embarrassed. "Callie, too, right Callie?" she reached over to stroke the cat. Callie purred with contentment.

The pheasant stayed close to the tree all morning, eating and walking around. She didn't seem bothered by the other birds who also seemed to have grown used to their rather large companion. A couple of doves and several sparrows were pecking at food on the ground and the little wren was merrily eating food on the table above her while a downy woodpecker hung on the feeder eating peanut butter and Maria could hear a catbird "mewing" in the tree.

"It's nice with so many different birds all happy together, isn't it?" Maria commented.

"Yes, very nice."

After lunch Mrs. Bird kept glancing at the sky. Suddenly, there was a loud rustling from the forest. They turned to see what was happening and were surprised to see a whole group of pheasants emerge! "Oh," said Maria. "Look, it must be her family!"

The birds cautiously approached the tree where the female pheasant was eating. She looked up to see who was coming, and as a male approached she ran over to join him. Soon all the pheasants were moving around, pecking at the ground, and almost tripping over each other. Suddenly they all took off towards the forest. One female pheasant hesitated for a moment, looking back at the cabin. Mrs. Bird nodded and Maria waved, and then the bird ran after the rest of her flock. "Bye Mrs. Pheasant," Maria called out as she disappeared into the forest.

"Oh, they all came for her! I'm sad to see her leave, but it's good she's with her family." Maria took out her notebook. "I have to write about it."

"Yes, pheasants usually gather together in flocks for the winter. It's nice they found her so she won't be alone."

Maria nodded, still writing. "I wish she could have stayed a bit longer."

"You saw the male?"

"Yes, he's very handsome and colorful! But I didn't get a photo," Maria added smiling ruefully. "It's OK, I think Mrs. Pheasant is beautiful!"

"Yes she is." Mrs. Bird looked anxiously at the sky. "Are you almost finished? It looks like rain will come soon."

"Yes, I'm done." Maria packed away her things. "I should go home. Callie is ready to go inside too!"

That evening as Maria was getting ready for bed her mother gently reminded her that they should probably go shopping for school clothes and supplies soon, possibly tomorrow if the rain kept up. Maria agreed, realizing she wouldn't be able to go to Mrs. Bird's anyway if it was raining. But as she lay in bed before falling asleep she felt sad. Shopping for school supplies meant summer was coming to an end, and then she wouldn't be visiting Mrs. Bird and Callie any more. She decided to talk to Mrs. Bird about it the next time they met. Maybe they could make a plan for her to visit on weekends after school started.

After this last bout of rain, which lasted all weekend and into Monday, the weather turned colder, especially at night. The sun was still warm but in the shade it was decidedly chillier when Maria made her way through the forest in the morning. But she was excited to see Mrs. Bird and Callie and her bird "friends" again and skipped along the path to keep warm. As she reached the cabin she saw the birds had been busy and there was not much left to eat. Mister Blue Jay was waiting for her and started up his squawking as soon as she arrived.

"Yes, yes, Mister Blue Jay, I'm here," Maria answered him. "Alright, here's some cookie for you," she broke off some pieces and put them on the bird table.

"Maria, you're here!" Mrs. Bird opened the door with a smile. "Oh, it was chilly last night! Has the sun warmed things up yet?"

"Yes, it's nice out here. Tell Callie she can come and sit in the sun!" Maria ran back to their table and got the chairs ready. "I'm so happy to see you after all that rain. Come on, we have to put more food out for the birds! Callie, come on out too!"

Callie was hesitating, obviously aware that the weather wasn't what it used to be. Mrs. Bird came out slowly, bringing food for the birds. The cat stayed determinedly on the front step, unwilling to risk getting damp or muddy outside.

"Callie, come and sit in the sun on your chair," Maria called out, and soon the cat joined her.

Maria was just going to say something about school going back when they were interrupted by a series of honks steadily increasing in volume. "What's that?" Maria asked, surprised.

"Ah, that's the geese," Mrs. Bird said looking up at the sky. "They're starting to gather, getting ready to go south for winter, where it's warm."

"They're very noisy!" Maria said with a laugh. "Are they announcing it's time to go to all the geese around here?"

"Yes, they are," Mrs. Bird nodded. "See, there's a small group flying over there," and she pointed above the forest. "They will fly around and others will join them."

"Oh, yes, I see them! They look small, but are they the same kind of geese I saw at the lake?"

"Yes, that's right."

"And they are all lined up!" Maria was turning to follow their flight.

"Yes, they make a V formation with a leader and all the others following in line. Then they switch after a while so no-one gets too tired having to lead all the way."

"Oh, and if they don't know the way they don't lead, right? I mean the ones who went to the south before can lead."

"That's right. They go to the same places every year, so the young ones learn by following," Mrs. Bird had a faraway look in her eye as she watched the group swing around and reorganize itself before heading away from them.

"But they won't go yet?" Maria said. "It's not winter yet. Won't they stay a bit longer?"

"Not yet, they are just preparing now. But it's starting to get chilly. And the sun is lower in the sky. They know it's time to go soon," Mrs. Bird was nodding her head. "You'll see some of the songbirds leaving too. Like the red-winged blackbirds and of course the robins."

"Oh," Maria looked sad. "It will be lonely without them!"

"You'll be back in school though, won't you, with all your friends?" Mrs. Bird looked at her with a smile.

"Well, yes. But I'll still miss all the birds," Maria hesitated.

"And don't you have a birthday coming soon? Won't that be fun?" Mrs. Bird continued.

"Oh yes, it's soon. We'll have a party the weekend after school starts. Which is fun, but it does mean school started so ..." Maria turned to stroke Callie.

"Maria," Mrs. Bird said abruptly. "I need to talk to your mother about something. Can you call her on your phone for me?"

"Oh, yes," Maria took out her phone. "Um, let's see. She has her lunch at noon. I can call her now." Her mother answered and Maria quickly explained there was no problem; just Mrs. Bird wanted to ask her something. She gave her the phone and went back to stroking the cat.

Mrs. Bird talked for a while on the phone, and soon gave it back to Maria. "Let's have our lunch now then," she said.

Maria readily agreed. As soon as all the food was set on the table and Callie had been given her piece, she turned to Mrs. Bird with her face brimming with expectation. "What did you need to talk to Momma about?"

Mrs. Bird laughed. "Well, I suppose I can't keep it a secret can I!"

Maria shook her head. "No, I want to know! It's not something bad is it?" she said, suddenly getting worried.

"No, not exactly."

"Oh, now I'm afraid," Maria looked at her. "Mrs. Bird tell me!"

"Alright, Maria. Now listen carefully and let me finish. You know how the birds are going to leave to go south for the winter, where it's warm?" Maria nodded. "Well, I'm going to go south for the winter too. I have a place in Florida and this cabin, well, it's just for the summer. I can't stay here all winter."

She stopped as Maria burst into tears. "No! Mrs. Bird, don't leave! You can stay with us, it's warm in our house. Callie too. I don't want you to go!"

"Thank you Maria that is very kind. Actually what I was talking to your mother about is having Callie stay with you."

Maria looked up hopefully.

"Yes, Maria. I want you to take care of Callie. I want her to live with you. That will be my birthday present to you, if you accept."

"Oh Mrs. Bird! Yes, yes, I love Callie! She can really live with me? Callie, you can live with me!" Maria was so excited she grabbed Callie and hugged her tight which the cat endured for at least two seconds before struggling to free herself. Then Maria bounded over to Mrs. Bird and hugged her. "Mrs. Bird that's amazing! I wanted a cat for so long! And Momma said yes, right?"

"She did indeed, Maria," Mrs. Bird said extricating herself from the girl's arms. "She told me you have a small yard out back so Callie will be able to go outside. But don't let her out at night, at least not at first. She has to get used to living with you first." Mrs. Bird was looking quite serious.

"Yes, yes, we'll make sure she's inside at night. She can sleep on my bed with me."

"I'm sure she will enjoy that!" Mrs. Bird smiled.

"But when are you leaving? Not yet, not soon?" Maria sat down again looking concerned.

"Well, I'm like the geese, just preparing right now. But it will be quite soon. Come and pick up Callie right before you go back to school, and then I'll be leaving."

"Oh, that's too soon," Maria sighed and a tear ran down her cheek. Just then a commotion started in the tree. Maria and Mrs. Bird turned and saw the blue jay squawking loudly. Several other birds joined in. "Oh, they don't want you to leave either!" Maria said laughing through her tears.

Mrs. Bird laughed too. "Well, you'll just have to get your own bird feeder and feed them at your house!"

"Oh yes, that would be amazing! I'll ask Momma if we can. Thank you Mrs. Bird, you have the best ideas!"

"You should get a suet feeder. You can hang it from a tree, like our peanut butter feeder. Suet is very good for birds in the colder weather. The woodpeckers will love it."

"Yes, alright. I don't know what suet is," Maria said slowly. "But probably the store with the bird seed has it. We don't have a big tree, but there is a branch from the neighbor's tree that hands over into our yard. Maybe we can put it there."

"I'm sure you will figure it out, and Callie will keep watch to make sure the squirrels don't eat all the food!"

"Right Callie, you'll have a job to do you know!" Maria looked over at the cat who was sitting a short distance away. She pricked up her ears at her name, but then began her cleaning session.

For the rest of the day Maria observed everything extra closely. She realized that soon the summer would be over, the cabin would be empty, no more Mrs. Bird, and the birds would leave too. She sighed. "It's been the best summer ever, Mrs. Bird. I wish you didn't have to go, but I'm so glad I met you."

"We're glad we met you too, aren't we Callie?"

The cat looked up but made no response.

"I hope she likes living with me," Maria said.

"Don't worry, everything will be fine," Mrs. Bird put her hand on Maria's. Her fingers seemed to have grown even more claw-like, Maria thought. And the old lady certainly didn't seem to like the cold or the wet. They smiled at each other, understanding that this parting was inevitable.

Maria's mother comforted her daughter when she came home after hearing of Mrs. Bird's plans. "A lot of people go to Florida to escape the cold winter. They're called snowbirds."

Maria nodded, trying to understand. Her mother willingly bought some things for the cat, as well as the suet holder and suet so that Maria could continue watching birds. The last few days of the summer passed very quickly. Her project was almost complete. Every evening she worked on her scrapbook, putting her photos together with the notes about each bird. Her mother was impressed and told her it was a wonderful achievement.

On the last day before school began, Maria went to Mrs. Bird's cabin with mixed feelings. Her mother had bought a cat carrier and she was going to bring Callie home, which made her feel excited. But it meant Mrs. Bird was leaving.

"I don't like long and sad farewells," Mrs. Bird said firmly as the time drew near. "So just take Callie and put her in the carrier and leave. Here, let me give you a hug, and that's it."

Maria complied, unable to resist letting some tears fall.

"Now, don't let Callie see those tears," Mrs. Bird patted her on the back. "Come on Callie, it's time for your new adventure!"

The cat seemed to understand and allowed Mrs. Bird to pick her up and put her in the carrier. She stared hard at Mrs. Bird and then looked away. "Maria will take good care of you," Mrs. Bird said. "Be good, both of you."

Maria had her backpack on her back and took the carrier in one hand. With the other she gave Mrs. Bird her last wave and set off down the path through the forest.

That evening Callie sat on the bed beside her while Maria worked on finishing her project. She talked to the cat, showing her the photos of all the birds and stroking her. It helped her not to cry. Suddenly she stopped. "What's this photo? I don't remember this bird!"

In amongst the photos of the birds was one of a large white bird. It was walking on the grass, not eating anything. "Who is that?" Maria asked, looking at Callie. The cat looked at the photo. Suddenly she became excited and snuggled her face against it, purring. "It's a snowbird," Maria said slowly. "It's Mrs. Bird, isn't it Callie?" The cat looked at her and snuggled against the photo again. "Oh, yes, Mrs. Bird is a snowbird!" Mrs. Bird had told her not to take her photo, but this one must have been taken by mistake, and it showed her as a big white bird. Maria put the photo at the end of her scrapbook, and wrote "Snowbird" under it. "Now I'm done!"

"Snowbird"

Later, when she and Jane were playing with Callie, Jane asked where she got the photo of the big white bird.

"It's on my phone, like all the other birds' photos."

"But where did it come from?" Jane persisted.

"I guess I took a photo of Mrs. Bird by mistake. She must have walked in front of the camera," Maria shrugged.

"No! You're kidding me!" Jane shook her head. When Maria didn't answer, she went on, "Anyway, I can't believe that witch gave you her cat!"

"She's not a witch!" Maria responded immediately.

"No, of course not. She's really a big bird!" Jane laughed, shaking her head again.

"Come on Jane, I'll show you!" Maria said suddenly. "Let's go see her cabin." Jane hesitated. "Unless you're afraid!"

Callie watched the two friends as they left. Maria looked back with a smile. "We'll be back soon, Callie."

When they arrived at the cabin Maria gasped. It looked so deserted. The bird bath was still on the ground, but it was all dirty. The bird table had fallen over and the feeder was hanging at a funny angle, empty of peanut butter. Jane looked around, unimpressed. Maria picked up the table and set it right. "It was much nicer here before," she said defensively. "Let's look inside."

Jane went up to the front door and tried the handle, but of course it was locked. They walked around and looked in a window. There was nothing inside. They tried another window, which Maria realized must look into Mrs. Bird's bedroom. It was empty of furniture, but there was a large collection of sticks in the corner. The girls looked at each other.

"It looks like a nest!" Jane exclaimed.

"Yes, doesn't it?" Maria agreed. "See, she's really a snowbird!"

"A witch, that's what she is. I told you!" Jane muttered backing away. "Let's go. This place is creepy."

They made their way back to the front and were just about to leave when there was a loud squawk. Maria turned and saw the blue jay on a branch above the bird table. He squawked again, and flew down to land on the table, fixing his beady eye on Maria.

"Mister Blue Jay!" she said. "Oh, I'm happy to see you! Here, I do have a piece of cookie in my pocket for you." She went over and put a piece on the table. He ate it and squawked again.

"Come on Maria, let's go. I'm getting cold!" Jane called out.

The blue jay fixed his eye on Maria and squawked again. "Alright Mister Blue Jay. You can come home with me too," Maria said softly and started walking towards Jane. She turned back and made a beckoning sign to the bird, and then the two girls headed off along the path that Maria had followed so many times. As they walked home through the forest there was a rustling in the trees and an occasional glimpse of a blue jay above them, flying from branch to branch.